The Saints
Reckoning

By

DW Bradbridge

First edition

© 2018 D. W. Bradbridge

Published by Valebridge Publications Ltd,
PO Box 320, Crewe, Cheshire CW2 6WY

Cover design by Electric Reads
Cover images:
John Beardsworth (cleric and soldiers)
Image of Shrewsbury - Panorama of Shrewsbury 1630-1650
(from a period painting in Shrewsbury Museum)

Typeset for print by Electric Reads
www.electricreads.com

Shrewsbury 1644

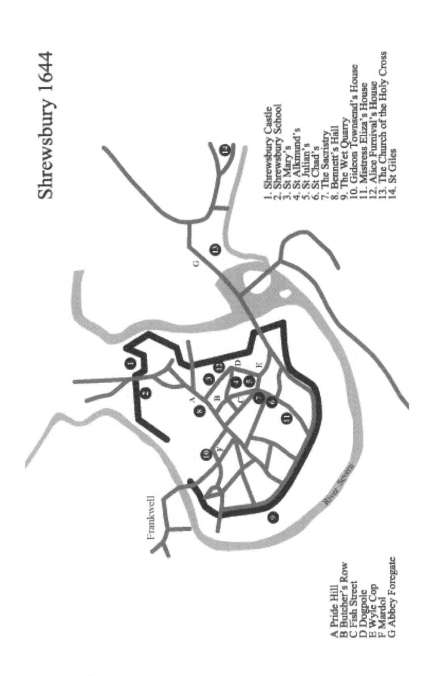

1. Shrewsbury Castle
2. Shrewsbury School
3. St Mary's
4. St Alkmund's
5. St Julian's
6. St Chad's
7. The Sacristry
8. Bennett's Hall
9. The Wet Quarry
10. Gideon Townsend's House
11. Mistress Eliza's House
12. Alice Furnival's House
13. The Church of the Holy Cross
14. St Giles

A Pride Hill
B Butcher's Row
C Fish Street
D Dogpole
E Wyle Cop
F Mardol
G Abbey Foregate

Frankwell

River Severn

Key Characters

In Nantwich:

Daniel Cheswis	Wich house owner, cheese merchant, and ex-constable of Nantwich
Elizabeth Cheswis	Daniel's wife
Cecilia Padgett	Daniel's housekeeper
Jack Wade	Daniel's apprentice
Alexander Clowes	Chandler, bellman, and Daniel's best friend
Marjery Clowes	Alexander's wife
Colonel Thomas Croxton	Deputy lieutenant responsible to Sir William Brereton, head of the parliamentary forces in Cheshire
John Davenport	Wich house owner and friend to Daniel Cheswis
Gilbert Robinson	Head briner in Daniel's Cheswis's wich house

In Northwich:

Sir William Brereton	Commander of the parliamentary forces in Cheshire
Sir Thomas Myddelton	Commander of the parliamentary forces in North Wales

Thomas Sudlow	A briner
Abel Sudlow	Tavern owner
Lieutenant Philip Saltonstall	Young parliamentary officer, and great-nephew of Myddelton
James Skinner	Daniel Cheswis's ex-apprentice
Matthew Tarbock	Skinner's friend

In Oswestry:

Colonel Thomas Mytton	Parliamentary officer and governor of Oswestry
Evan Davies	A blacksmith
Hester Davies	Evan's wife
Millie Davies	Evan and Hester's daughter
Lizzie Davies	Evan and Hester's daughter
Ellis Davies	Evan and Hester's son
Jack Morgan	Landlord of The Bell Inn
Jack Hipkiss	Sergeant in the Oswestry garrison
Charlie Hipkiss	Jack's Hipkiss's brother

In Shrewsbury

Alice Furnival	Printer and Daniel Cheswis's first love
Jem Bressy	Royalist spy
Sir Fulke Huckes	Royalist officer and former governor of Shrewsbury
Colonel Robert Broughton	Governor of Shrewsbury

Thomas Bushell	Manager of the Royal Mint in Shrewsbury
Richard Halton	A merchant
Ben Collie	Print worker
Jakob de Vries	Print worker
Cornelis Smits	Carpenter
Joseph Finch	Farmer
William Stubbs	Son of cookhouse owner
Gideon Townsend	Worker in the mint, Parliamentary spy
Faith Townsend	Gideon's sister
Greaves	Landlord of The Sacristry
Maredudd Tewdwr	Schoolteacher
James Logan	Minister of the Church of the Holy Cross
Leach	An apothecary
Edwin Hodgson	A farmer
Mistress Eliza	Owner of safe-house
Andrew Harding	Minister of St Julian's Church
Nicholas Prowd	Minister of St Mary's Church
Mr Lentall	Minister of St Chad's Church
Abel Hook	Gaoler at Shrewsbury Castle
Martha Hook	Abel's wife
Richard Wollascott	A tanner

In Montgomery:

Edward, Lord Herbert	Owner of Montgomery Castle
Thomas Lloyd	Guard

Chapter 1

*W*hen Millie eventually summoned up the courage to leave the safety of The Bell Inn, she had expected to find them waiting for her, but the streets were empty. There had been six men, arrogant strutting soldiers all, except for the young lad with the withered arm, who had seemed strangely embarrassed to be in the company of the others. Three Shrewsbury men, two foreigners, and the boy, all guilty of abusing her in a most vile and unwarranted manner.

The ringleader of the group, a thickset brute of a sergeant called Hipkiss, had thrust his hand up her skirts as she tried to serve them their ale, and they had laughed at her, a drunken, lecherous cackling that belonged in the gutter. But the mirth had abruptly ceased when she took one of the pewter tankards from the table and cracked the sergeant square across the jaw with it, sending him sprawling helplessly from his chair, covered in beer.

Fortunately for Millie, the landlord, Jack Morgan, had seen what had occurred and had quietly hustled her away to safety behind the bar, leaving his two burly sons, Dai and Will, to eject the furious soldiers. The two foreigners, both Dutchmen, had threatened to come back and set fire to the place, but Jack's suggestion that such an occurrence would precipitate the involvement of Colonel Lloyd, the town's governor, had been *enough to persuade them to keep their peace, and all six men had left the inn glaring and snarling like chained dogs, before heading off up Church Street towards the garrison.*

It was well past ten when Millie emerged from the side door of the inn and crept furtively along the narrow alley which opened out into the main road heading to the south of Oswestry. She would have left it until later had it not been for the fact that the Royalist guards manning the New Gate usually raised the drawbridge at eleven, and she had no wish to be stranded on the wrong side of the town's defensive walls.

It was a dank and depressing March evening, one of those which felt colder than it actually was. There was a touch of fog in the air, and, as she quickly scanned the almost deserted street, she could only just make out the bulk of St Oswald's Church to her left. The ruined steeple, destroyed in order to prevent the castle from being overlooked in the event of a siege, loomed out of the darkness towards her like a jagged claw.

As she pulled her coat around her shoulders, Millie shivered. She pressed her hand against the handle of the meat knife she had taken from the kitchen and secreted inside the lining of her bodice. Reassured, she stepped out into Church Street, turned right, and strode purposefully towards the New Gate, where torches burned brightly in the sconces, illuminating the guards protecting the gateway. Candles flickered enticingly in the windows of one or two of the houses that lined the road, but, for the most part, those who lived outside the town walls had retired for the night.

Millie walked up the middle of the road, her shoes echoing on the cobbles, and breathed a sigh of relief as she walked through the gateway into the town. Several of the guards nodded to her as she passed, accustomed to seeing her walk home at such a late hour.

Inside the walls there was a little more activity. Up ahead, next to the cross which marked the centre of the town, a tavern was still turning out the last stragglers, those too drunk to find their own way home. A goodwife flung open the door of one of the houses lining the left side of the street and threw a bucket of slops into the channel that ran down the middle of the thoroughfare, causing the young rector of St Oswald's to jump to one side as he passed by on his way back out of the town, surely heading towards his own rooms next to the church.

It was then that Millie saw the men loitering by the wall opposite the smithy owned by her father and behind which her own house stood. The burly sergeant was leaning with his back to the wall, staring at her intently, whilst the rest of the men whispered among themselves. Two of them were smoking pipes, but they put them out when they saw Millie approaching. She gasped at the realisation that the men knew exactly where she lived and had been waiting for her.

Putting her hand once again to the knife hidden in her bodice, Millie quickened her step and headed straight for the door to the smithy. As the men started to head towards her, the rector spun round and looked quizzically in her direction, but then he seemed to change his mind and turned away, crossing the drawbridge and disappearing into the night.

Millie opened the workshop door, slipped inside, and fumbled for the bolts that would guarantee her safety – but she was too slow. No sooner had she started to slide the first bolt into place than the door shook violently and burst open, throwing her back against the wall of the smithy. She felt strong hands grabbing her by the wrists, restricting her movement, and suddenly she found herself staring at the malevolent, beery grin of the sergeant.

"So, flax-wench," he growled, breathing stale tobacco fumes into her face, "it seems you are just as stupid as I thought. Did you truly believe I would let a lowly slattern such as you get away with striking an officer of His Majesty, the King? You shall pay for this dearly and no mistake."

Millie turned her face to escape the stench and gave the sergeant a look of distaste.

"Officer?" she scoffed. "Do not dissemble with me, sir. You're no officer. You're naught but a poxy sergeant and a drunken one at that. Go back to your billet and sleep it off before you get into more trouble than you're already in."

The sergeant's Adam's apple bobbed nervously in front of her eyes as a ripple of uncertain laughter emanated from behind his shoulder. But then she felt the flat of his palm strike her cheek, and the laughter stopped as her head exploded into stars.

"You are a feisty one, I'll give you that," he snarled, "but it's time you learned what feistiness can bring you."

She felt his body pressing against hers, squashing her against the wall and forcing her to smell the stench of onions and stale beer on his breath. His hand wandered up the back of her thigh and started exploring the inside of her skirts, and with increasing panic she began to realise that there was more at stake than just a beating. She wriggled to the left and tried to escape the sergeant's grasp by ducking underneath his arms, but he was too strong for her, and grabbing her around the waist, he lifted her off her feet and started to carry her across the workshop towards an open space, behind which stood an anvil perched on top of a tree stump.

Suddenly, she found herself being dumped unceremoniously on the dusty floor of the workshop. The wind was knocked out of her, and she was unable to move before she felt his weight on *top of her, pushing her head against the base of the tree stump. Forcing herself to ignore the jeers and laughter of her tormentors, she twisted her head to her right and tried to work out a way to free her right wrist from the sergeant's iron grip. As she did so, she caught a slight movement out of the corner of her eye, from the dim corner of the smithy where a broken cart stood, its rear axle resting on a wooden block and its buckled wheels lying loose on the floor. Straining her eyes in the dark, Millie realised with horror that staring back at her from between the front wheels of the cart was the terrified face of a person she knew well.*

What her younger brother Ellis was doing in the smithy at such an hour she had no idea, but there he was, motionless in the gloom, his right hand grasping a set of clinch cutters, presumably grabbed at the last minute as a makeshift weapon. When Ellis saw that Millie had seen him, he nodded briefly at the tool in his hand and then at the five soldiers, who were standing at an angle facing slightly away from him, and who therefore could not see where he was hidden.

Millie gave a brief shake of her head. With the best will in the world there was no way that a slender, sixteen-year-old youth such as Ellis was equipped to take on half a dozen seasoned soldiers, all fuelled with drink.

Suddenly, she saw her opportunity – taking his left hand away from her right wrist, the sergeant started to fumble with the buckle of his belt in an attempt to lower his breeches. Quick as a flash, Millie reached inside her bodice, extricated the meat knife, and with a wide swing of the arm, speared the sergeant's right hand, which had been gripping her left wrist. With a piercing shriek, the sergeant rolled over onto his back, pulled the knife from the back of his hand and flung it away.

"Fuck! Bitch!" he spat. "Jesus, you will pay for that."

Millie tried to get to her feet, but two of the soldiers grabbed her by the arms and pushed her with venom onto her back so that she couldn't move. She then felt her skirts and shift being removed and a ripping sound as the shift was torn into a dressing strip for the sergeant's hand.

"That's a pretty cunny you have there, girl," mocked the sergeant as he bound his hand. "It will make a fine plaything, just you see."

There was a ripple of laughter from the rest of the soldiers, but at precisely that moment there was a guttural roar from the corner of the workshop as Ellis emerged from behind the broken cart, brandishing the clinch cutters, which he swung at one of the soldiers, catching him on the side of the knee.

Howling in agony, the soldier collapsed onto his side, but before Ellis could swing the clinch cutters again, one of the two Dutchmen grabbed the end of the tool and wrenched it from the youngster's grasp. There was a second or two when no-one moved, but then Ellis bolted for the door and raced out into the street, slamming the door behind him.

"Snel, Corni, laat hem niet wegkomen," snarled the Dutchman to his fellow countryman. "Catch him, and he's yours. He's more to your taste than the girl, anyway."

Without a word, the second Dutchman, younger and slimmer than the first, nodded at his colleague and disappeared out of the door in pursuit of the youth.

That left five of them to rape her. The sergeant went first, then the greying, middle-aged man who had seemed to be second in command, and then the remaining Dutchman. Even the soldier who Ellis had hit with the clinch cutters had a go once the pain had subsided in his knee. The only one who did not indulge was the young lad, who shook his head abruptly when offered his turn.

"Please yourself, Will," said the sergeant, *"but don't think it will make any difference. You're just as implicated as the rest of us."*

The lad said nothing, but when she looked up towards him, Millie caught his gaze and thought she detected a look of apology in his eyes.

It's too late for that, she thought, as she lay sobbing, crumpled on the ground, her privy parts sore and stinging.

"What now?" said one of the soldiers, just out of her eyeline.

"We need to get out of here," said the Dutchman, *"before anyone decides they want to investigate."*

"Aye," said the sergeant, after a brief silence, *"but there's one thing we must do first. Come, give me a hand."*

Millie heard nothing for several seconds, and she wondered whether the soldiers had gone. But then she became aware of the sound of scraping and pushing coming from somewhere behind her head. She was too traumatised to care about the implications of the soldiers' exertions, and, in truth, she would have gladly welcomed death at that moment. Little did she know how close it was.

Fortunately for her, she did not realise what the soldiers were doing until the very last moment, when she happened to glance upwards and saw a shadow creeping towards the edge of the tree stump. Suddenly, realisation dawned, and her mouth opened in a silent scream as the anvil toppled over the edge and started to plummet towards her.

Chapter 2

Colonel Thomas Croxton raised a cynical eyebrow and levelled a penetrating stare in my direction. As he did so, the candles illuminating the walls of the Booth Hall flickered in their sconces, casting an uneasy light on the scene in the colonel's office, a portent, I thought, of the storm that was about to descend upon me. I smiled nervously at the young officer, knowing full well that such pleasantries would cut no ice whatsoever.

"Now let me get this straight," began Croxton, brushing breadcrumbs from his immaculate black doublet and leaning authoritatively across his desk. "Jem Bressy, the well-known Royalist intelligencer, a man who is very close to the top of the list of delinquent spies who we would wish to apprehend, quite bizarrely and coincidentally turns out to be instrumental in helping you rescue your housekeeper's granddaughter from the clutches of her kidnapper, the murderer Abraham Gorste. What is more, this happens at the precise time when the location of the chest full of plate, silver, and gold, buried by Abbot Massey of Combermere Abbey, becomes known to you."

I glanced askance at my friend and Nantwich's bell ringer, Alexander Clowes, who had also been summoned to the Booth Hall to face the colonel's wrath, but he merely pursed his lips and shuffled uneasily on his chair.

"That is correct, sir," I admitted.

"Then forgive me if I am a little slow on the uptake," said the colonel, scratching his forehead in mock puzzlement, "but can you please explain why you failed to arrest Bressy, and why, having seen him escape and knowing that he also sought to identify the location of Massey's treasure, you did not make damned sure you got back to Nantwich before he did? Instead you roll in here at noontime the following day, by which time Bressy has long since removed the treasure and ridden halfway to Shrewsbury, having secured his booty and the undoubted gratitude of Prince bloody Rupert." The corner of Croxton's mouth twitched involuntarily, his fingers drumming the table with irritation as he fought to keep his anger under control. "You will forgive the direct questions, Master Cheswis, but when he finds out, Sir William Brereton will be asking the same information of me."

I had not worked under Croxton for long, but I knew him well enough to know that his mood did not usually stray this close to incandescence, and I realised I would have to tread carefully.

In truth, I did not blame Croxton one jot for being so vexed. Indeed, until now his response had been positively restrained. Two days previously, Alexander, my apprentice Jack Wade, Amy and I had been led back into Nantwich by a beaming Roger Wilbraham, the prominent local merchant and landowner who had also been present at Combermere, only to discover that Bressy had already dug up the treasure in Ridley Field and made himself scarce. Under the circumstances, it would not have surprised me in the least if I had been dragged into Croxton's office on the spot. The fact that Croxton had not done so was a surprise, but a welcome one nonetheless, for it had given me the opportunity to talk to Alexander in private, in order to make sure we got our story straight.

"It is truly regrettable that I was not able to return to Nantwich with more haste," I said, with as much contrition as I could muster, "but both Amy and I were suffering from shock and exposure. Amy, in particular, was in no fit state to ride. Furthermore, the coroner from Whitchurch made it clear he required me to provide him with a witness statement. Had I failed to do so, your assessor Mr Folineux may well have found himself placed under a charge of murder and would be languishing today in a cell in Shropshire rather than serving you in the sequestration of delinquents."

This much at least was true. Abraham Gorste, who had kidnapped my housekeeper Mrs Padgett's granddaughter in an attempt to force me to disclose clues that would help reveal the whereabouts of the aforementioned treasure, had cruelly bound Amy to the inside of a water tank at Combermere and opened the sluice in a last-ditch attempt to force me to reveal what he wanted to know. The ruse had worked, and I had capitulated instantly, but Gorste had not counted on the sudden appearance of sequestrator Marc Folineux, who had seen Gorste's action and killed him outright by striking him over the back of the head with an oar from the murderer's rowing boat.

Croxton, however, was no fool, and he was never going to be satisfied with me passing off my concern for Amy's welfare as a reason for my failure to prevent the treasure from getting into Royalist hands.

"Master Cheswis," he said, a touch of exasperation entering his voice, "I am fully cognisant of the nature of your relationship with Amy Padgett, that she is like a daughter to you, and I understand your desperation to free her from her incarceration, even if it was a foolhardy endeavour to attempt to do so with only your apprentice for company, but that does not explain your lack of urgency after Amy's safety was secured. You say it was she who gave you the final clue to the location of Massey's treasure. Why then did you not leave Amy in the safe hands of the Cotton family at Combermere and ride back here with all haste? And what about you, Mr Clowes?" he added, turning his attention to Alexander. "Even if Mr Cheswis was in no fit state to ride back to Nantwich after his ordeal in the water tank, you, sir, certainly were. Why did you not ride back in his stead?"

Alexander glanced at me uncertainly and opened his mouth to speak, but the first question at least was something for which I was well prepared. I shot my friend a warning look and answered the colonel myself.

"In retrospect, sir, we may have made the wrong decision," I conceded, "but at the time, we could not possibly have known that Bressy had deduced where the treasure was buried. The missing clue to its location was carved onto the engraving belonging to my wife, which had been in Gorste's possession, and he was already dead by this time. As you say, it was Amy who remembered the 'clue word' from the engraving, but only after Bressy had already disappeared into the night. I concede in hindsight that he must already have searched Gorste's quarters and found the engraving there, but we could not possibly have known that."

This, of course, was only partially true, for Bressy had indeed been present next to the water tank when Amy had revealed the final clue, but I was in no position to admit that to Croxton. I could not possibly reveal that I had been forced to make a pact with Bressy, giving him free reign to pursue the treasure in return for his help in saving Amy's life. I just thanked God that the sequestrator Folineux had not also been there at the time, he having been lured away from Bressy and into the house by Alice Furnival a few seconds beforehand, a fortunate twist of fate. All I had needed to do was make sure that Amy was not questioned about the matter. But who, I reasoned, could possibly think of interrogating a child about such things? My conscience pained me at the tangled web of deceit I had been forced to spin, and to my own side too, but there had been no alternative.

Croxton gave me a thin smile of acknowledgement, but he was not to be diverted from seeking answers to all of his questions.

"And you, Mr Clowes," he repeated, "you were about to speak. What do you have to say for yourself?"

Alexander pulled his fingers nervously through his thick shock of sandy hair and tried to prevent himself from shrinking backwards in his chair.

"I had only just arrived on the scene with Roger Wilbraham when Daniel disappeared in search of Amy," he said. "I had no idea Bressy had been present until much later in the evening, when Daniel was able to speak to me in confidence, but by this time it was already dusk, and I had no wish to risk injuring our horses by attempting to ride back to Nantwich in the dark. The roads hereabouts are too uneven for that."

Croxton rose to his feet, walked thoughtfully over to the window, and opened the shutters a little wider. It was a dull, overcast day in Nantwich, and the light was having difficulty penetrating the inner confines of Croxton's office.

"Then tell me this, Master Cheswis," he said, his voice hardening. "Marc Folineux's account of this episode is that Bressy introduced himself as a cousin of Thomas Cotton, and neither you nor Alice Furnival, who was also present, contradicted him in this regard. Mistress Furnival I can understand. She is a known Royalist informant, and Bressy was a close colleague of her late husband. Her reasons for dissembling are clear. However, you also said nothing. Pray explain why that was the case, and why, for that matter, Alice Furnival was there in the first place?"

"Mistress Furnival's presence at Combermere is easy to explain," I said, grateful for the opportunity to draw Croxton's attention away from my own actions. "She was at Combermere to help Sir Fulke Hunckes persuade Thomas Cotton to allow the secret library in his summerhouse to be used as a repository for Lord Herbert's own library, currently at his home in Montgomery Castle. His Lordship was concerned his valuable collection of books might fall into parliamentary hands should the castle be taken by Sir Thomas Myddelton. Hunckes thought protecting the library might help persuade Herbert to declare his support for the King.

"As for myself," I continued, "I had thought you had understood my actions. Firstly, Bressy was armed, and I was not, so he was going to get away in any circumstance. Secondly, he had just saved Amy's life, and whatever there is to be said about him, I was grateful for that action. Thirdly, of course, however handy Mr Folineux may be at wielding an oar behind someone's back, he is no fighter, so I thought it prudent to allow Mistress Furnival to lead him to the safety of the house. Bressy can always be pursued, and the treasure may be recoverable."

Croxton sighed in exasperation and turned from the window to face me. "Very well, Mr Cheswis," he said, "I have heard enough. Let us cut to the chase. There are those who might consider your abject failure to recover the treasure an indication of either disloyalty or incompetence on your part." Croxton paused to let the words sink in.

"You mean Folineux?" I ventured. "I fear he has taken a dislike to me from the outset."

"I mean no-one in particular," riposted the colonel, his voice hardening, "and I certainly do not take advice on military matters from a sequestrator. Personally, I do not have you for a traitor, not after what you did at Lathom House and in Bolton, but there are some aspects of this matter which do not sit well with me. You will be pleased to know, however, that I have decided to offer Clowes and yourself the opportunity to redeem yourselves."

At that moment, there was a knock at the door, and in strode Croxton's young clerk Ezekiel Green, carrying a tray on which were balanced three cups of cordial. Now I was beginning to get really worried. I had not anticipated an easy time from Croxton, but a tray of drinks was not among my list of expectations.

The colonel reached for one of the cups, took a large draught and smiled at me, a glint of steely insistence in his eye. "I'm glad you mention the fact that Abbott Massey's treasure is recoverable, Mr Cheswis," he said, "for that is precisely what you will be doing. Bressy, no doubt, will be heading for Shrewsbury, with a view to depositing his haul at the King's mint, which is housed in the undercroft of a largely derelict mansion house. I am sure it will not surprise you to learn that Sir William Brereton has an informant in place there, and he will be able to facilitate your access."

I stared at Croxton for a moment, not sure whether I was hearing him correctly. "Wait a minute," I said, with wide-eyed incredulity. "What do you mean by 'access', exactly?" Are you telling me you want us to break into a guarded property in the centre of a Royalist stronghold and rob the mint?"

"Or disable it," said Croxton, evenly. "Either way will do."

There was a momentary silence whilst I tried to take in what the colonel was saying, the quiet broken only by the sound of Alexander's chair scraping across the floor as he recoiled in shock. I stared aghast at Croxton, but it was my friend who spoke first.

"Colonel Croxton," he said, his voice tinged with desperation, "the treasure has gone. Why take us away from our families and send us on a wild goose chase from which we may not return? We are intelligencers by default only. You know that. We have neither the aptitude nor the training for such a task."

"That, Mr Clowes, is where I beg to differ," insisted Croxton, jabbing a finger across the table in Alexander's direction. "Apart from your duty to put right your failure in allowing Bressy to escape with the treasure, you have shown yourselves thus far to be adept at this kind of work. You worked well under cover in Chester and at Lathom House, and your determination to complete a task to which you are committed is not in doubt, as shown by your success in rescuing Amy Padgett."

"But sir," persisted my friend, "is this absolutely necessary? I have a young family, and Daniel's wife is with child."

Croxton raised an eyebrow at this latest piece of news, but I could tell from the look in his eye that he was not to be dissuaded.

"Hush, Alexander," I said, putting my hand on my friend's arm. "There is nothing to be gained from this." I turned to Croxton and returned his stare. "Tell me about the mint," I said, wearily.

For a moment, I thought I saw the briefest flicker of satisfaction cross the colonel's face, but if I did, the young officer hid it well. Nodding briefly, he reached inside the drawer of his desk and extracted a roll of thick paper, which, when laid out flat on the surface in front of him, measured perhaps two feet by one foot six. It was, I noted, a map of Shropshire.

"By John Speed, the famous cartographer, himself a Cheshire man by birth," explained Croxton. "Speed is long since dead, and the map is now thirty years old, but it serves its purpose. Take a look in the top right-hand corner, if you will."

I peered at the six-inch square to which Croxton was pointing and was able to identify a detailed plan of Shrewsbury, depicting the abbey, the River Severn, and the town centre. I noted how the river almost encircled the town, leaving only a narrow sliver of land to the north, from which the centre could be accessed without crossing the river. Croxton gestured to us to come closer and pointed a thin finger at precisely this spot on the map.

"The castle is here," he said, "protecting the town at its most vulnerable point. The town walls run around the castle to the north, whilst to the east the land falls away sharply and steeply to the river. To the immediate west is the castle gate, and the school, beyond which, once again, you will find the River Severn. The town is located to the south.

"The mint is currently located in an old stone mansion called Bennett's Hall, which lies on Pride Hill, the main street leading through the town from the castle. It was once a fine house of some standing, but it suffered a catastrophic fire about a hundred years ago, leaving only the stone shell. Since then, a number of wooden cottages have been built inside the old stone structure as well as a number of traders' workshops. The mint itself is managed by an engineer called Thomas Bushell, who in his younger days was a gentleman-in-waiting to Sir Francis Bacon, attorney general and the late lord chancellor. In sixteen thirty-seven, Bushell successfully petitioned the King to allow him to set up a mint in Aberystwyth, which he operated successfully for five years until war broke out, when he was ordered to relocate the operation to Shrewsbury.

"Particularly noteworthy is the fact that the coins made in Shrewsbury have hitherto been made primarily out of melted plate, which makes them of inferior quality to those once made in Aberystwyth. As a result, Bushell has been forced to import silver from Wales to improve the standard of the coinage. Bushell does not, as far as we're aware, currently use gold."

I nodded sagely. "So that means Bressy's haul is only going to be of use if it consists largely of silver, in which case it will be valuable indeed."

"Correct," said Croxton. "You catch on quickly, Mr Cheswis. We are not sure if Bressy is aware of this, but we assume he must be. It means that any gold, jewellery or plate that was included in Massey's treasure will need to be disposed of somewhere else."

"And where would he do that?"

"I think that is the least of our worries," said the colonel. "The first task is to ascertain when Bressy shows up at Shrewsbury with the treasure. I despatched a rider on Saturday to alert our man within the mint, and he has instructions to return with news as soon as Bressy presents himself at Bushell's door."

"I see, and in the meantime…?"

"In the meantime, we cannot afford to wait. You and Clowes are to proceed with all due haste and make contact with our man in the mint. His name is Townsend, and you will find him of an evening in an inn called The Sacristry. It is located next to St Chad's Church."

"And by 'all due haste' you mean…?"

"By tomorrow at the latest," said Croxton. "But do not worry. I am fully aware that you cannot simply ride into Shrewsbury unannounced. Your best bet is to ride south as far as Oswestry with Sir Thomas Myddelton, who plans to join with his brother-in-law Thomas Mytton, the governor of Oswestry, before mounting a push into Wales. You will be safe with them. From there you can join with some of Mytton's men, who will be able to get you into Shrewsbury."

I groaned inwardly. I had resigned myself to the fact that Alexander and I would be called upon to rectify the issue of the lost treasure, but I had hoped for a little more notice than this.

"And where will we find Sir Thomas Myddelton and his men, Colonel?" I asked.

Myddelton, the de facto commander of the parliamentary forces in North Wales, had spent much of the previous year with Sir William Brereton, trying to secure his help in making inroads into his Royalist-dominated homeland, with mixed success. He had been a regular visitor to Nantwich, but I had not seen either him or Brereton for several days.

"Ah, therein lies a temporary, albeit not insurmountable, difficulty," admitted Croxton. "Sir Thomas is currently in Northwich with Sir William. There is a threat to Tarvin and some of the other villages thereabouts from Prince Rupert, who looks to reassert himself in the area. But no matter – it means you can be the one who breaks the news of what has happened to Massey's treasure to Sir William, which, in all honesty, is as it should be. I will provide you with the necessary documentation and a letter to Sir William from myself, and you can ride to Northwich first thing tomorrow morning."

And so it was agreed. There was nothing more to be said on the matter. Alexander and I were dispatched back to our respective families to break the news of our impending departure and to cogitate on the latest chapter of our seemingly endless debt of service to Croxton, to Sir William Brereton, and to the blessed Army of Parliament.

❦

As it turned out, Elizabeth was not in the least surprised that I had been ordered to pursue Bressy and recapture Massey's treasure. Indeed, having had most of the weekend to consider the price to be paid for securing Amy's safe return, and having accepted that the only reason why Amy had been taken in the first place was Elizabeth's unknowing status as custodian of one of the clues to the location of Massey's treasure, we had both come to the conclusion that there was no price too high for the girl's safety, a girl who had become an integral part of our own family, and that we would have to accept any resultant cost, inconvenience or danger with good grace.

She shed a tear, of course, as most women are apt to do, but it was only when she realised that I would be expected to depart on my circuitous route to Shrewsbury as early as the following day that her features tightened, and she embarked on a silent frenzy of cleaning, cooking and organising that only ceased when Mrs Padgett arrived shortly after lunch.

"You must stop this right now, Mistress Cheswis," said my concerned housekeeper, upon finding my wife on her knees in the kitchen up to her elbows in a bucket of soapy water. "This is my domain. If you don't stop this nonsense, there will be little left for me to do, and then where will we be? This is work that you are paying me for."

"There you go, my dear," I said, grateful for the intervention. "You must listen to Mrs Padgett. She knows what is for the best."

Elizabeth said nothing, but my housekeeper nodded vehemently.

"She will not listen to me," I added. "She is as stubborn as an ox."

"Master Cheswis is in the right of it as usual," said Mrs Padgett. "But wait," she added. "This has not come out of thin air. What is it that ails you?"

In retrospect, I own that my subsequent explanation did not help matters much. I do not, at the best of times, consider myself particularly adept at dealing with emotional matters, but on this occasion my contribution was positively disastrous, for all I managed to achieve was to transform a room containing one emotional but relatively stable woman into one containing two such creatures, both in floods of tears. And if that were not enough, there was then a sharp knock at the front door, and a furious Marjery Clowes strode in, berating me for allowing her husband once again to be dragged into a dangerous mission that he had no reason to be involved in.

"Marjery," I said, in exasperation. "I fear the days are long gone when anything I say or do has any bearing on whether Brereton or Croxton decide to call on Alexander's services. It seems that we are now viewed as a team, and they will continue to call on us as long as the war rages and perhaps afterwards too. There is little we can do about it."

With that I left the three women to console themselves and headed for The Red Lion, where I found Alexander waiting for me, his head buried in a tankard of ale.

ભ

By the time I returned to our house on Beam Street later that evening, dusk had already begun to fall, and I was starting to wonder what kind of reception I would receive from Elizabeth, having left her on her own all afternoon.

After chewing the cud with Alexander for a couple of hours, it had occurred to me that, if I was expected to leave for Northwich the following morning, then I had better put my affairs in order at the wich house, especially as a kindling was scheduled for the following week.

I had found Jack Wade in the yard, covered in sweat and stripped to the waist, loading a barrow of salt onto a cart with the help of Gilbert Robinson, my foreman.

When they had finished their work, I despatched Wade back to Beam Street to advise Elizabeth that I would be late home and spent the rest of the afternoon with Gilbert, discussing the engagement of briners to cover the three-day kindling. In addition to my own wich house, Robinson was contracted by three other wich house owners including my good friend, John Davenport. All of these owned businesses located along the length of Wood Street and tended to employ regular teams of jobbing briners to complete the work. As such, it took little more than a few forays into neighbouring properties, and all the necessary arrangements for the kindling were in place.

"You left it a little late this time, though," chided Gilbert, as I thanked him for his efforts. "Young Jack does a grand job. He catches on quick, but he is still a young lad, and he cannot manage the wich house on his own. If the truth be told, Master Cheswis, you are spending too much time away, too much time selling cheese and bothering yourself too much with whatever it is you do for Sir William Brereton. You know how it is. If you are not here to control matters, you run the risk of not being able to complete a kindling, and if that happens you will have to sub-contract to other wich houses, or worse. If it comes to the attention of the rulers of walling, you may lose part of your walling allocation."

Gilbert spoke the truth, and I knew it. Although I had been freed from my onerous duties as one of Nantwich's constables, it seemed that the whole of this time and more was now being taken up by the demands of Brereton and Croxton. In principle, I was due to be paid for any time spent in the service of the army of Parliament, but the rate of pay was less than I could earn from my own business, and I had not yet seen one penny of the amount due to me. With a wife, family, housekeeper and apprentice to support, I was beginning to wonder how we were going to make ends meet.

"You are right, Gilbert," I said, "but my hands are tied. Is there anything you can suggest? Do you have any spare time on your hands that you can use to help me run this place?"

Robinson wiped his bare arm across his forehead and smiled. "Perhaps," he said. "It depends. I have a little money saved up – not much, but enough to buy a small share in your wich house, if you were to sell it to me – take me on as a partner, as it were. If you were prepared to do that, then there would be an incentive for me to spend more of my time at this place."

"I'm not sure–" I began, but stopped myself short, for what Gilbert was suggesting was not so unreasonable. I had long felt that life as a briner was not one which appealed to me in the long term. That was why I had chosen to develop my alternative business as a cheese merchant. And after all, was Robinson not an expert in this field, a man with salt in his blood? Would he not be an ideal partner?

"Just think about it, Master Cheswis," said Robinson, "and let me know."

My mind, therefore, was whirling with a myriad of conflicting worries as I made my way across the town bridge, through the beast market, and back up Beam Street: how to console a distraught and newly pregnant wife, whose husband would now be away for an unspecified length of time, how to recover Massey's treasure from Bressy and return in one piece, and whether to accept Gilbert Robinson's proposal with regards to the wich house.

As if to reflect my mood, a soft rain had begun to fall on the streets of Nantwich, turning the mud, horse excrement and other detritus into a foul, malodorous mulch that clung to the boots like clay. In truth, when I returned home I was expecting to find the atmosphere similar to that which I'd left, but I was surprised to find Elizabeth busying herself in the hall, laying out the clothes and provisions for my journey neatly on the table. When she heard me enter, she looked up, smiled, and embraced me, holding me tightly around the waist.

"Husband," she said, "I owe you an apology. I had no right to behave in the way I did earlier. You have put your life at risk for this family and continue to do so."

I reciprocated the embrace and inhaled the sweet scent of my wife's hair, wondering when I would be able to enjoy that smell again.

"Hush, my love," I whispered, "do not torture yourself."

"It's just that I have already lost one husband to this war, and my son a father. I do not want to lose a second husband, nor for this new child to suffer the same fate as Ralph," she added, tapping her belly lightly with the flat of her hand.

"What will happen is God's will alone," I said, simply, "but I swear to you, I will exercise the utmost care."

"Especially in Shrewsbury," said Elizabeth, looking up at me out of the corner of her eye, "and whatever you do, stay away from that widow. She has designs on you and is nothing but trouble."

So that was it. Elizabeth's sullen behaviour earlier in the day had not just been because of the danger facing me in Shrewsbury. She did not trust me in the presence of Alice Furnival. My cheeks burned with shame as I held Elizabeth tightly, not just because, with my marriage less than three months old, I could not command full confidence from my wife as to my fidelity, but because of the sudden realisation that deep down, when all was said and done, I did not trust myself either.

Chapter 3

Northwich – Tuesday August 20th, 1644

It is no more than half a day's journey from Nantwich to the neighbouring salt town of Northwich, and so Alexander and I were able to take a leisurely ride along the banks of the River Weaver and enjoy the feel of the late summer sun on our backs. The road was good, and, this being Parliament territory, there was little risk of encountering a Royalist patrol. We therefore made good time, and it was still early afternoon when we passed through the undulating pastures to the south of Northwich and approached the confluence of the Rivers Weaver and Dane. As we did so, the first of the tenements and wich houses that lined the north bank of the Dane came into view.

We had barely reached the Dane Bridge, which marked the entrance to the town, when a couple of pickets waved us down in a strangely flustered manner and asked to see our papers.

"What is your business here?" demanded the first, a broad-built, muscular fellow in his twenties.

"We have been sent to you by Colonel Thomas Croxton in Nantwich, as our papers make clear," I explained. "We have business with Sir William Brereton."

The second picket, an older, slimmer man to whom the other clearly deferred, studied our paperwork and frowned.

"This is not the most opportune moment to be visiting Northwich," he said, handing me back our passes. "Many of our number are busy engaging the enemy at Tarvin, and Sir William is likely to be indisposed for most of the day. You may have to wait some time."

I acknowledged the picket's comment with interest. "There is a battle going on at Tarvin?" I asked.

"More a skirmish, if the truth be told," admitted the picket, "but it is a fight nonetheless, and one which has been brewing for several days. On Sunday, we heard news of a Royalist detachment of foot and horse that was approaching Northwich from the direction of Chester. On the way, they raided some poor farmer and took his cattle without paying. Sir William sent out a party of soldiers to chase them off, and there was a skirmish not far from here at Sandiway. However, the malignants were too strong for us. Our party was chased away and fifteen of our number were taken as prisoner. The only blessing was that one of our musketeers, who had been hiding under a hedge, managed to shoot their officer, who was dragged back to Chester on a bier. Those who were there said he appeared to be mortally wounded. We have since heard his name was Marrow."

"You mean Colonel John Marrow, the officer who was defeated at Oswestry not long since?"

"The very same. Or at least so I believe. A gallant officer by all accounts. Shame he chose the wrong side."

I nodded gravely. This war, I had come to realise, was full of brave men convinced of the legitimacy of their cause, who had lost their lives fighting against their own countrymen. I thought of Thomas Sandford, the brave firelock who had been instrumental in the Royalists' capture of Beeston

Castle, but who had lost his life in the previous January's attack on Nantwich, and I thought of Newcastle's brave whitecoats, who had fought to the last on Marston Moor, all on the opposite side to myself, but worthy of respect for their bravery nonetheless.

"So, tell me," I asked, dragging myself away from my thoughts. "How has it come to be that they fight today at Tarvin?"

"After Sunday's skirmish, the Royalist detachment made a beeline straight for Tarvin. Sir William, however, suspected that their design was to head for Lancashire, so he and Sir Thomas Myddelton rode to Frodsham to intercept them before they crossed the river. Finding them not there, he then received intelligence as to their true location, so he made haste for Tarvin with the majority of his men, sending a couple of messengers back here with orders to put the town on full alert. We now wait with trepidation for news of what has transpired. There are many here who have headed straight to church to pray for salvation, for if the King's party prevails, the outlook for Northwich looks bleak. We will not be able to hold them the other side of the Weaver for long, I fear."

Alexander gave me a weary look and shrugged. "It seems we have little choice," he said. "We will have to wait for Brereton to return."

I agreed. "I trust there is lodging to be had in the town?" I asked the picket, who smiled sympathetically.

"With the town full of soldiers, there are few billets that are not spoken for," he said, "but if you follow me, I will take you to an inn, which may be able to accommodate you. There you can rest until Sir William returns. You can even stretch your legs around the town if you feel so inclined, although if I were you I would stay this side of the Town Bridge, which straddles the Weaver to the west of the market square. If the malignants break out of Tarvin and decide to attack us, it is that direction from which they will come."

I thanked the elder of the two pickets and allowed him to grab hold of Demeter's reins and lead us across the Dane Bridge, leaving the other picket to maintain his vigil at the entrance to the town.

"My name is Thomas Sudlow, a briner here in town," said my guide, as he led me towards the ramshackle collection of wich houses, which fought for space around Northwich's single brine pit on the north bank of the Dane.

"A briner?" I said. "Then we have something in common. I too have interests in the salt trade, a wich house of six leads in Nantwich."

"Then you are indeed a fortunate man," said Sudlow. "In Northwich, most of the wich houses only have four leads. Very few of us have six. If you only have four pans in which to boil your brine, that makes for a less efficient process in my experience. Small wonder that Nantwich's salt business is twice the size of our own."

I smiled in acknowledgement, but begged to differ. "What you say may well be true, but it depends on how many kindlings you can get. These days it seems our rulers of walling do not have enough kindlings to go around."

"We are all in that boat, I believe," agreed Sudlow, ruefully, "and this war does not help. Tell me, is this your first visit to our town?"

"It is."

"Then I shall be pleased to show you something of our salt-making area. We have to pass through it to reach your accommodation."

Once across the bridge, Sudlow turned right down a narrow lane, which was lined on either side by a seemingly endless row of wich houses that, as in Nantwich, were open-ended wooden sheds with wattle and daub walls and thatched roofs.

"This is Seath Street," explained Sudlow. "My own wich house is located along this road. The High Street runs parallel to this, but on the other side of it there are two other streets similarly lined end-to-end with wich houses, as well as Horsemill Street, which is the street running perpendicular to this, and on which you would emerge if you were to follow this street to its end. Behind Horsemill Street are the Crum Hills."

"The Crum Hills?"

"Aye, all the deposits from hundreds of years of salt-making are piled up behind the wich houses to the east of the town, but there is a reason for this. The Crum Hills are important, for they form a natural barrier and protect the town from flooding should the Dane decide to burst its banks, as it is occasionally prone to do. They were built precisely for this purpose."

I thanked Sudlow for his explanation and surveyed the scene around me. I was surprised to note that there was little sign of activity in the town's salt-making area. I did notice a stream of smoke coming from one of the buildings, indicating a kindling was in progress, but other than that it was as though the threat of attack had forced everyone back into their homes.

"It is quiet here," I opined, as I watched a solitary briner walk out of the wich house with the smoke coming from its chimney and adjust a theet, which ran from the back door of the wich house in the direction of the brine pit.

"Aye, that it is," agreed Sudlow. "Any salt worker with any sense will have gone back home. Most of the briners live to the east of here in the township of Witton, so if Northwich is unfortunate enough to be attacked from the west, it is likely they will escape the worst of it."

Sudlow led us a hundred yards up the street until we reached the brine pit. From there we turned left down a narrow path overgrown with brambles, which led us between two wich houses before emerging into a wide thoroughfare lined with houses, taverns and shops. Sudlow pointed to a less than salubrious-looking hostelry with the sign of a white horse hanging over the doorway, where a slim, fit man of middle years with short greying hair was sweeping out the detritus from the previous night's drinkers.

"My brother, Abel," explained Sudlow. "He will see you right."

At the sound of his brother's voice, the landlord looked up from his work and cast a suspicious eye in our direction.

"Customers," explained Sudlow, before his brother could open his mouth. "The chamber round the back is still free, is it not?"

"It depends," said the landlord. "Are they paying?"

Not wishing to end up having to sleep on the floor of some stable, I dismounted, took out my purse, and proffered some coins in the landlord's direction. "Will that suffice?" I asked.

"Aye that will do, but dinner's extra, and you'll have to share. One of you will have to take the floor, as the chamber that's free only has one pallet. How long will you be staying?"

"That I cannot tell," I said. "I will let you know tomorrow. I presume you have stabling here?"

"Aye, round the back. The horses will be safe enough there, though you'll have to see to them yourselves, for the moment. Our stable lad hasn't shown up for work yet, the malingering little runagate. I expect he's cowering in the church with the rest of the town. As for me, King's men or Parliament men, it makes no difference to me. All soldiers drink beer, regardless of their allegiance."

Although I expected nothing better, the room allocated to us by Abel Sudlow was barely adequate. It was sparsely furnished, with a single truckle bed and a simple wooden chair and table. There was also a faint odour of mould in the air, which made me start sneezing so that I was forced to open the window and let in some fresh air.

As if my mood could not be made any worse, I drew lots with Alexander for the bed and lost, so I was forced to lay out my things on rushes on the floor.

Towards five o'clock I decide I could stand the place no more, so I left Alexander snoring on the bed and took a stroll through the market square towards the bridge spanning the River Weaver. I was rewarded with the sight of a column of horses approaching the town from the west, at the head of which, to my great relief, I was able to identify the colours of Sir William Brereton and Sir Thomas Myddelton. As they grew closer, the cornets at the head of the column flourished their colours, and the tenseness of the watching crowd began to dissipate, as people began to realise that Parliament had secured a victory, and Northwich was safe, at least for another day.

Behind the cornets, riding side by side, were the two contrasting figures of Brereton and Myddelton themselves; Brereton, slight of build and sober in both dress and demeanour, rode on the right of the column, surveying the growing crowd, his pinched features betraying little. To his left, riding a fine black gelding, was the more substantial frame of Sir Thomas Myddelton, who acknowledged the enthusiastic cheers of the onlookers, his fist clenched in a victory salute. Despite wearing his hair short, just below his ears in the Puritan style, Myddelton was somewhat more ostentatiously dressed than his senior commander and seemed to swagger on his horse as he rode onto the bridge.

I positioned myself on the right of the column to make myself visible to Brereton. The commander looked at me in surprise as I caught his eye, and he waved the column to a halt.

"Well, well, Master Daniel Cheswis," he said, eyeing me with curiosity. "I would not have expected to see you here. What brings you to Northwich?"

"I am here with Alexander Clowes, sir," I said, shuffling uneasily, aware that the eyes of the crowd were boring into my back. "I have a communication from Colonel Croxton and news of the task on which we have been most recently engaged."

"Good news, I hope," said Brereton.

"I doubt you will find it so," I admitted, ruefully. "There are some matters which need to be discussed."

Brereton pursed his lips and gave me a penetrating stare. "Then perhaps we had better do so, sir," he said. "I have some military matters to discuss with my officers first, but have yourself and Clowes present yourselves at my quarters in two hours' time, and we shall see what manner of disaster you have to report."

ଓଌ

The sun was already low in the sky by the time Alexander and I made our way reluctantly across Northwich's cobbled market square, past a row of solidly built wooden stalls, and presented ourselves to a group of bored-looking guards standing sentry by the entrance to the substantial coaching inn located on the corner of a narrow lane leading down to the River Weaver.

It had come as no surprise to discover that Sir William Brereton and his senior officers had all secured lodgings at The Swan, the establishment's less important residents having been swiftly re-housed in other nearby hostelries to make way for the commander and his entourage, for the inn's central location and proximity to the Town Bridge dictated its role as Brereton's operational centre on the occasions he was present in Northwich.

It also helped that the inn was only two doors away from the town's House of Correction, as became immediately apparent when the inn's front door was flung open to reveal two Royalist prisoners being roughly manhandled in the direction of the gaol by a row of eager red-coated soldiers – pikemen by the look of their build – and a fresh-faced lieutenant with straw-coloured hair, dressed in a smart black jacket with an orange sash tied round his waist.

The soldiers continued gleefully to propel the sorry-looking prisoners (one of whom was holding his arm gingerly, the other sporting a cut lip) towards the gaol, but the lieutenant stopped in his tracks and looked us up and down.

"Ah, you must be Cheswis and Clowes," he said. "You are expected. Please follow me."

The lieutenant could have been no older than twenty, but he bore an air of authority, perhaps borne of privilege, which made him appear much older. He led us through the inn and into a small ante-room just off the hallway.

"You may wait here awhile, until Sir William is ready to receive you," he said. "In the meantime, I understand you have brought correspondence with you. I will take that, if I may. Sir William wanted to read it before he talks with you."

I reached inside my doublet and handed the young officer the letter I had been carrying from Croxton.

"Thank you," said the lieutenant, examining the seal on the envelope to make sure it had not been opened. "Pray be seated. I will return for you presently." He then left us alone in the room, closing the door behind him.

In the event, it was fully twenty minutes before we were ushered into a larger and better-appointed chamber on the opposite side of the hallway. Brereton was sitting thoughtfully at a large oak table studying Croxton's letter, but he was not alone. Peering over his left shoulder and wearing an expression fit to freeze the gates of hell was Sir Thomas Myddelton.

"You may leave us now, Philip," said Myddelton to the young lieutenant. "You know what is expected of you. You may report back here when you are ready."

"It will be done, sir. I will not be long." The young officer bowed slightly and retreated out through the door, leaving Alexander and myself to face the wrath of the two commanders.

"My great-nephew," said Myddelton, by way of explanation. "A fine young officer, but you will be able to judge that for yourself, for you will be seeing rather a lot of him in the coming days, thanks to your ineptitude."

Alexander opened his mouth to say something, but I grabbed him quickly by the elbow, which was enough to assure his silence. The last thing we needed was to create even more trouble for ourselves. Brereton must also have realised that unnecessary words were about to be spoken, for he coughed meaningfully and contemplated us sternly over the top of his hat, which was sat on the table in front of him.

"Well, gentlemen," he began, "it is a predicament of some magnitude that you have brought to me, a shambles no less, but fortunately for you it is one which Colonel Croxton feels you should be given the opportunity to put right."

"Sir, it is most regretful–" I began, but Brereton cut me off in mid-stream.

"Save your apologies and excuses, Master Cheswis," he said. "You rescued your housekeeper's daughter, who you perceive as family, I understand that. The loss of the treasure was unfortunate, but now we must recover it or at least make sure the King suffers a loss of similar magnitude."

"This could put back our progress in Wales and the Marches by months," snapped Myddelton. "Prince Rupert has been sore pressed for resources, and such a windfall will make a significant difference to him."

"Indeed," said Brereton, dismissing Myddelton's point with a wave of the hand, "but let us stick to the point, shall we? Croxton has devised a plan, of which he says you, Master Cheswis, are already aware."

"Yes, sir. We are to travel with Sir Thomas's forces as far as Oswestry, where we are to seek the help of Colonel Mytton to provide us with the means to enter Shrewsbury undetected. From there we are to seek out your agent in the mint, who has been tasked with ascertaining how much of Jem Bressy's haul is made up of silver and therefore able to be processed by the mint. We are then to collude with your man to recover what silver we can, and, if that proves to be impossible, to deliver a blow to the King by helping your agent to destroy the mint. Although it hasn't been specifically said, I presume we are also tasked with trying to locate the whereabouts of Bressy and recovering any part of his haul consisting of gold, jewellery or other valuables."

Brereton nodded with satisfaction. "You summarise matters most succinctly," he said. "Thomas Bushell's mint has been of concern to us for some time. It has been operational now for two years and is of key strategic importance to the King. Your task, therefore, is not a matter of choice between two alternative outcomes. Not only must Abbot Massey's treasure be recovered, so also must the mint be put out of action on a permanent basis."

"You would entrust Alexander and myself with such a task?" I asked, astounded.

Brereton shrugged. "It seems I have little choice. Time is of the essence, and resources are thin. Not only that, you are one of the few people who knows what Bressy looks like. He is a most elusive fellow. Just make sure you don't fail me this time."

I gave Brereton a wan smile and glanced at Alexander, whose face was drained of colour. "And how do you propose we achieve such a task, sir?" he asked. "We are scarcely qualified for the kind of covert operation which you propose."

"Oh, I beg to differ, Master Clowes," said Brereton, evenly, "but you need have no fear. Our man Gideon Townsend has many years' experience in such matters. He is a veteran from the war in the Low Countries and Germany, and he knows what he is about. He has been in situ in Shrewsbury for more than a year, watching, waiting, reporting, building contacts and infiltrating the Royalist elite in the town.

"He now reports that the King is considering relocating the mint to Bristol, so any opportunity we might have to shut down the operation threatens to disappear, unless we act quickly. We had already been considering sending in some additional agents to help Townsend complete his mission, so your involvement with the case of Abbot Massey's treasure and the pursuit of Jem Bressy comes at an opportune moment."

"So, when do we ride for Oswestry?" I asked, trying to get to the point.

"Ah, therein lies the difficulty. Sir Thomas was set to ride tomorrow, and you were supposed to accompany him. However, he will now be somewhat indisposed, at least for the next few days."

"Indisposed?"

"Yes, our skirmish with the Royalists today has changed a number of things. We dealt Prince Rupert a severe blow in Tarvin. In addition to securing the village for Parliament, we captured forty-five of his men and killed one of his most senior officers. You can be sure the Prince will not take such a defeat lying down. Tomorrow he will be back, and we must protect what we have gained. Sir Thomas and his men will be required to remain here and defend Tarvin, at least until I can send for reinforcements from Nantwich to help garrison the place. That will take a few days. In the meantime, I have

43

asked Sir Thomas's great-nephew, Lieutenant Saltonstall, who you have just met, to gather together a small group of dragooners to escort you to Oswestry."

"It would not be safer to remain here until Sir Thomas is ready to march?" I asked.

"I'm afraid not. Apart from the loss of valuable time, for you to remain here would put you at risk of capture, should things not go well for us tomorrow. This is something we cannot countenance. So you will depart at first light and make full haste for Oswestry, where Colonel Mytton will receive you."

At that moment, there was a knock on the door, which Myddelton opened to admit his great-nephew and a column of perhaps ten red-coated dragoons, some young, some rather longer in the tooth, but all exuding an air of battle-hardened experience. I breathed a sigh of relief. We would be in good hands, at least as far as Oswestry.

"Volunteers to the man, sir," explained the young lieutenant to his great-uncle as the men filed into the room and lined up against the wall.

It was only then that I became aware of a familiar face among the volunteers. I had not noticed him at first, for he had been part-obscured by his colleagues, but the look on Alexander's face confirmed my suspicions. There was no mistaking it. The grinning features of the last soldier through the door, perhaps a little gaunter than I had known them, the result, no doubt, of six months hard campaigning, belonged to someone I knew well. I smiled in recognition, for the young man next to the doorway was none other than my erstwhile apprentice and, it would seem, reformed Royalist, James Skinner.

Chapter 4

*L*ord Edward Herbert of Cherbury sat at a desk in the oak-panelled library at his home in Montgomery Castle and stared out of the window at the soldiers patrolling the castle's inner ward. There were but two of them in view, good men both, but Herbert knew that despite the strength of the fortifications at Montgomery, the small retainer of men that he had kept to protect his home would be woefully inadequate to prevent a determined force from entering and garrisoning the castle, should either side in this unfortunate conflict show serious intent to do so. And what would become of his beloved books then, he wondered. In his heart, he knew the answer.

He contemplated the shelves of carefully preserved volumes of poetry, religious tracts and philosophical works, and shuddered. In truth, when Sir Fulke Hunckes, the governor of Shrewsbury at that time, and that flighty young widow – what was her name? – Furnival, that was it – had suggested storing the books in a secret vault at Combermere Abbey, near Whitchurch, he had thought he had found the ideal solution. With his books safely out of the way and in secure storage, he had considered he might have been able to follow his instinct and declare his support for the Royalist cause. Hunckes had even offered him further financial inducement to hand the castle over to the King, money derived from a mysterious *source of funding, which Hunckes and Furnival had been rather vague about. But when it emerged that the secret vault under Thomas Cotton's summer house had been used as a prison for a Nantwich housekeeper's granddaughter, the whole scheme had been compromised, and the conspirators forced to flee back to Shrewsbury.*

Despite his disappointment at the failure of the plan to use Combermere as a repository for his valuable book collection, this was not what was bothering Lord Herbert on this particular day. Despite his legendary eccentricities, the old baron was a pragmatist, his belief in divine intervention having led him to the acceptance that the opportunity offered by Hunckes and the Furnival woman had already passed him by, and for good reason. God had simply willed it so.

Herbert had since prayed that when the next challenge came, God would intervene and guide him to make the right choices. Which was why he was now sat in his library shuffling papers about his desk, the particular documentation in question being the constituent parts of a letter from his Highness, Prince Rupert of the Rhine, once again asking for financial support as well as access to the castle, in order to garrison it for the King.

In truth, it grieved him not to be able to support his monarch in the way he would have liked. After all, both his sons were already fighting on the King's side. But Herbert knew to his own cost that opposing the will of Parliament could be a dangerous game. Two years previously, he had been imprisoned for daring to suggest that the words 'without cause' should be added to a resolution that the King had violated his oath by declaring war on Parliament. After this experience, he had decided that his best chance to survive the conflict and sustain the least damage to himself or his property was to take no further part in the war and refrain from supporting either side.

This second approach from Rupert was difficult to ignore, of course, but he felt obliged to take into account the prevailing state of play in Cheshire, North Wales, and the Marches. Since his defeat at Marston Moor, Rupert was no longer perceived as invincible, and, ensconced in Chester, he was finding it increasingly difficult to raise funds and forces. At the same time, it had become clear that Sir Thomas Myddelton's design was to cut a swathe through Shropshire and the Welsh Marches. Shrewsbury was safe for the moment, but Oswestry had fallen, as had Welshpool. The Red Castle would be next, and then it would be Montgomery's turn. And if Myddelton came knocking on his door, perhaps also with Sir William Brereton in tow, he did not want to have to explain why he had been funding Royalist forces in the region.

No, Herbert would claim ill-health on this occasion, which was near enough to the truth. He seemed to suffer constantly from gout and had developed a serious eye condition, which he feared might ultimately threaten his sight. He was becoming an old man, he realised. Surely his decision to decline support on these grounds would be accepted, especially if he phrased it in the right way.

But then Herbert had a thought. There were also other reasons why he should sit and wait. Firstly, on his return to Shrewsbury, Hunckes, who had been quarrelling over military matters with the commissioners of array for weeks, had been replaced as governor by Colonel Robert Broughton, whilst overall military command had been placed in the hands of Sir Michael Ernle, and with Ernle directly responsible to Prince Rupert, surely he could expect a courtesy visit from the new commander in the not too distant future.

There was one other thing which was gnawing away at his mind. What, he wondered, had happened to the surprise windfall that had been expected by Hunckes and the Furnival woman? Both had kept him in the dark as to the source and exact nature of that funding, and his host Thomas Cotton had also seemed deliberately vague. But Herbert was no fool. He had noticed the comings and goings of Roger Wilbraham and the cheese merchant from Nantwich, and he had spoken to the sequestrator Folineux, who had killed the kidnapper and murderer Abraham Gorste, and who had spoken of a mysterious man with jet black hair, who had helped save the young girl imprisoned in the summer house. According to the sequestrator, this man had subsequently masqueraded as a cousin of the Cottons and finally vanished into the night.

Herbert could not shake the suspicion that this unknown person was somehow involved in the plan to secure the promised funding, and the one person who seemed to know more about him than most was not Hunckes but the mysterious Alice Furnival. Come to think of it, why had she been involved in the Royalist approach to him in the first place? After all, she was ostensibly no more than a printer's widow.

And crucially, was it not so that on the day Hunckes and Furnival had returned to Shrewsbury from Combermere, Hunckes had done so with a face like thunder, whereas the Furnival woman had worn a strange half-smile, as though the events of the previous day had been a triumph of sorts, not the disaster they appeared to be?

Lord Herbert dipped his quill into his pot of ink and began to draft out his response to Prince Rupert. He knew now what *he was going to do. He would seek out Alice Furnival and get to the bottom of what had really happened at Combermere, for was it not possible that the money promised to him for his support had been secured after all? And if this were the case, surely an alternative solution could be found to secure the safety of his beloved books. Herbert completed his letter, sealed it, and called for his steward.*

Chapter 5

It took two full days to ride to Oswestry. The weather was good, being fine and sunny with a hint of freshness in the air, but we took a somewhat circuitous route through the Shropshire countryside, with a view to avoiding any potential Royalist scouts out of Shrewsbury who might wish to betray our position.

Our guide, Lieutenant Saltonstall, proved to be an able and efficient young officer, somewhat stand-offish and very aware of his status perhaps, but for all that he was more than able to command the respect of the small band of volunteers he led. It was also clear that, despite his youth, he had managed to attain a position of some trust within his great-uncle's regiment.

"I was very fortunate," he explained to me as we rode through the village of Ellesmere on the second day of our journey. "I am nothing more than a third son from a minor branch of the Saltonstall family, but my grandfather was a favourite brother of Major-General Myddelton's wife. It is more than forty years since their father, Sir Richard Saltonstall, was Lord Mayor of London, but our name still has some sway, I'm glad to say. Sir Thomas was kind enough to secure me a commission, and he has rather taken me under his wing. I have much to be grateful to him for."

"You seem ambitious for success," I suggested, to which the young officer offered a smile.

"What else am I to do?" he asked. "My father was also a third son, and was apprenticed to a goldsmith at my age, a field in which he eventually made his name and a good living, but you can only trade off a family name for so long. Fulfilling a meaningful role in my great-uncle's regiment is my best opportunity to make a name for myself in my own right."

"Assuming, of course, that Parliament ultimately prevails in this conflict," I pointed out.

"Everything in this life is a gamble," riposted Saltonstall, with the kind of nonchalance that can only be found in the young. "But at the moment my great-uncle's home at Chirk is occupied by the malignants. If he succeeds in his quest to remove Prince Rupert and his army of brigands and papists from Wales, then there is every chance that I shall be justly rewarded."

I began to wonder whether Saltonstall's obvious ability might be tempered by a youthful impetuousness, which, unless checked, might eventually prove to be his undoing. Alexander, meanwhile, who was not one to give undue deference to privilege, and who had been listening to Saltonstall with raised eyebrows, leaned over the neck of his mount and called over to the lieutenant.

"Aye, but only if your ambition does not get you shot first."

I could see Saltonstall reddening at Alexander's remark, and I stepped in to diffuse the situation before my friend could open his mouth again.

"I think what Alexander is saying is that war has a nasty habit of turning on you and biting you where it hurts the most, but Sir Thomas certainly seems to trust in your abilities."

"I should hope so," said Saltonstall, sending a contemptuous glare in Alexander's direction, "and more than you know, for what you have not yet been told is that I will be accompanying you to Shrewsbury to help you complete your mission. And don't worry," he added, seeing the expression on my face, "I was fully briefed by Sir William and my great-uncle whilst you were waiting to see them. You will both be acting under my command. All will be explained when we arrive in Oswestry."

We rode the last few miles in silence, arriving outside the Beatrice Gate to the north-east of the town as the sun was dipping behind the outline of the castle, which straddled the defensive walls on Oswestry's northern side.

Oswestry was a fair town, but one which appeared to have suffered much from the war. Although the arched Beatrice Gate, with its twin gatehouses adorned with the lion rampant crest of the Fitzalan family, appeared relatively intact, the wall encircling the town had been badly damaged, with breaches in several places.

The townsfolk appeared war-weary, as you might expect given their experience over the previous few months, and I did not perceive too much support for Mytton's force among the local populace – but then again, I suspected that any military force which consumed the people's food, occupied their houses, and brought with them the threat of being besieged or attacked would not have been particularly welcome. Indeed, I heard later that a good eighty clubmen had been forced to surrender their arms when Mytton had captured the town in July.

Alexander and I were billeted in the house of a blacksmith called Davies, who received us hospitably enough. Indeed, he purported to be a Parliament sympathiser himself, although I suspected he would have gladly supported anyone who would guarantee him an income. A short, wiry man in his forties, Evan Davies seemed to spend most of his time hidden away in his workshop, surfacing only to eat and sleep. In truth, he seemed to walk around as if something were permanently on his mind, and I began to wonder what had blighted his life so as to cause such a fog of despondency.

"Anyone from a town suffering like this one has, they've a right to behave in that way," opined Alexander, when I commented on it the morning after we arrived. I couldn't argue.

Davies and his family lived in a modest workers' cottage, which adjoined his smithy, this being located a few yards from the cross in the centre of Oswestry. His wife, who gave her name as Hester, was a large, buxom woman of cheerful demeanour, who spent most of the day fussing over us like a mother hen.

"With my Millie and Ellis now gone, and Lizzie old enough to take on her fair share of duties around the house, who else is there for me to concern myself with?" she smiled, when I tried to point out we were perfectly able to take care of ourselves.

Millie and Ellis, it seemed, were two of the Davies's children, who for some unexplained reason were no longer at home. When I asked what had become of them, Mrs Davies merely frowned and changed the subject, something in her expression telling me that I should not push the matter.

Lizzie was the family's only other offspring, a taciturn and seemingly shy young girl of about fifteen. Russet-haired with a face full of freckles, she was on the cusp of womanhood, a fact which had not escaped the notice of James Skinner, who was also billeted with us, and who spent the majority of our first day in Oswestry trying to engage the girl in conversation, an uphill battle, or so I initially thought. By early evening he appeared to be making some headway, and both he and the girl removed themselves to the Davies's backyard and sat in a corner where they could not be heard.

Skinner, in fact, seemed to have undergone a remarkable transformation in the seven months since he had been captured by Jem Bressy and spirited away to Chester after January's battle near Nantwich. Gone was the hangdog demeanour and evasiveness that had characterised his brief time as my apprentice. What had emerged was a confident young soldier, who had completed his journey into manhood and was living the life he yearned for, that of an adventurer.

I had not seen him since May on that fateful day in Bolton, when Skinner had turned a blind eye to Alexander and I hiding from a vengeful Royalist force in a bedchamber at Henry Oulton's house, Green Acres. I owed Skinner my life that day, the second such time the youth had stepped in to save my skin, and I did not intend to forget it. I'd known from my brother Simon that he and many of his colleagues in Henry Tillier's regiment of the Royalist army had been captured at Marston Moor, and that he had turned his coat in order to avoid incarceration as a prisoner of war, but that suited the lad just fine. He was still only sixteen, but in those few short months James Skinner had grown up.

"I was lucky," Skinner had related during our ride through the Shropshire countryside. "I was pulled out from what was left of our company by your brother, who recognised me in the crowd, and he arranged for my recruitment into Lieutenant-Colonel Lilburne's troop of dragoons together with my friend Matthew Tarbock, who also rides with us today, and we were taken to Lilburne's camp near Doncaster."

Skinner pointed out a squat, sandy-haired lad with an engaging smile, who rode a few yards behind us. Perhaps two years older than Skinner, he acknowledged us by removing his Monmouth cap in salute.

"Matt is a good Cheshire lad from Northwich," explained Skinner. "His family are grocers in the town. We served together with Simon as part of the troop of two hundred dragoons that helped the lieutenant-colonel take the castle at Tickhill without a shot being fired, and against the Earl of Manchester's orders too. That earned Lilburne a talking to, I can tell you. A public dressing down by the earl in front of Parliament men and Royalist prisoners alike. But Freeborn John could not care less. He is his own man and sees Manchester as a vacillating fool. Lilburne can be a dangerous man to be associated with, I believe."

I nodded in agreement. The man certainly had a knack for finding trouble. I had heard it said that if the lieutenant-colonel was put in a room on his own, John would fight Lilburne, and Lilburne would fight John. I worried what would happen to Simon if Lilburne got it wrong one day.

"And how fares my brother?" I asked.

"He is enthused by Lilburne and his ideas, as you yourself know," said Skinner. "The lieutenant-colonel has also accepted Simon as a kind of protégé, which suits him well.

He is, however, downcast that he appears to have lost the love of his betrothed, Rose Bailey. He swears he will be back in Nantwich after the campaigning season is over, when he intends to put things right with her."

This was news to me, but I cannot say I was surprised. Simon was never a man to take a setback lying down, and the loss of Rose Bailey's affections to the tanner's apprentice Edmund Wright would, I knew, be viewed by Simon as no more than that – a setback, which could be rectified at a stroke once he returned. I was not so sure myself, but I made a mental note to prepare myself for a reckoning sometime around Yuletide.

"So, tell me, how did you end up back in Cheshire?" I asked, changing the subject.

"We arrived back in Cheshire a couple of weeks ago," explained Skinner, "after we were given the option of transferring to the garrison at Northwich. It was Matthew's chance to return home and the opportunity of a relatively quiet life, so I followed him. But you know me, Master Cheswis, a quiet life is not really for me, and when I saw you on the town bridge talking to Sir William Brereton two evenings ago, I made a few enquiries and made sure I was around when Lieutenant Saltonstall came asking for volunteers to escort you to Oswestry. It didn't take much to persuade Matt to come along too. He has paid his respects to his family, so now he feels free to join us."

In truth, I was pleased to see Skinner again and grateful that he had chosen to ride alongside me to Oswestry. It was unfortunate, I mused, that he would be travelling no further with us. This was eventually confirmed on the following Tuesday afternoon, fully five days after our arrival in Oswestry, by which time I was beginning to wonder whether we would ever get to Shrewsbury at all, when a beaming Lieutenant Saltonstall presented himself at Davies's smithy to inform us that our presence was requested by Colonel Mytton in order to brief us on the details of our passage to Shrewsbury and how our cover would be maintained once we got there.

We had seen little of Saltonstall since our arrival, a fact which suited us fine, especially Alexander, who held the lieutenant for an arrogant brat, the worst kind of inexperienced young officer, whose attitude, borne of privilege, was liable to get him and those around him into trouble. As if to confirm my friend's thoughts, we quickly learned from Skinner that, since our arrival in Oswestry, the lieutenant had used his influence as a relative of Sir Thomas Myddelton to secure the very best in accommodation and had spent the previous five days gallivanting around the town's taverns with a small group of young officers of a similar age and background.

"I thought two years of war had straightened out most of his type," mused Alexander one evening. "They are now mostly either battle-hardened junior officers or dead. It seems I was wrong."

I had smiled sympathetically at my friend's views, but, if the truth be told, I was not so sure myself, for behind Saltonstall's pretentious exterior, I thought I detected a steely-eyed determination, which would stand us in good stead, should times ever get difficult. I resolved, therefore, to reserve my judgement, until I could assess the young lieutenant more objectively.

Saltonstall, Alexander, and I were received by Mytton in a reception room belonging to an inn in the square below the castle walls. The colonel, who enjoyed a reputation as a shrewd and efficient officer, was a slightly built man with delicate features. He sported a pencil-thin moustache, but the rest of his face was clean-shaven, save for a similarly narrow vertical line of beard on his chin. His oddest feature, though, was his hair, which was flat on top, including a fringe, which hid half of his forehead. Below his ears his locks cascaded into a jumble of curls, which made him look as though his hair had been flattened by the wearing of his hat. He bade all three of us take a seat and gestured towards Lieutenant Saltonstall.

"I understand you have already made the acquaintance of my brother-in-law's great-nephew," he began. "You will be glad to hear that he has devised an excellent cover story to explain your presence in Shrewsbury."

Alexander cast a startled look in my direction. Saltonstall said nothing, but the smug half-smile on his face filled me with apprehension. I had not been aware of a family connection between Mytton and Myddelton, but it certainly explained the ease with which the lieutenant was able to get Mytton's ear.

"My wife and Sir Thomas's wife are sisters," he explained, as though reading my thoughts. "I have never made Lieutenant Saltonstall's acquaintance before, but it is gratifying to see he is making such progress."

Mytton and Saltonstall were too busy looking at each other to catch Alexander rolling his eyes, which was just as well, I thought.

"I will be pleased to hear the lieutenant's plan, sir," I said, trying my utmost not to reveal my reservations.

"It is quite simple," said Mytton. "We have created passes for you as guests of Richard Halton, a Shrewsbury merchant of some standing. His main business is in silks, wines and spices, which he imports via Bristol, but he also buys some tobacco from the New World, which comes into Chester and Liverpool. Halton is a Parliamentarian by nature, but he has been careful to conceal his sympathies, which has allowed him to continue to trade in Shrewsbury more or less unhindered.

"Halton has relatives in Ruthin, not far from Sir Thomas Myddelton's seat at Chirk, who are also involved in the import and export trade. You are therefore to pose as representatives of this branch of his family. Lieutenant Saltonstall is to pose as Percival Halton. He is real enough – a cousin of our Shrewsbury merchant, but he still resides in Ruthin. He is a sickly youth, perhaps two years younger than Lieutenant Saltonstall, and has not often been seen outside his own environs. As such, the lieutenant is unlikely to be identified as an impostor. You, Master Cheswis, will be the family's clerk and bookkeeper, whilst Mr Clowes will be the lieutenant's personal assistant.

Alexander scowled at Saltonstall, but addressed Mytton. "Excuse my ignorance, Colonel," he said, "but if Lieutenant Saltonstall has dreamed up this plan over the last two days, how is Richard Halton to be made aware of our arrival?"

"A good question, Mr Clowes," acknowledged Mytton. "A fast rider was despatched to Shrewsbury first thing this morning. In all probability Halton is being briefed as we speak."

I gave Mytton a reluctant nod of approval. I was not sure what operating under the young lieutenant's command was likely to bring, but I could not deny the plan was well thought out.

"What happens when we arrive in Shrewsbury?" I asked.

"Your first job will be to make contact with our agent, Townsend, who frequents an inn called The Sacristy, which is attached to St Chad's Church. We will give you the necessary code words before you leave."

"And Lieutenant Saltonstall will accompany us on this task also?"

"A young man like him will only attract attention, if only that of the local cutpurses, so no, this will be a task for Mr Clowes and yourself. Saltonstall will remain at Halton's until a more discreet meeting can be arranged."

"And Halton's role in this?"

"He has none," emphasised Mytton, "other than that of being your host. And so it must remain, particularly when viewed from the outside. It is imperative that if your cover is compromised, not a shred of suspicion fall on the shoulders of Richard Halton."

Chapter 6

And so it was decided. Half an hour later, fully equipped with all the necessary passes and information, I left Alexander to drown his sorrows in a tavern and made my way back towards our quarters near the Cross, not sure whether our new alter-egos of Humphrey Jakes, bookkeeper, and William Black, servant, would give us the protection we needed or whether they would help launch both us and Lieutenant Saltonstall into a whole new circle of danger that did not bear imagining.

Indeed, as if to mirror my concerns, as soon as I came within sight of the Davies's smithy, something happened that was to change the entire course of our mission to Shrewsbury.

It was a busy day in Oswestry, and the area around the Cross was teeming with townsfolk going about their daily business. Suddenly, from amongst the crowd, I caught sight of James Skinner weaving his way quickly towards me through the throng. When he reached me, I could see that the lad was in a considerable state of agitation.

"You must come quickly," he said, without waiting for me to ask what was troubling him. "Mr and Mrs Davies have received a letter, which has vexed them both most grievously. I have told them their problem is something you might be able to help them with, so they sent me to find you."

I put my hand on Skinner's shoulder to try and calm him somewhat. "Slow down a moment, James," I said. "I cannot imagine what manner of letter would require my input, but let us take a slow stroll back, perhaps via a side lane or two, and you can explain the nature of things."

Once Skinner had regained his composure, he was able to tell me a tale of sadness and horror that explained both Evan Davies's haunted demeanour and why the family had no difficulty offering billets to the three of us, despite the family's relatively modest accommodation. It appeared that Evan and Hester Davies's eldest daughter, Millie, had been raped and murdered earlier in the year, in the most heinous manner imaginable, by a group of Royalist soldiers.

"There were six of them," explained Skinner, "most of whom attacked her in the smithy late at night after she had returned from work. It was the father who found the body. It is small wonder that he is in such a state."

"God's Blood!" I exclaimed. "That is more than enough for any man to bear, but I don't understand. What does a letter have to do with this?"

"The letter," said Skinner with a grimace, "purports to be from Millie's younger brother, Ellis, who disappeared the night Millie died. Ellis, I am told, can be a quiet soul when the mood takes him, often preferring his own company to that of others, but he doted on Millie. He had apparently taken the habit of retiring to the smithy on his own in the evening – Lord knows what for. But it was assumed that he was there when Millie was attacked, witnessed the killing, and was then discovered, killed and dumped in a ditch somewhere, but no corpse has ever been discovered."

"Of course not. Why would the murderers kill the boy and go to the trouble of removing his body when they left Millie lying dead on the floor of the smithy? Easier to leave them both there."

Skinner shrugged. "I suppose so," he said. "I had not thought of that. Anyway, today a letter has arrived from Ellis, who says he is in Shrewsbury, is close to identifying the killers of his sister, and will return to Oswestry once he has assured his own revenge and that of his family."

"Assuming someone doesn't string him up first," I said. "But tell me, you came looking for me. What role am I expected to play in this?"

Skinner wrapped his arms around his body and looked away furtively. "I might have mentioned to the Davies that you were about to travel to Shrewsbury and that they might want to ask you to seek out Ellis in order to persuade him to return home before he does something that might be considered foolhardy."

"You did what?" I hissed. "What on earth did you do that for? They are not supposed to know about our movements." I then caught the imploring look in his eyes and sighed. "Oh, I see, this is about the girl, isn't it? You want to impress her?"

Skinner reddened and smiled sheepishly. "There may be something in that," he admitted. "I might also have let slip to Lizzie something about your reputation for solving mysteries of this kind. If Ellis truly wishes to identify Millie's murderers, perhaps you can be instrumental in helping him to bring them to justice."

I looked aghast at Skinner. "However do you know about that?" I demanded. "You have not seen me since January, other than for a few seconds in a room in Bolton."

"I would have thought that was obvious. Your brother Simon related to me how you solved the murders carried out in January in Nantwich, as well as the story of your activities at Lathom House. Your most recent exploits at Combermere have been described to me by Master Clowes since we have been here."

I removed my wide brimmed hat and brushed my hair back with my fingers as I considered Skinner's words. I had not deliberately tried to forge a reputation for myself as someone who might solve crimes such as this. Indeed, I had actively tried to avoid it. Somehow, though, the crimes seemed to have developed a habit of finding me. In all honesty, I had to admit that the story related by Skinner intrigued me, but my instinct told me that becoming involved in an investigation in a Royalist-controlled town where I had no influence and where I was supposed to be engaged in a covert operation on behalf of Parliament was a disaster waiting to happen. I made one last effort to avoid the inevitable.

"James," I said, "you have to know I cannot carry out such an investigation in Shrewsbury. Firstly, I have no authority there, and secondly, there are people in the town who would recognise me – Alice Furnival for one and Sir Fulke Hunckes for another. Jem Bressy is probably also there. If any of those people realise I am out and about in Shrewsbury, I am liable to be arrested – and Alexander too."

Skinner looked downcast at my response, but he was not giving up. "Perhaps it may not come to that," he said. "It may be just a case of persuading Ellis to come home.

Please, Master Cheswis, all I ask is that you step inside and listen to what Mr and Mrs Davies have to say. See, we are almost there."

Skinner and I had just emerged from a side lane opposite the Davies's front door, and my erstwhile apprentice gestured meaningfully towards the entrance. I exhaled deeply and thought about it for a moment. How could I possibly say no to Skinner? After all, I owed the lad a debt of gratitude for saving my life on two occasions. I looked reluctantly at the front door of the smithy, groaned inwardly, and succumbed to Skinner's wishes.

The whole of the Davies family, or what remained of it, were sat together at the table in their modest living quarters. Lizzie looked expectantly at us as we walked in through the door, and I noticed Skinner give her the briefest of nods. Evan Davies looked as though he had seen a ghost and did not move, but Hester was more animated and rose immediately to her feet.

"Master Cheswis," she gushed, "we are so grateful to you for agreeing to help us locate our son. We thought he was dead. We have no idea how we are going to repay you."

I glanced over at Skinner, who looked even more sheepish than before, but there was nothing to be gained by embarrassing him in front of the Davies family, so I decided to play along with his game, at least for the time being.

"James has told me the story of the loss of your daughter," I began. "First, I must offer my condolences. Even in these times of violence and betrayal, I cannot begin to imagine how traumatic that must have been for you."

Hester Davies acknowledged my expression of sympathy with a grateful smile, but said nothing more other than to bid me take a seat, so I pulled up a chair and quickly got to the nub of the matter.

"Mr and Mrs Davies, I may or may not be able to help you in the matter of your son. I cannot promise anything, but perhaps I had better take a look at the letter you received today."

Evan Davies reached inside his shirt and pulled out a piece of paper, which he unfolded and laid out flat on the table. I studied the letter closely, which was written in an untidy scrawl and filled with spelling mistakes.

> *Deer Father, Mother*
>
> *I am safe inn Shrowsbury. Do not wory about me. I saw what happend to Millie and new I must needs flee. I have fownd the men who kild Millie and have sworn to avenge her deth. Please God I will succeed.*
>
> *Pray for me and send my love to Lizzie*
>
> *Yor son*
>
> *Ellis*

I folded up the letter and handed it back to Davies. "This is your son's hand?" I asked.

"I cannot say for sure. I have never been taught my letters and therefore take no notice of such things, but my wife swears the letter is genuine."

"My father was a school teacher," explained Hester. "He taught me to read, and I taught Ellis accordingly. He has still progress to make, but for a blacksmith's son to know his letters, that is not so usual."

"That is true," I acknowledged, "and it has certainly come in useful here."

"Indeed. We have God to thank for the fact that he is still alive. We thought we had lost him."

I smiled sympathetically and contemplated the family as they waited expectantly for me to speak. The expressions of surprise and hope in their faces were plain to see, but it was clear that confusion was the overriding emotion. I suddenly became acutely aware of the degree to which the family were expecting that I would be able to track down their son, and wondered what manner of exaggerated story Skinner had told of me.

"Mistress Davies, pray tell Master Cheswis what you know of what happened on the night Millie was murdered," prompted Skinner, taking the words out of my mouth.

"Millie worked at The Bell Inn, which stands near the church, just outside the town walls," said Hester. "Jack Morgan, the landlord, said there was an unpleasant incident the night Millie was killed."

"An incident? What kind of incident?"

Hester glanced at her husband and wrung her hands in anguish. "The Bell Inn attracts an unruly sort on the best of nights, but on this particular occasion there was a group of soldiers, who were particularly the worse for drink. There were six of them, so I'm told. One of them thought it would be all right if he put his hands up Millie's skirts, so she hit him with a tankard."

"She was a feisty one, our Millie," cut in Evan Davies with a rueful smile. "Wouldn't take no shit from bastards like that, begging your pardon. That's why she was good at her job."

"So what happened next?" I asked.

"All hell broke loose. Millie had to be rescued and hidden away until order was restored, and the soldiers were kicked out. Jack Morgan says he has not seen them since."

"And did anyone recognise them?"

"If they did, nobody was saying anything. Colonel Lloyd, the Royalist officer in charge, said there was nothing to investigate, that it was nothing more than a tavern brawl and refused to take the matter further. The bastards closed ranks. There was nothing more we could do."

I nodded, unsurprised. Prince Rupert's forces did not have the best of reputations for the way in which they treated the local populace. Such a story was commonplace, and, unfortunately, both Evan and Hester Davies knew it.

"I presume the landlord managed to get a suitable description, though?" I asked.

"Oh aye," said Davies. "Jack said the leader of the group was a sergeant – a big muscular fellow. There were two foreigners also – both Dutchmen, he thought, and a young lad, who had something wrong with his arm."

"And how can you be sure it was these men who committed the crime?"

"Because several passers-by reported seeing six men loitering outside here that same night. A couple of people also saw Ellis running like the wind down the street and through a gap between the houses. He was being pursued at speed by an adult. That's how we know Ellis was in the smithy when Millie was murdered."

"You know what they did to her, don't you?" breathed Hester, her voice shaking with emotion. "They raped her on the floor of the smithy and then killed her by dropping the anvil on her face. She was such a beautiful girl, but when we found her, we could only recognise her by the clothes she was wearing."

Davies got out of his seat and put his arms around his wife to comfort her. I could see Skinner aching to do the same to Lizzie, who had been sat the whole time white-faced in silence, but convention dictated he refrain from doing so. Instead he turned to face Evan Davies.

"But you *do* know the name of the sergeant, don't you?" he prompted. I glanced in surprise at Davies and then recalled that Skinner had told me that '*most*' of the perpetrators remained unidentified.

"Hipkiss," said Davies, through clenched teeth. "That was his name. Jack Hipkiss. But unfortunately, the man died in the battle at Whittington on the second of July before he could be brought to justice, and with that disappeared the chance of identifying the rest of them too."

"I see," I said. "Perhaps you'd better explain how you know this."

Davies sat down again and took a mouthful from the jug of ale on the table in front of him.

"Hipkiss has a younger brother," said the blacksmith, "Charlie Hipkiss, an honest and godly man by all accounts, and also a sergeant in the force led by Colonel Marrow that was defeated at Whittington. Charlie came to us a couple of days before the battle to say he had been approached by several townsfolk, who thought they had recognised him as the man who had accosted Millie on the night she died. It was not him, of course, they simply bore a passing resemblance to one another, but Charlie had put two and two together and had approached his brother, who had admitted that he was guilty of assaulting Millie in the tavern, although, of course, he denied murdering her.

"Charlie told us he had tried to persuade Jack to turn himself in and defend himself against the murder charge, but he refused. We would have had the man arrested and forced to reveal the identity of his accomplices, but two days later he was dead. We have no idea who the other five men were, or indeed whether they remained in Oswestry until the town was taken by Parliament. Now it seems they may well have found their way back to Shrewsbury."

"So it seems," I agreed, "but tell me, how do you consider I might be of help in this matter?" At this juncture, I noticed Skinner starting to look somewhat uncomfortable, and I wondered what was causing him to become so discomfited. Everything was soon to become clear.

"We ask one thing, Master Cheswis," said Hester Davies. "A favour, nothing more. We wish for you to locate Ellis and persuade him to stop this folly of seeking revenge. We have already lost a daughter. We do not want to lose our son as well. Jack Hipkiss is dead, and little more is to be done about it. Persuade him to come home, we beg of you."

"I would be happy to do that," I said, "but I don't know your son, and I have no way of recognising him."

"Of course not," countered Hester, "but Ellis says he has identified the men who murdered Millie. There is but one other person who might have some kind of idea as to who these people might be."

"Hipkiss's brother."

"Precisely, and if he has also returned to Shrewsbury, then you might be able to track him down."

"And how would I do that?"

Skinner coughed to attract my attention, and I began to feel a deepening sense of foreboding.

"Forgive me, Master Cheswis," said Skinner, "but there is something which I have learned from Mistress Davies, which might help you be successful in that enterprise. It seems that when Charlie Hipkiss came here, he revealed not only that he was a Shrewsbury man, but also the nature of his trade."

I looked in puzzlement, first at Hester and then back at Skinner. "And what trade was that, James?" I asked.

Skinner offered me a nervous smile and then delivered the hammer blow which confirmed that it was my destiny to seek out the killer of Millie Davies. "Charlie Hipkiss was employed in a printer's workshop," he said, "and to my knowledge, Shrewsbury has but one of those."

Chapter 7

*T*homas Bushell inspected the contents of the wooden chest displayed on the table in the drawing room of Alice Furnival's spacious Shrewsbury town house and nodded his appreciation.

"A fine collection of silverware," he said. "Of that there is no doubt. Coin, tableware, decorative plate – it's all there. It would be a shame to melt it down." Picking out a goblet from the chest, he examined the fleur de lys emblem engraved on the side and looked quizzically at the other three occupants of the room. "Also, very unusual," he added. "At least two hundred years old. Looks like it might have once belonged to a monastery. Where did you get it, if you don't mind me asking?"

Sir Fulke Hunckes, until recently the governor of Shrewsbury, cast a quick glance at his host and pursed his lips. Alice Furnival, for her part, merely ran her fingers through her blonde curls and smiled nervously, but it was the third person, the athletically built man with jet black hair called Bressy, who spoke.

"That, Mr Bushell, is of no consequence to you. Suffice it to say that these valuables were recovered by fair and legitimate means – they are not stolen – and they are to be put to the best use in the name of his Majesty King Charles." Bressy articulated himself clearly and politely, but his voice was edged with steel, and it occurred to Bushell that this enigmatic stranger, introduced to him by Hunckes and Furnival, both respected residents of Shrewsbury and unquestioned supporters of the King, was not likely to be a man who would take being crossed lightly. Nonetheless, he put the goblet back in the chest and gave Bressy a thin smile.

"That may be the case, Mr Bressy," he said, unable to keep the irritation from his voice, "but I'm afraid I have to tell you I am unable to take the contents of this chest into my possession."

Hunckes, a broad-shouldered man in his forties with a well-groomed, greying beard and the beginnings of a paunch, looked sharply at Bushell. "That is not what you said when Mistress Furnival and I broached the existence of this treasure," he began. "You told us you needed silver to turn into coin to pay the troops."

"Silver, yes, but I told you that two months ago. Times change."

Hunckes gave Bushell a look of disbelief and brought his fist down hard onto the table, causing the contents of the chest to rattle slightly. "Times change?" he growled. "What the devil is that supposed to mean? We risk our lives to bring you this treasure only for you to tell us that you won't accept it. Pray tell us why this is so."

"Not won't – can't," said Bushell, evenly, the hint of a smile touching the corner of his lips, "and I would request that you retain a modicum of civility, if you wouldn't mind. It is not my fault."

Hunckes glared and leaned across the table until his face was level with Bushell's. "No? Then whose is it?" he demanded.

Alice stepped forward and placed her hand on Hunckes's arm. "I think Sir Fulke would merely like to know what has changed, and what we are supposed to do with all this silver," she said, smiling at Bushell.

"*Then let me explain,*" *said Bushell, straightening his doublet as though Hunckes had grabbed him by the collar. "Firstly, the mint has thus far only been able to process silver. This chest contains plenty of silver, that is true, but there is also gold and gemstones as well as some plate, so, with the best will in the world, we would not have been able to use everything. Some of it would need to have been sold elsewhere.*

"*Secondly, Sir Fulke, you are no longer governor of Shrewsbury, so I must take my instructions from other sources. More to the point, though, I have received orders from the King that the mint must be relocated with immediate effect. He wishes that we re-establish the mint in Bristol, so we are now busy dismantling the moulds, with a view to sailing them down the Severn at the earliest possible opportunity.*"

"*But why would he do that?*"

Bushell shrugged. "I cannot say. I am no politician, nor am I a military strategist. Perhaps he feels Shrewsbury is not so strong for the King as you might like to think, or perhaps he feels the mint is vulnerable to attack by Parliament and wishes to remove it out of harm's way. Who knows? All I can say is that it is not the first time I have been ordered to move production to a more convenient location. You will be aware, I'm sure, that the mint has only been located in Shrewsbury since the start of the war. Before that it was in Aberystwyth on the Welsh coast. Safely in the King's territory, but too far from where it was needed."

"*That much is true,*" *conceded Hunckes, stepping back from Bushell and stroking his beard thoughtfully. "So what do you propose we do?*"

"*I will be happy to take the silver once the mint has been re-established in Bristol,*" *said Bushell, "but that might take a couple of months. In the meantime, I would suggest that Mr*

Bressy, who does not strike me as a man short on initiative, finds an alternative repository for your haul until such a time as I am ready."

"Oh, marvellous," said Bressy, his voice heavy with sarcasm. "And where do you suppose I will find such a place?"

Hunckes and Alice glanced at each other and exchanged brief nods of agreement.

"I think I know such a place," said Alice. "We have suspected all along that we might have to pay Lord Herbert for his support. If we move quickly, we can get the treasure to Montgomery Castle where it should be safe in the interim. Once the mint has been moved to Bristol we can pay Herbert with the gold and other valuables for his support in garrisoning Montgomery for the King, and we can transfer the silver to Bristol for processing into coin."

Bressy looked at Alice and nodded slowly before snapping shut the lid to the chest and locking it securely. He then addressed Hunckes and Bushell.

"Mistress Furnival is right," he said. "If you can help me with this chest, I will be on my way. I have but one choice. Today, gentlemen, I must needs ride for Montgomery."

Chapter 8

Our last night spent under the Davies family's roof was not one which I recall with a great deal of pleasure. When I was not being kept awake by Alexander snoring like a hog, I tossed and turned, wondering which part of God's plan for me dictated that I be continuously thrust into the path of Alice Furnival. That I might at some time run into my former betrothed during the pursuit of Jem Bressy and the treasure he had dug out of Nantwich's Ridley Field was an occupational hazard I was prepared to accept, but the fact that I had effectively promised to seek out and interview one of Alice's employees in connection with yet another murder case, my involvement with which I had not wished for, made me ever more convinced that my fate was somehow inextricably intertwined with that of my first love.

My mood therefore, heavily affected by lack of sleep, was somewhat on the grumpy side when Alexander and I presented ourselves at dawn, with our horses, at Colonel Mytton's quarters, ready for our ride to Shrewsbury. The sight which greeted us there did little to improve my state of mind, for Lieutenant Saltonstall had seen fit to dress himself up in an ostentatious costume consisting of a -bright red and black slashed doublet with matching breeches and a new wide-brimmed hat with a feather in it.

"Sweet Jesus!" exclaimed Alexander, ignoring Saltonstall's beaming smile. "I thought we were supposed to be inconspicuous while we were in Shrewsbury. Dressed like that you'll have the whole town wondering who you are."

"Just trying to look the part," said the lieutenant, defensively, his smile fading into an expression which made him look like he had been slapped across the face.

"But you look like a bloody popinjay," said Alexander. "Just make sure you don't go into any tavern dressed like that, that's all I'm saying. You'll either get yourself robbed or arrested."

Saltonstall, clearly affronted, narrowed his eyes and glared at Alexander. "You don't like me much, do you, Clowes?" he said.

"Liking you has nothing to do with it," came the response, "but I do wish to increase my chances of getting out of Shrewsbury in one piece."

I sighed wearily and decided to intervene to put a stop to their bickering. "Don't take Alexander's comments to heart," I said. "He means well but could just use some lessons in civility." This earned me a sullen glare from my friend, but I ignored him. "There is some truth in what he says, though," I added, "perhaps if you were just to lose the feather–"

"I shall do no such thing. I am playing a member of a leading merchant family and shall portray myself in that image in a way I see fit. Now let us make haste. We must be on our way if we are to make Shrewsbury in good time."

If Saltonstall's mood had been soured by Alexander's comments, they were not improved when I pulled my horse to a halt no more than a hundred yards outside Oswestry's New Gate and hailed a balding, thick-set fellow, who was hauling barrels into the tavern on the left-hand side of the street. Above the doorway, suspended from a pole, hung the sign of a bell.

"Jack Morgan," I shouted.

"What's it to you?" replied the man, without turning around.

I was not expecting such a degree of brusqueness, but I persevered nonetheless. "My name is Cheswis, and I have been a guest of Evan and Hester Davies these past days. Yesterday they received word from their son in Shrewsbury."

This was enough to make the man turn around abruptly and eye me with a mixture of suspicion and incredulity.

"You mean Ellis? He disappeared the night poor Millie was killed, and was presumed dead. Are you telling me he is still alive?"

"I am indeed. Or at least that is how it seems. We are travelling to Shrewsbury ourselves today and have been asked to seek him out and bring him home. I would talk a while with you, if I may."

It was only part of the story, but it was enough to make the landlord scratch his head in wonderment and invite us inside.

"You can't go in there," protested Saltonstall. "We have no time for idle chatter with innkeepers."

"We have ample time," riposted Alexander. "If you can't stomach waiting for us, then you are welcome to ride on, and we will catch up with you later, although I would not fancy your chances of avoiding the local cutpurses dressed like that."

If there was one thing about Saltonstall, it was that he knew when he was defeated. Grumbling loudly, he dismounted and tied his horse to a post outside the tavern before sulkily following us inside.

The interior of the tavern was dimly lit and reeked heavily of tobacco and stale beer. At the far end of the bar, a servant girl was sweeping the floor with a stiff brush, but she scuttled away into the kitchen when she saw us enter. Morgan gestured towards a table near to the bar and poured out four mugs of ale, before sitting down beside us.

"Millie was a good girl," he began. "She was conscientious in her work and knew how to handle the customers. Our family was devastated when she was so cruelly murdered, but can it be true? Ellis is really alive?"

"I cannot be sure," I admitted, "but it would help if I could ask you a few questions about the night Millie died."

Morgan's eyebrows immediately narrowed at this request, so I gave the innkeeper a brief explanation of the content of the letter written by Ellis, including the fact that the boy claimed to have worked out the identities of his sister's killers, as well as our total ignorance of exactly where in Shrewsbury Ellis was to be found.

"So, you see," I said, "any information you can give me about what happened here that night might help me in our quest to locate him before he puts himself in any danger."

Morgan took a long draft of beer and wiped his sleeve across his mouth as he considered my words. "Very well," he said, at length. "They were sat at the table over there." He gestured towards a round table in a dimly lit corner of the room. "A bunch of loud-mouthed braggarts they were. All spoke with Shrewsbury accents except for two foreigners, both Dutchmen, I think – one about thirty and the other a younger and slimmer man, perhaps in his early twenties, who they called Corni."

"Corni?"

"Probably short for Cornelis, if he was a Dutchman," offered Saltonstall, who had now begun to show an interest in the proceedings. I shot the lieutenant a look, but he merely smiled back in the superior manner, which, I was beginning to realise, was his wont.

"Pray continue, Mr Morgan," I said.

"The leader of the group, a burly domineering fellow, was sat on the left as I viewed them, facing the bar so that his sword hand was free," explained Morgan.

"This was the sergeant who died at Whittington, I presume?"

"Jack Hipkiss, yes, although I only found out his name later."

"And who else was there?" I prompted.

"Next to Hipkiss was a short, stocky man in his forties with dark hair. Hipkiss called him Ben, if I recall, and seemed particularly friendly with him. Then came the two Dutchmen, then a fifth man, who I can't remember anything about, and finally a young chap, who had something wrong with his arm, as though it was shrivelled or something. He was different to the rest and seemed oddly discomfited by the whole thing."

"You have a good memory, Mr Morgan," I said, impressed with the detail of the landlord's descriptions.

Morgan smiled in acknowledgement. "It pays to notice things," he said. "In my trade, that is a necessity, I would say."

"Just so," I concurred. "So, what happened to start the disturbance?"

"I think you must know this already," said Morgan, "but no matter. I will tell the tale again. I was stood behind the bar when the sergeant called for more ale, so I sent Millie over with new tankards. As she put them down on the table the sergeant saw fit to stick his hand up her skirts, so Millie picked up one of the tankards and hit him across the jaw with it, showering him and his friends with beer and nearly knocking him from his stool.

"I rushed around the bar, but my sons, Dai and Will, were quicker. Dai took a punch to the face himself, but they managed to grab hold of the sergeant and propel him through the door and into the street before he could do anything. Meanwhile, I ushered Millie out of the way, and she hid behind the bar. The sergeant's friends made some noise and some threats, especially the Dutchmen, but after a few minutes cursing they left too. That's the last I saw of them."

"You never saw them again, not even in town?"

"No, they were not stupid. They kept themselves well away from here. Probably frequented another tavern from that day forward, or maybe even fled the town. Can't say I was sorry."

"What about the sergeant's brother?"

"Charlie Hipkiss? Yes, I saw him once. He walked past here a couple of days before Oswestry fell. I mistook him for the sergeant, so I accosted him and threatened to call the constable. Turns out several other townsfolk took him for the sergeant too, but it all counted for nothing. A couple of days later the Royalists had all been chased from the town, and less than two weeks later Jack Hipkiss was dead, cut down on the battlefield at Whittington."

At this point Saltonstall leaned forward and smiled enigmatically at Morgan. "That is most interesting, landlord," he said, "but if the malignants were chased out of Oswestry two weeks before the battle, and the engagement took place two miles outside of Oswestry, how can anyone be certain that Hipkiss actually died on that day? Indeed, how can it be that this is known at all?"

Alexander opened his mouth to say something, but I laid my hand on his arm to silence him. I had to admit that Saltonstall had a point, so I turned my attention once more to Morgan.

"You know how it is after a battle," said the innkeeper with a wry smile. "All manner of scavengers crawl out of the woodwork. When it became known that Marrow had been defeated, many folk came out from the town to loot the bodies of the dead. Some of these people – I will not give their names – reported seeing Hipkiss's corpse lying stripped and naked on the battlefield. Knowing it to be the body of a murderer, they bore it back to Oswestry where it was identified by Hipkiss's brother."

"Charlie Hipkiss? I thought he also served under Marrow. What was he doing in Oswestry?"

"He was wounded and captured when the siege was broken by Colonel Mytton, but on hearing that he had tried to get his brother to turn himself in to face justice, Mytton freed him on the grounds that he did not take up arms against Parliament again. He went back to Shrewsbury, I believe."

◌

As we left The Bell I had the strange feeling that Morgan had told me something significant, but I could not work out what it was. Perhaps it was merely the fact that the innkeeper had given me the names of two of Hipkiss's accomplices – Ben and Corni – although I had no idea how I was supposed to use that information. Whatever it was, it weighed on my mind for much of the journey to Shrewsbury.

Fortunately, neither Alexander nor Saltonstall seemed particularly disposed to idle chatter, and so I was left to my thoughts, whilst the lieutenant concentrated on making sure our mounts were pushed forward with expediency, at a speed guaranteed to recover the time lost talking to Jack Morgan. As a result, the sun was still relatively high in the sky when the striking red sandstone edifice of Shrewsbury Castle appeared on the horizon.

We entered the town from the north, through the narrow strip of land between two bends of the River Severn that connected Shrewsbury with the rest of Shropshire. We rode along a street of shops and houses set underneath the imposing bulk of the castle, which rose impressively to the left, whilst on the right, opposite the castle gates, stood the large stone building that housed Shrewsbury School. It was from here, I had been told, that the Furnivals operated their printing press.

Apart from a couple of strange glances given to Saltonstall by the armed guards on the gate, we had little difficulty getting into the town, for the paperwork provided by Colonel Mytton had been good. It was not long before we were drawing up outside Richard Halton's residence, an impressive half-timbered building located behind St Mary's church on the edge of the escarpment, which fell sharply down to the river bank. Halton himself, a plump, jovial man in his fifties with greying bushy whiskers that hung languidly over his clean-shaven chin, had been alerted to our arrival and was there at the gate to welcome us. He glanced furtively up and down the street as we approached, betraying a nervousness that was not lost on Alexander, who cast a worried glance in my direction.

Saltonstall, who affected not to have noticed Halton's demeanour, leapt from the saddle to shake our host by the hand in the manner of a long-lost friend, but Halton himself had not failed to realise that we had understood his discomfiture, and made a point of apologising to us.

"Forgive me, gentlemen," he said, "I am not used to such subterfuge."

I nodded sagely and ushered our host towards his front door. "Then let us retire to where we are less visible," I suggested, "so that we can put your mind at rest."

Halton nodded his acquiescence and summoned a young groom, who led our horses to stables located round the side of the house.

Saltonstall, eager to demonstrate his authority to anyone who might be watching, shouldered his way between myself and our host and laid his arm around Halton's shoulder, leading him into a long hallway. Once inside, Halton extricated himself from the young officer's display of false bonhomie and pointed towards a door at the end of a corridor. I could see Alexander was trying hard to stifle a grin, so I shot him a warning glance and gestured for him to follow our host into the hallway.

Halton led us through a well-lit and finely furnished reception room, which opened out at the back of the house onto a paved area. This, in turn, led to a lawn perhaps twenty yards long, bordered by fruit trees. A path weaved its way across the grass to a picket gate, behind which a jumble of vegetation obscured the line of the town walls and the steep bank which fell away towards the river.

Halton opened a set of doors and pointed towards a wooden table and chairs, which had been positioned at the edge of the paved area overlooking the garden.

"We can sit here a while," he said. "It is secluded enough, and it is a fine day after all."

I glanced doubtfully at the fences bordering Halton's garden, the other side of which lay gardens belonging to the adjoining properties.

"You must not worry about my neighbours," insisted Halton, reading my thoughts. "The house on one side is occupied by a young widow and her family, whilst the other is currently empty. We are safe enough from prying eyes here."

"Then let us talk awhile," I said, drawing out one of the chairs from under the wooden table, positioning it in the shade and facing the property to the north of Halton's home.

With the day beginning to draw towards early evening, the sun had disappeared behind the gable end of the house, plunging half of the paved area into shade, although the majority of the garden still basked in the late summer sunlight.

"Tell me, Mr Halton," interjected Saltonstall, in an attempt to take control of the conversation, "what is your understanding of our role here?"

Halton sat down on one of the chairs alongside me, prompting Alexander and Saltonstall to do the same.

"Lieutenant, the details of that are not my concern. The less I know about what you are doing in Shrewsbury, the less I will be able to betray to the governor should my position ever be compromised. All I have been told is that you are supposed to be my young cousin Percival, although I have to say you look very little like him, and that you have two companions, a clerk and bookkeeper called Jakes and a manservant called William Black. More than that I do not wish to know. All I ask is that you are discreet and that you do not stay longer than is necessary. I cannot afford to be revealed as a Parliamentarian sympathiser."

"I assure you we will cause you as little disturbance as possible," I cut in, earning myself a glare from Saltonstall, "but in the first instance I must needs locate a place they call The Sacristy. Perhaps you can help us."

"The Sacristy?" snorted Halton. "A veritable den of papists, Armenians and other assorted reprobates. A tavern these days, and so-called because it is attached to St Chad's Church, which means it is easy to find. Just follow the church spires. There are four churches within Shrewsbury's town walls, all within a stone's throw of each other. The nearest to here is St Mary's, then St Alkmund's, then St Julian's, and finally the oldest and largest of the churches, St Chad's, a fine church, albeit with a minister with rather too much of a penchant for the kind of idolatry associated with the Laudians for my liking. Why, may I ask, would you wish to visit a place such as The Sacristy?"

I had begun to realise that Halton was not a man in which to confide too many details of our purpose in Shrewsbury, lest he found himself in a position where he was forced to betray us. It was clear that he had been recruited by Mytton not because of any great aptitude for intelligence work, but because of his social status in Shrewsbury and his ability to provide suitable cover for people like Alexander, Saltonstall and myself. He obviously knew very little about the colonel's undercover operations in the town, and it was better that it remained that way.

"I am sure that Parliamentary command in Oswestry is indebted to you for looking after us whilst we are here in Shrewsbury," I said, "but it would truly be in everyone's best interest if you did not ask too many questions about who we are meeting here and why."

Halton gave me an apologetic smile, his face reddening slightly. "Of course," he said, "forgive me my curiosity, it was just–"

At that point our host's voice faltered, his attention distracted by something over my right shoulder. I glanced over at Alexander, whose face had frozen, and a sense of foreboding began to creep over me. I turned around slowly on my chair, and my heart sank, for on the other side of the fence, wearing a dark blue dress edged with lace, and a smile I could have sworn was tinged with amusement, was Alice Furnival.

"Good afternoon, Mr Halton," she said.

For a moment, I feared Halton was going to dry up completely, but after a couple of seconds he returned the greeting, albeit somewhat hesitantly and with the hint of a stammer. Fortunately, the situation was retrieved by Saltonstall, who stepped forward and introduced himself.

"Percival Halton of Ruthin," he announced, removing his hat and bowing, "and this is Mr Jakes, my bookkeeper, and Mr Black, my manservant."

"Mistress," said Alexander and I in unison.

Alice arched an eyebrow in my direction, but responded to Saltonstall. "My name is Alice Furnival," she said. "You must be Mr Halton's young cousin, if I'm not mistaken. And

I see from your attire and demeanour that you can be no other than a King's man, and that can be nothing but a good thing. Shrewsbury is a Royalist town, but there are still too many Roundheads here for my liking."

Alice's gaze shifted momentarily towards me, forcing me to shuffle my boots involuntarily.

"That is undoubtedly so, mistress," acknowledged Saltonstall, "but since Oswestry fell, this town must be full of young men eager to serve his Majesty's cause."

Alice smiled. "There are plenty of soldiers, that is true, and a fair number of young gentlemen like yourself, keen to show their loyalty to the Crown, but, as in every place in this country, treachery and treason lie not far below the surface. It always pays to keep your eyes open. But tell me," she probed, "if you bring your accountant with you, it cannot be the war that brings you to Shrewsbury."

"Business," I interjected, keen to assert some semblance of control over the conversation and only too aware that Saltonstall had absolutely no idea who Alice was. "Like his cousin, Mr Halton trades in exotic goods from the Orient and the New World. They have some trades to conclude, hence my presence also."

"But I hope to find time to enjoy some of the entertainment Shrewsbury has to offer, whilst I am here," added Saltonstall with a grin, overplaying the rakish young cavalier card a little more than was necessary, although Alice did not seem to notice.

"You are here long?" she asked.

"A few days perhaps."

"Then I wish you good business. I am sure we will meet again before you leave." Alice nodded at Halton and disappeared behind a wall, back into her own house. I realised with a start that her last words, whilst addressed to Saltonstall, had been meant for me.

"Perhaps we should continue this conversation later," I said, hurriedly, "and better it be inside your house, where we cannot be overheard. In the meantime, I would take a walk with Mr Black. We have some things we need to do."

"If you plan to visit The Sacristry, I would come too," said Saltonstall, adjusting the feather in his hat and placing it back on his head.

"No, you will not," I whispered, lowering my voice so that Alice would not be able to hear should she still be lurking behind the wall. "Mytton expressly ordered that you were not to accompany us there."

"Have you forgotten who is in charge here?" riposted the lieutenant. "And anyway, what harm can it do?"

I was about to respond to that in no uncertain terms when Alexander grabbed me by the arm. "Perhaps he is right, Daniel. At least if he's with us we can keep an eye on him."

I considered this for a moment, and I had to admit there was a modicum of sense in what my friend said. I sighed and strode back through the doors into Halton's reception room.

"Very well," I said, "but that hat stays here, and if I hear one word that threatens to compromise our cover, we will disown you. Is that clear?"

"Of course," sniffed Saltonstall. "I would expect nothing else. Now let us be about our business."

Chapter 9

I must confess I felt somewhat uncomfortable as we skirted round the back of St Mary's Church, towards the escarpment which fell away towards the River Severn, for we looked a somewhat incongruous threesome. Halton had loaned Saltonstall a less conspicuous hat, but he still looked every inch the young cavalier, whilst Alexander's discomfiture at wearing the attire of a manservant was plain to see. For my part, I was dressed in a sober black outfit in the Dutch style, which would normally have marked me out as a puritan, but it was one which I felt was in keeping with my role as a man used to handling the monetary affairs of a young merchant.

When we reached the main street, I could see the spire of St Alkmund's Church straight ahead and realised there were fewer than a hundred yards between the two places of worship, but instead of aiming for the church we turned north in front of St Mary's and headed towards the junction with Pride Hill.

As we did so I noticed that we were attracting curious stares from the throng of townsfolk going about their early evening business or returning home from their work. With a start, I realised the problem – we were walking too slowly and without obvious purpose. There was no reason for a young gentleman to take his manservant on a casual stroll, so I had a quiet word in Alexander's ear, and he fell back ten paces, in order to avoid the impression that we were together.

As we reached the junction with Pride Hill, Saltonstall pointed to a substantial stone building of two storeys on the opposite side of the road.

"Bennett's Hall," he said, matter-of-factly, "the site of the mint moved here from Aberystwyth. The mint itself is in the undercroft, but the rest of the building has been converted into individual workshops or workers' cottages."

I looked closer at the house and realised it had once been a very fine residence indeed. The outer red sandstone walls were dressed with lines of attractive white stone, but the areas around the windows were marked heavily with black, the result of fire damage when the hall had been destroyed years previously. There was no roof on the building. Instead you could see the timber and thatched roofs of the cottages and apartments that had been constructed inside the original walls. Looking from the north-west of the house, I could see that the front of the building was occupied by two large apartments covering the two storeys, whilst the rear was filled with a mixture of smaller units.

"A shame to see such a magnificent building brought so low," I said.

Saltonstall snorted. "Maybe. I was thinking more that the jumble of cottages built inside the shell make it easier to break into."

I nodded. "That may be so, but let us see what Mr Townsend has to say on the matter. It may not come to that."

From Bennett's Hall, we followed the road south for a few yards before turning left into a narrow lane lined with butchers' stalls, which eventually led into an open space in front of St Alkmund's churchyard. From here a series of lanes led away downhill in between half-timbered buildings with stone shingle roofs. I looked across the churchyard and realised that St Alkmund's was built on the highest point in the town.

As I took in the relative peace and quiet of the churchyard, I noticed the beginnings of a commotion by the door to the church, which had been flung open to reveal two figures, who staggered out of the dimly lit porch into the sunlight. The first was a youth of no more than twelve or thirteen, who, judging by the rags he was wearing, had been sleeping rough. He was being held by the collar by a middle-aged man wearing a cowl, who I took to be the minister of St Alkmund's. My first assumption was that the churchman had found the youth sleeping under the pews and was in the process of ejecting him into the streets. However, when I heard the terrified-looking youth pleading with his captor, I realised something was amiss.

"I did not do it, sir, I swear," whimpered the boy, who was wriggling to try and get free.

"You can explain that to the constable," replied the minister, in a tone which suggested something other than anger. I looked more closely at the man and realised he was white with shock.

Suddenly, the youth twisted his body around and aimed a kick at the minister's shins, causing him to howl with pain and topple over onto his back. The youth took the opportunity to break free from the minister's grip, and with surprising agility he vaulted the church wall, disappearing down a flight of steps into one of the dark alleys that led away from the church.

Saltonstall and I quickly ran over to the minister and helped him to his feet. The churchman rubbed his shin gingerly and smiled at us in gratitude.

"What on earth was that about, minister?" I asked. "A vagrant, perchance?"

"W-worse than that," stammered the minister. "The boy has committed the gravest of sins – murder, and in the Lord's house too."

"Murder?" I said. "What do you mean?"

The minister did not need to answer this question, for whilst I was talking to him, Saltonstall began to open both sides of the double doors to the church. As he did so, the lifeless body of a man fell backwards into the porch, the corpse's head hitting the stone floor with a sickening crack.

I leant over the body and put my hand to the man's neck, but there was no sign of a pulse.

"He's dead," I announced.

"I think that is fairly self-evident," muttered Saltonstall, with more than a hint of sarcasm.

I was about to say something, but then I caught sight of the pool of blood the man had been lying in. I ran my hand over his torso and saw that his dark coat had been punctured by a single wound just underneath his heart. I unbuttoned the coat and saw that the man's white shirt was saturated in blood.

"He was killed by the boy," announced the minister. "I found him here, leaning over the corpse. It could only have been him."

I looked at the churchman doubtfully. "Are you sure? This man has been run through with a sword. Did the boy have such a weapon when you came upon him?"

The minister shrugged. "I saw nothing," he conceded. "That much is true. I was alone in the vestry when I heard noises from within the church, as though there had been a scuffle. I came out to investigate and found the boy leaning over the body. What am I supposed to think? And why did he run if he is not guilty?"

"For the same reason as anyone looking like a vagrant would run if found alone with the body of a man stabbed through the heart. Who would believe that he had not intended to rob him?"

The minister did not answer, for he had noticed something about the victim. Bending forward, he put his hand towards the man's mouth, and then I saw it too – a small section of silver chain protruding from between the victim's lips. The minister took hold of the chain between his thumb and forefinger and pulled gently. Slowly, more chain appeared, until a small silver item fell out of the man's mouth onto the stone floor. The minister let out a gasp of horror.

"A crucifix!" he exclaimed. "It is sacrilege, no less. What manner of a crime do we have here?"

"I could not say," I admitted, equally shocked. "Who is this man, anyway?"

I looked closely at the body, but there was little clue as to his identity. The man had been slim and looked fit, in his mid-thirties with short, dark hair, and he had been wearing common workers' clothes. Beyond that, there was little distinguishable about him.

"His name is Jakob de Vries," said a familiar voice behind me.

I froze and looked up to see Alice Furnival standing among a small crowd, which had begun to gather outside the church, attracted no doubt by the commotion.

"A Dutchman, he was employed by a wheelwright on Pride Hill, but he also worked in my print shop from time to time, as and when demand allowed."

I looked around at the growing multitude of curious onlookers and cursed silently for having let myself be dragged into such a vulnerable situation. The last thing I needed was to be quizzed by the local authorities as a key witness in a murder trial.

"Come, Mr Jakes," said Alice, as if she were reading my mind, "the constable has arrived. Let him do his work."

I nodded dumbly and rose to my feet. I noticed Alexander had held himself back from the crowd and was gesturing to Saltonstall to join him.

"I will follow you presently, Mr Halton," I said. "I'm afraid I have some business to attend to." With this I extricated myself from the crowd and left the minister to the constable. Saltonstall eyed me curiously but obeyed me nonetheless and followed Alexander out of the churchyard.

Alice, meanwhile, attempted to draw me away around the side of the church, back in the direction of St Mary's, but I positioned myself on the periphery of the crowd and waited to see how the constable handled the situation.

At that point, there was a further commotion, and a young man with fair hair pushed his way through the crowds to where the corpse was lying, almost knocking the constable over in the process.

"Mijn god, Jakob, wie heft dit gedaan?" he exclaimed, clearly distraught.

I looked aside at Alice. "Another Dutchman?" I asked.

"Yes, his name is Cornelis Smits. He is a carpenter by trade. Much younger than Jakob, but he comes from the same town in Holland, so I hear. Jakob was like a brother to him."

Corni! Now I was beginning to understand. How many people of that name could there be in Shrewsbury? The young Dutchman must be one of the six men who had raped and murdered Millie Davies, which meant that the dead man must be the other Dutchman mentioned by Jack Morgan. But what of the young man caught kneeling over De Vries's body? Could that have been Ellis Davies? If so, I had to ask whether I had been wrong about the youth killing the Dutchman.

Perhaps I had failed, after all, in stopping Ellis exacting revenge on those who had killed his sister. However, if this were the case, what had happened to the murder weapon? Had there been an accomplice who had got away? I could have been wrong, but I had the impression that the boy was just as shocked as the minister at the violent murder. And what about the crucifix found in the victim's mouth? That was very odd. On reflection, I found it hardly likely that a young boy barely into his teens would think to carry out such a bizarre act. The act of placing a cross in the victim's mouth was almost like a religious ritual.

I was shaken from my thoughts by Alice, who grabbed me by the arm and led me away from the church and into a narrow alleyway next to a baker's shop.

"What are you doing?" she snapped. "You'll get yourself arrested."

"You seem to be showing a considerable interest in following me about," I countered. "Isn't that what you want?"

Alice's face tightened, and she slapped me hard across the cheek. "Of course not," she said, bristling with anger. "I know why you are here, but I would never wish for you to be arrested as a spy. You need to leave here now and get yourself back to Nantwich."

"You know I can't do that."

Alice puffed out her cheeks in frustration. "You are wasting your time here, Daniel. The treasure Bressy secured in Nantwich is already in a safe place far from here."

"And why would that be, Alice? I thought the plan was to have the silver melted down into coin in the mint."

Alice gave me a cold stare, but I could tell from her reaction that she had made a mistake. "Daniel," she said, "take my advice and get yourself out of Shrewsbury. I will not betray you, but I cannot guarantee the same for your bellman friend and the young dandy, whoever he is – and as for Mr Halton, he is an agreeable gentleman. I would not wish to see him suffer for housing a group of Roundhead spies. Think about it." She then gathered up her skirts and stomped off back towards the house.

⚬

It would not have been the most prudent of moves to have retraced my steps to St Alkmund's, so I followed Alice as far as St Mary's and then turned right down the street known as Dogpole until I reached the main thoroughfare that led down to the bridge across the Severn. From here I cut through a narrow passageway between half-timbered cottages and then up a hill, which seemed to be heading in the direction of the most distant of the church steeples that dominated the Shrewsbury skyline.

With relief, I eventually emerged into a square next to the impressive bulk of St Chad's Church. The Sacristy was marked out by the crowds of men drinking and smoking, which had spilled out onto the cobbles. The clientele, I noticed, was largely different from that of most taverns. There was, of course, a fair smattering of soldiers, both officers and otherwise. However, there was more than a fair share of well-dressed young men, amongst whom I realised Saltonstall, in his current attire, would not have looked wholly out of place. Perhaps, I mused, the lieutenant's decision to dress as a well-to-do young cavalier was not such a bad idea after all.

Weaving my way through the crowds, I noticed that Saltonstall was already in earnest conversation with a group of young men his own age, one of whom was brandishing a copy of *Mercurius Aulicus*, the Royalist newssheet. Alexander, meanwhile, was propping up the bar with a tankard of ale and observing the lieutenant warily at a respectful distance. He grimaced as I entered and beckoned me over.

"God's Blood, Daniel," he whispered. "Are you mad? What on earth do you think you are doing associating with that woman? You will get us all arrested."

I felt myself reddening and exhaled in exasperation. "What am I supposed to do Alexander? She appeared out of nowhere at Halton's and again at the church. I cannot very well ignore her, can I?"

"That is a matter for debate," replied my friend. "Because of this our cover story is now worthless. We will now be in considerable peril if we remain in Shrewsbury for a moment longer than is necessary."

"She says she will not betray us."

"And you believe that? She is a royalist spy. Daniel, listen to me, you do not think logically when you are in that woman's company. She is naught but a scheming witch and cannot be trusted."

"It seems there are many you do not trust, Alexander," I said, nodding in Saltonstall's direction, and immediately regretting my words.

Alexander stared at me with furrowed eyebrows, and I thought he was about to continue the argument, but he looked at me intently for a moment longer and then changed the subject.

"We will talk about this later," he said. "In the meantime, your man is at the other end of the bar," He indicated a thick set figure with thinning, straggly hair and a short, greying beard, who was perched on a bar stool nonchalantly eating a slice of mutton pie.

I looked nervously at Alexander. "How do you know that's him?" I asked.

"Because our bloody companion was foolish enough to march right up to the bar and ask the landlord, who told him that if he, a stranger, didn't know who Townsend was, then he as sure as hell was not going to identify him. Fortunately, I managed to stay far enough out of the way to make sure the landlord didn't realise that I came in here with him. I also noticed the glance the landlord gave to our man at the end of the bar. My guess is that is Townsend, so off you go. Make yourself known to him. I'll stay here and try and make sure our young friend stays out of trouble."

I gave a tight-lipped nod of assent to Alexander before buying a tankard of ale and moving closer to the man at the bar.

"Good evening, friend," I ventured, "you appear to be drinking on your own. May I join you?"

I was rewarded with an even stare and a single upturned eyebrow. "Well now, that depends. It's a free country, at least for the time being, and I'm as willing to share a pitcher of ale as the next man, but it pays to be wary of strangers in places such as this. What is your business in Shrewsbury, may I ask?"

"God's business," I replied, "and that of my brother, William."

A smile touched the corner of the man's lips as he recognised Brereton's field word. "Gideon Townsend," he said, taking my hand in a vice-like grip, which belied his otherwise easy-going demeanour.

I winced slightly as I extricated my hand. "Humphrey Jakes," I said, keeping my voice low so only Townsend could hear, "at least for the moment. Chief bookkeeper to Percival Halton."

"The young chap over there?" he said, nodding to where Saltonstall was conversing loudly with his new friends, the clunk of pewter upon pewter as tankards were raised drawing the attention of several tables nearby. "Not exactly inconspicuous, is he?"

"He is here by command of Colonel Mytton," I whispered in explanation. "His presence is not of my choice, I assure you."

Townsend smiled knowingly. "He'll get himself in trouble if he's not careful. At least your mate has the good sense to keep quiet."

I glanced over to Alexander, who was still propped across the bar, his head bowed over his tankard. "He will be loud enough if needed," I said, "but tell me, you have news for me of the mint?"

"Indeed I do, most of which is not for discussion here. The walls have ears. What I can tell you, though, is that everything has changed. The King has commanded Thomas Bushell to relocate the mint to Bristol, where he feels it will be more secure. Consequently, I will be spending much of the next two days helping to dismantle the equipment for shipment down the Severn."

I stared aghast at Townsend. "So that means—"

"Precisely. There are alternative plans, but let us not draw attention to ourselves. Finish your ale at your leisure. Then we can retire to the safety of my rooms, where we can talk about such matters in more privacy."

Townsend's suggestion was a good one, and there is little doubt that I would have taken him up on that offer, had it not been for the fact that at that very moment all decisions in that particular regard were taken out of my hands.

My first realisation that something was wrong was when a young man with long, brown curls and a blue doublet emerged out of my peripheral vision, strode over to where Saltonstall was standing, and clapped him heartily on the shoulder.

"Phillip? It can't be, can it? Phillip Saltonstall? I knew I recognised that voice from somewhere. What the devil are you doing in Shrewsbury?"

The lieutenant swung around in astonishment, and I saw a look of panic enter his eyes. "Edmund," he said, with enough hesitation to put his newly-made friends on their guard. "What a surprise."

"Indeed," said the new arrival, "and such a pleasure to see you here in Shrewsbury. And to think, I was told you had been fighting for the damned Roundheads –

one of Brereton's boys, I'd heard – just goes to show how misinformation can spread."

Saltonstall hesitated, just for a split-second, but it was enough to seal his fate.

"Wait a minute," interjected one of the young cavaliers with whom he had been drinking. "He said his name was Halton. Are you saying we have an impostor here?"

"Tush," said the young man with the blue doublet. "His name is Saltonstall. I've known him for years. We were at school together."

"And you say he's a crophead to boot? I'd say that means we have a spy in our midst."

The lieutenant's eyes flicked towards me in a desperate plea for help. "Now wait a minute," he began, but that was as far as he got.

At that moment Alexander hurtled across the room and dived headlong at the young man in blue, sending him sprawling across the table around which the young cavaliers were sat, whilst beer, food and tableware flew in all directions.

"Steal my purse, would you, you thieving bastard!" screamed Alexander, placing his left forearm across the young man's throat whilst reaching inside his doublet and extracting a small pouch of coins.

"What are you talking about?" gurgled the young man, spraying spittle over Alexander's arm. "That is my purse! Are you so in your cups as you cannot tell what is yours and what is not?"

Saltonstall, meanwhile, who had promptly recognised Alexander's action for what it was, tried desperately to make a bid for the door, but got his legs tangled up in one of the chairs that had been deposited on the tap room floor and was promptly jumped on by two of the cavaliers. I gaped in horror at the chaos that had ensued around me, but was brought to my senses by a hand holding me firmly by the wrist.

"Quick, come with me," urged Townsend, "while you still can."

I needed no second bidding. As inconspicuously as I could, I followed Townsend around the back of the bar, through a side door into a storeroom, which in turn led into a passageway outside the tavern. As I emerged onto the street in front of the church, I could still hear Alexander's shouts from inside the taproom and momentarily thought about turning back to help.

"Don't even think about it," hissed Townsend, pushing me into a doorway, where we would not be seen. "Your friend can look after himself." And then, as if to prove a point, Alexander suddenly burst through the front door of the tavern pursued by two of the cavaliers, who staggered to a halt when they saw my friend neatly vault the wall into the churchyard and disappear among the gravestones.

"Leave him," panted one of them. "He'll not get far. We have the other one, after all."

◌

Gideon Townsend lived in a modest worker's cottage on the road called Mardol, which was the main route out towards the Welsh Bridge, the village of Frankwell and, beyond that, Wales itself. For my purposes, the location was advantageous, for not only was it the opposite end of town to Halton's house, but it was also accessible from an overgrown track that ran behind the houses and through a jumble of vegetable patches, pigsties and ramshackle workshops, which meant that it could be approached relatively easily without us running the risk of being seen. We were welcomed by a homely woman in her forties with mousey brown curls, who introduced herself as Faith.

"It's not as you think," said Townsend, once I was settled. "Faith is actually my sister, but folk hereabouts think we are man and wife. We prefer it that way. A married couple attracts less attention than a middle-aged bachelor and his sister living under the same roof."

I looked at Faith Townsend again, and this time I saw the family resemblance, something about the eyes and the bridge of the nose, but it would not have been immediately apparent to someone who did not know.

"We have been in Shrewsbury since the start of the war, when I secured work at the mint, after it was moved from Aberystwyth," explained Townsend.

"So, you were sent here specifically to work on Brereton's behalf?"

"That is correct. We are from Wem originally, a town full of good men, and strong for Parliament too. In truth, I shall be glad to see the mint moved to Bristol. It means Faith will be able to move back to our home town, and I will no doubt be given some new, more amenable task by Sir William."

"That is assuming three things," I said, morosely, "firstly that nobody saw you leading me out of the side door of The Sacristy, that no-one remembers seeing me talking to my friend Alexander, and, most importantly, that no-one associates me with Saltonstall, for if that happens we will be lucky to get out of this place alive."

Townsend furrowed his brows. "There is a chance of that?" he asked.

"Of course. I was seen walking through the town earlier with Saltonstall, and what is more, a man was murdered at St Alkmund's only a short while before I arrived at The Sacristy. We were both present when the body was found. Someone will surely remember that."

Townsend looked at me quizzically, so I explained what had happened outside the church.

"Then we may be lucky," said Townsend. "The constable will be otherwise engaged at the moment, which means he will be less likely to be interested in us, or your friend. Let us hope he is good at hiding himself. He will need to be if one of those cavaliers persuades the authorities to raise hue and cry."

"And what about Saltonstall?"

"He will be locked in gaol, or the castle if he's considered important enough. I presume if he has given his surname as Halton, you were receiving the hospitality of Richard Halton? You said you were the younger Halton's bookkeeper."

I nodded glumly. "And Alexander was supposed to be his personal manservant. William Black was the name he was using."

Townsend nodded. "And I presume Jakes is not your real name either – but no matter. It is better I do not know your true identity. One thing is certain, though. You cannot go back to Richard Halton's tonight. Even if he has managed to preserve his freedom, a watch will have been put on the place. If you show up there you will be immediately arrested."

I collapsed back on my chair with a sigh and began to contemplate the unholy mess I had managed to create for myself. One of my associates had been arrested whilst the other, my best friend, was presumably hiding in St Chad's churchyard or somewhere down by the river bank in fear for his life. Meanwhile, I had come close to being arrested myself, I had somehow managed to get myself embroiled in a murder investigation about which I knew precious little, and whilst all this had been going on, Bressy had disappeared off the face of the earth, leaving me little prospect of recovering Massey's treasure. However had I managed to get myself into such a predicament?

"There is one small mercy, though," said Townsend, a hopeful smile lighting up his face, "At least there is no-one here who knows you and can identify you to the authorities. So long as this is the case you will be safe here with me."

I smiled wanly and tried to look Townsend in the eye. In truth, it was not an easy task, but I owed the man a degree of honesty, so I took a deep breath and told him about Alice.

If there was one thing I learned very quickly about Gideon and Faith Townsend, it was their remarkable capacity for making you feel a lot better about yourself when there was not much to feel better about. Gideon's face was a mask of concern when I told him about the history of my relationship with Alice and her sudden appearance whilst I was speaking to Halton earlier that evening, but his expression became more contemplative when I explained how Alice had made a point of explaining that she would not betray me to her Royalist paymasters, and when I began to relate the background to my somewhat hasty promise to the Davies family to find their missing son, Ellis, and the curious but growing connection between the group of murderers and Alice's print works, his response was much more upbeat.

"Hang on," he said, "so you are telling me that Charlie Hipkiss, the brother of the ringleader of this group of rapists and murderers, works for Mistress Furnival, and the young Dutchman Jakob De Vries also worked from time to time for her?"

"That is correct," I confirmed.

"And you have mentioned that Ellis, in his letter to his parents, made it clear that he had located all five of Millie's murderers who were still alive. Is it not likely that all five are still in contact with each other? De Vries's friend Corni certainly was. But what about the other? Perhaps more of them are associated in some way with Mistress Furnival's print shop. If that is the case, and this young lad Ellis is roaming around Shrewsbury with revenge on his mind, surely it is in her interest to work with you to help stop him. The reverse of the deal is that she facilitates a way to get you out of here in one piece, and perhaps Saltonstall as well, although how we achieve that I have no idea."

"And Alexander?"

"We don't know where he is at the moment, so let us deal with one thing at a time, but yes – his safety must also be brought into the equation."

And so Gideon Townsend and I made the decision to seek out Alice the following day. The question of how safe it was going to be to do that was answered a few moments later when there was a loud knock at Townsend's back door. I was surprised when Faith disappeared and returned a few moments later with the landlord of The Sacristry. The strength of Brereton's network of collaborators never ceased to amaze me. The man explained that Saltonstall had, indeed, been arrested and locked up in the castle, but of Alexander there was no sign. Richard Halton, it appeared, had displayed an aptitude for quick thinking which I had not thought him capable of, talking himself out of a tight corner by explaining that he had not seen his cousin Percival since he was a scrawny teenager, and had on this occasion unfortunately been hoodwinked by an imposter. This, it seemed, had been enough to prevent Halton being summarily arrested, but, as expected, a watch had been placed on his house in anticipation of either of the imposter's accomplices making an attempt to return.

They did not seem to worry Townsend too much, but then again, neither did the other major headache, now under significant time constraints, namely what to do about Brereton's orders for the destruction of the mint.

From my perspective, with Bressy having failed to leave Massey's treasure in Bushell's safekeeping for processing into coin, there seemed little point in me being involved at all. I knew nothing about the workings of the mint and had come to the conclusion that there was little I could do that could not be managed by Townsend himself.

"But the fact is you are here and are acting under Brereton's orders," argued Townsend, vehemently. "Not only that, we have a narrow window of opportunity to complete this. I cannot do it by myself."

The mint, Townsend explained, was located in the undercroft of Bennett's Hall, the burned-out manor house I had viewed with Alexander and Saltonstall earlier that day. The fact that the mint was constantly guarded from the outside, together with its underground location under solid stone floors, meant that the workshop was both relatively secure and out of sight. There were, however, ways by which a resourceful intruder could gain access unnoticed. Several of the ground floor workshops at the rear of the house had access to a shared cellar, which was adjacent to the mint. This was, admittedly, separated from the mint by a stout wooden door, which was permanently locked. However, Townsend had not only managed to rent one of the workshops, he had also managed to fashion a copy of the key to the wooden door.

"There is one main problem, though," he explained. "The last of the silver in our stockpile was not coined until today. We now have to dismantle the melting and casting equipment and pack it ready for transportation down to the river. We don't anticipate this process to be completed until Friday sometime. A barge with an armed guard has been arranged for Saturday, so our one and only opportunity to complete our mission is during the night of Friday to Saturday."

"And how do you propose we do that?"

Townsend smiled and rubbed his hands together, warming to the task. "It is quite simple," he said. "The first thing you must understand is that this mission is not about destroying the melting and casting equipment. It is heavy and cumbersome to move for one thing, but also not difficult to replace. No – the key to everything is the destruction of the dies, which were made six years ago when Bushell was commissioned by the King to open his mint in Aberystwyth. They are unique, because the dies all carry a special plume of feathers design, which marks them out as coming from here, rather than from the Tower Mint in

London. More importantly, the dies were all supplied from London, which is now under the control of Parliament, so you see, if we destroy the dies, we remove the King's ability to mint coins entirely.

"The plan," he continued, "is as follows. On Friday evening, we go to the workshop early enough not to arouse suspicion – that is you, I, and your friend Alexander – assuming, of course, that he has managed to escape the attentions of the authorities. The workshop has been laid out as a tailor's workshop and is full of various fabrics and yarns, which will come in handy, as will become evident.

"We then wait until the small hours, when we enter the mint by means of the cellar and remove the dies. The piles and trussels, that is the lower and upper dies, are kept together, but in separate boxes according to coin type. There are five boxes in total, holding the dies for half-crowns, shillings, half-shillings, half-groats and pence respectively. The boxes are heavy enough, so they need to be removed quickly and silently, which is why your help and that of your friend is needed.

"We then carry the boxes through the rented workshop and out into the yard at the back, where Faith will be waiting with a horse and cart. Once the town starts to wake up, a tradesman's cart will not attract much attention hereabouts, especially if it is piled high with fabrics. The dies will then be smuggled out of town via the Welsh Bridge and eventually dumped in the Severn, where they will be well out of the King's reach. They will be gone before Bushell even realises they have been stolen."

I had to admit, it all seemed straightforward enough. The only problem was that we would have to wait forty-eight hours before Townsend's plan could be put into action. There was little I could do about Saltonstall's incarceration in the castle, and so I had to hope that Alexander had been resourceful enough to evade capture. In the meantime, I realised there was plenty to keep me busy. After all, I had a murder to solve.

Chapter 10

I should have slept soundly that night, but, in truth, I did not. Despite the comfortable bed I was given in a spare chamber overlooking the pathway to the rear of the house, I spent most of the night tossing and turning, only too aware that Alexander and Lieutenant Saltonstall would be spending the hours of darkness in considerably less comfort than myself. Indeed, the first tinges of dawn had begun to illuminate the eastern sky by the time I finally succumbed to exhaustion and slept a dreamless sleep.

I was woken by the smell of eggs and the welcome sight of sunlight streaming in through the window, and I realised it must already be mid-morning. I pulled on my shirt and breeches and staggered downstairs to find Faith Townsend hard at work at the stove. Her brother, it appeared, had already left for the mint.

"It seemed as though you needed the rest," she said by way of explanation, "and, in truth, the more time you spend here rather than roaming the town, the safer we will all be."

I gave her a bleary-eyed nod and sat down at the kitchen table.

"Here," she said, as she placed a trencher of bread and eggs in front of me and poured me a mug of small beer, "have some breakfast."

"You and your brother put yourselves at great risk for me, mistress," I said, taking a bite out of the hunk of bread, "I am grateful for it."

"It is nothing, Mr Jakes. It was part of God's plan to bring you to our door, so it is our duty to preserve your well-being." She gave me a brief smile and continued busying herself around the kitchen. Her expression was one of openness and hospitality, but I sensed there was more to it than that.

"You are of the Puritan faith," I ventured.

She smiled. "I have *faith*, that is true," she said. "Faith was the name that was bestowed upon me by my parents, and I have faith in God's ultimate purpose for us, although I have long since given up wondering what the exact nature of that purpose is. What will be, will be, but I always try to do what I believe He would want me to do."

I nodded in sympathy, but was curious as to the tone of resignation in her voice. "Tell me," I asked, "what made you follow your brother here and immerse yourself in Brereton's world of intelligence and subterfuge. Was there nothing for you in Wem?" I could tell I had hit the mark, for she stopped in her tracks momentarily, as though her thoughts were somewhere else, before visibly pulling herself back to the present.

"Oh yes," she said, "there was a different life once. I was married, you know, with two children – a boy and a girl, Stand-Fast and Verity, but one winter's day – it would have been in sixteen thirty-five – the youngest, Verity, she was just four years old, developed a cough and a fever, and a week later they were all taken by the Lord. First Verity, then the boy, and finally my husband, Nehemiah. I prayed for them, and plenty prayed for me, but it was Gideon who took me in, gave me a roof over my head and helped me come to terms with God's will. It was hard, but each day I thank the Lord that he has given me this new purpose in life. But in truth I am only flesh and bone. I now find myself secretly praying that we will soon fulfil our purpose here, and we may return to Wem, and I chide myself for that."

"You should not feel guilty for wishing such a thing," I said. "I fervently hope that your wishes come to pass and that my role in this present venture may make a small contribution towards achieving that."

I felt truly sorry for Faith Townsend. With a young wife of my own and a child on the way, I dared not think how I would feel if they were to be taken from me by a fever.

"You seem like a good man, Mr Jakes," ventured Faith, dragging me away from my morbid thoughts. "You are married, may I ask?"

"Yes, very recently in fact, and my wife, Elizabeth, is with child."

"Then you are truly blessed, and I wish you Godspeed with your venture today – but one thing, if I may. I could not help overhearing your conversation with Gideon last night."

My eyes shot upwards to meet Faith's, for I knew what was coming.

"I know of this Alice Furnival," she said, hesitantly. "She is recently widowed, and I got the sense all was not finished between the two of you, perhaps not intentionally, but there is something there nonetheless. I pray God gives you the strength to resist any such folly, for it could mean the end for all of us."

I looked at Faith and smiled. I tried to keep the worry and – what was it? Guilt? Yes, guilt – out of it, but I could not be sure if I succeeded, for Faith had struck at the heart of things. Why, I mused, did Alice always turn out to be at the very centre of everything?

ᘓ

The walk across town to Alice's house was fraught with tension, for I could not be sure whether the witnesses to Saltonstall's arrest had identified me as an accomplice. Even if they had not, I considered it likely that Halton's interrogation had revealed that the young lieutenant had arrived in Shrewsbury with two accomplices, not one, and hence a watch would have been put out for me.

Fortunately, Gideon Townsend had laid out a set of workers' clothes for me, so at least I would be less conspicuous than in the sober yet smart attire I had donned to play the role of Percival Halton's bookkeeper. Nonetheless, I avoided the main streets as much as I could, cutting through Butchers Row and past St Alkmund's. As I passed the church I glanced over to the doorway where Jakob De Vries had been murdered and noticed the flagstones had been scrubbed clean, although a faint, brown stain remained stubbornly visible, a grim reminder of what had happened here the previous day.

I had not had time to ponder on the curious circumstances of the Dutchman's death, but did so now. The young boy caught leaning over De Vries's corpse, I conceded, could very well have been Ellis Davies, and he certainly had the motive to kill De Vries, assuming, of course, the Dutchman was indeed one of Millie's murderers. Several things did not fit in though. Firstly, no-one had actually witnessed the moment the murderer struck. Secondly, De Vries had been killed with a sword, and the young suspect had no such weapon on his person. Granted, the boy's decision to flee would no doubt be interpreted as proof of guilt by some, but it seemed equally likely to me that the boy had simply fled in terror. Most interesting, though, was the curious fact that the murderer had found time to insert a crucifix into his victim's mouth. That, I considered, was not the act of a young man bent on revenge, but something altogether more calculating and sinister.

I was still pondering this fact when I emerged onto Alice's street. Two men, I noticed, were lurking outside Halton's gate, but there was nothing for it. I marched up to Alice's front door and rapped loudly on the knocker. This elicited a curious look from one of the men, but after a few seconds his attention reverted to the pipe he had been filling with tobacco.

It was Alice herself who opened the door. As she did so my heart lurched involuntarily as it was wont to do when I was in her presence. Alice, for her part, looked me up and down in amusement as she took in my new disguise.

"My, my," she whispered, casting a furtive glance towards the guard outside Halton's gate, "you and your friends certainly seem to be creating a stir. One of them is in the castle being interrogated by the governor as we speak, whilst the other is the subject of an intensive search. You had better come in before you get yourself arrested."

I stepped gratefully into Alice's hallway and closed the door behind me.

"By the way, you look like a vagrant," she added. "Where on earth did you get those clothes?"

I ignored the question and watched as a flash of irritation passed over Alice's eyes, but she fought to keep a straight face.

"Very well, I cannot expect you to betray your colleagues so easily, but why are you still in Shrewsbury, Daniel? There is nothing for you here, only danger."

"Believe me," I said, "I would be gone in a flash, you can be sure of that, but you know I cannot leave without finding out what has happened to Alexander. In the meantime, however, I come to you on an entirely different matter. It concerns the Dutchman who was murdered outside St Alkmund's yesterday."

Alice arched an eyebrow. "That was a shock, I grant you, but what does that have to do with you?"

"My interest relates to the young boy who was seen running away from the scene of the killing. I believe he may be a young man called Ellis Davies. He is from Oswestry and has been missing since March, when his sister was raped and murdered by a group of six Royalist soldiers. One of the perpetrators was a man called Jack Hipkiss, who died in the battle at Whittingham in July. His brother, I believe, works for you."

"Charlie Hipkiss?"

"The same. Ellis's parents received a letter from their son a few days ago saying he had identified the rest of his sister's murderers and would avenge her killing. That's the last we heard. However, we suspect that two of the murderers were Dutchmen, one of whom was called Corni. That description fits the murdered man De Vries and his friend, who appeared yesterday. As De Vries also worked for you, I wondered whether a discussion with Charlie Hipkiss might help us identify the rest of the murderers and help us find Ellis before he gets arrested."

Alice looked puzzled. "Why would that be a problem? He killed De Vries after all, or do you not think so?"

"It is possible," I conceded, "but it is too simple an explanation, and some things do not add up. In particular, the boy did not have any weapon on him that could have been used to murder De Vries, and then there is the conundrum of the crucifix that was found in the victim's mouth. That is not the kind of thing a young boy would do."

Alice thought about this for a moment, and then gestured for me to follow her into a large reception room.

"You may visit me at the printing press tomorrow if you are still here," she said. "I will make sure Charlie Hipkiss is available. In the meantime, please be seated, there is something I would like to show you."

I made myself comfortable on a settle and waited for Alice, who disappeared into another room. The Furnivals' house was well appointed – a fine oak dining table with ornate chairs, wood panelling on one of the walls, with tapestries and a couple of landscape paintings on the others. The room I was in, like the equivalent in Halton's house, opened out into a terrace overlooking the rear garden.

I wondered whether, if things had been different, I would have eventually been able to have provided her with this kind of lifestyle. Maybe one day, I thought. A successful cheese merchant may aspire to such a lifestyle, given the right amount of good fortune, but a lowly wich house owner with no more than six leads? I did not think so.

I was jolted out of my reverie by Alice's return. She was holding a small envelope, which she handed to me.

"I received this letter on Monday," she said. "I think you should read it."

Puzzled, I took the letter from her and turned it over, examining it with interest. The envelope was of good quality and had been sealed with red wax. It was addressed to Alice as the proprietor of the Royalist newssheet she had inherited from her dead husband, Hugh Furnival. I opened the envelope, extracted the letter from inside, and studied it carefully. The message, written in bold but neat handwriting, was short and concise.

JDV Matthew 2652

I shrugged, none the wiser. "What do you think it means?" I asked.

Alice walked over to a writing desk underneath a window and picked up a book, which I immediately recognised as a copy of the King James Bible.

"At first I thought JDV Matthew must be a name," she said, "but I know of no such person. I then wondered whether Matthew might, in fact, be a biblical reference. The significance of the message, however, did not become clear until I re-read it yesterday evening. Read it yourself, and you will see what I mean."

I took the bible from Alice and opened it at Matthew Chapter 26, Verse 52, and what I read made my hair stand on end.

Then said Jesus unto him, put up again thy sword into his place, for all they that take the sword shall perish with the sword.

"That is exactly how the Dutchman died," I said. "Most interesting, I agree, but on its own, this means nothing."

Alice exhaled with exasperation and jabbed a finger at the letter. "But there is clearly more to it than that," she insisted. "Look at the initials. JDV obviously refers to Jakob De Vries."

"Perhaps," I conceded, "but who on earth could have composed such a thing? And for what motive? Surely this letter could just as easily relate to something entirely different, or nothing at all. If it had not been for the unexplained initials, you would not have associated it with the murder at all."

"That is true, and I would be inclined to agree with you were it not for one small thing."

I looked up just in time to see Alice thrust the second envelope in my direction. It was, I noticed, identical to the first, and contained a similar sheet of paper, which I unfolded gratefully.

"It was delivered first thing this morning," Alice pointed out. "Obviously designed to make sure I took a good look at the first one again."

I nodded in acquiescence and took the second envelope from her. "BC Luke 1244," I said, reading the message out loud. "Are you familiar with your gospels, Alice?"

"Of course, the verse in question is well-known enough, although I do not understand why it has been sent to me, nor what it means in this context."

I quickly flicked through the pages of the bible until I came to the relevant passage. What I read did not make me any wiser.

Consider the ravens, for they neither sow nor reap, which neither have storehouse nor barn; and God feedeth them: how much more are ye better than the fowls?

"What do you make of it?" asked Alice. "And what relevance are the ravens? Are we to believe that this is a warning someone is going to be killed by a flock of birds?"

"I rather doubt it," I replied, thoughtfully. "That would indeed be bizarre. The ravens more likely have some kind of abstract significance. More important, though, is how the letter has been constructed. If we accept the theory that Jakob De Vries's death was connected to the rape and murder of Millie Davies, then perhaps so is this. And if we are to believe that JDV refers to De Vries, then we must ask ourselves, who is BC? At the moment, Alice, all roads appear to lead to your print shop, so tell me, who do you know with these initials?"

Alice thought about this for a moment. I noticed a change in her expression, which suddenly became a couple of shades paler.

"I know someone," she said. "A good friend of the Hipkiss family, who will almost certainly have been in Oswestry in March. His name is Ben Collie."

"Ben Collie," I echoed. "Ben and Corni were the two names given to me by a witness to the original disturbance that preceded Millie's murder. Ben Collie and Cornelis Smits. And you say he works for you?"

"Indeed, for many years in fact, but not since the start of the war. Like Jack and Charlie Hipkiss, he fought on the King's side, and he was also a member of the Royalist garrison at Oswestry, but he found his way back to Shrewsbury after the defeat at Whittington, and I re-employed him."

"What kind of a fellow is he?" I asked.

"That is what I cannot understand," mused Alice. "Ben has always been quiet, helpful and respectful. A good worker. I find it hard to believe he could have been involved in something such as this."

"War does strange things to a man," I offered. "I cannot say whether that is the case with him. One thing is certain, though. His life may be in danger. He will need to be warned."

"Of course, but I'm afraid I cannot do anything about this today. It is also not safe for you to be seen about town, so I suggest you go back to wherever it is you are hiding and present yourself at my workshop tomorrow afternoon, when I hope we will be able to get to the bottom of the matter."

I arose from the settle and stepped over to the window, from where I was able to stare out over the gardens and contemplate Alice's suggestion.

"Very well," I said at length, "I see I have little choice in the matter. I will meet you at your workshop tomorrow. In the meantime, what is the best way out of here? I do not wish to run the gauntlet of the governor's men unless I absolutely have to."

At that moment, and as if to answer my question, my eye was caught by a sudden movement from among the trees behind the picket fence at the end of the lawn. Alice must have seen it too, for she glided over to the doorway to the terrace and opened it, a slow smile spreading across her face. As soon as she did so, I was amazed to see a somewhat bedraggled Alexander emerge from the undergrowth, neatly vault the picket fence, and sprint across the grass and terrace before bursting breathlessly through the door into Alice's reception room.

"Good morrow, Master Clowes," said Alice, scarcely able to keep the amusement from her face. "Congratulations on escaping the attentions of the governor's search party. I trust the pigsty you slept in was comfortable enough."

Alexander scowled and wiped some of the mud from his breeches. "There is an old quarry," he said, "outside the town walls on the common ground above the bend in the river. Fortunately, I managed to reach it before the hue and cry went up. It offers good cover in the shadows between the rocks, but as you can see, it is not the cleanest or driest of places."

My friend was not exaggerating. Having removed and lost his coat in The Sacristy, he was down to his shirt and breeches, both of which were streaked with what looked like clay.

"So how did you find your way back here?" I asked.

"That was the simple bit. I waited until it was light, and then I walked along the river bank as far as the English Bridge and followed the crowds walking into the town to begin their day's work. I figured no-one would be on the lookout for a fugitive who was beef-witted enough to want to seek a way back into the town, and I was right. I then made my way across numerous back gardens and woodland until I could see Mistress Furnival's house and that of Mr Halton. I assumed you would eventually find your way to one of those places, so I hid amongst the undergrowth and the trees until you appeared. I have seen no sign of Halton, though, nor Saltonstall for that matter."

I explained briefly to Alexander what had happened to the lieutenant, described Halton's fortunate escape, and informed him of the fact that the house was now being watched from the front by the governor's agents.

"So, we cannot simply walk out of here together?"

"That, my friend, is the nub of it," I agreed.

During this exchange, Alice had been looking on thoughtfully, but now she spoke. "Gentlemen, do you think we could come to some kind of an understanding?" she asked.

Alexander gave me a look, but it was clear he was in no mood for arguing.

"We have little choice in the matter. What do you propose?" I asked.

"An agreement," said Alice, "that protects all our interests, but need not go beyond the walls of this room. As I see it, your immediate priority is to make sure that you are both able to leave Shrewsbury in one piece."

"That is true," I conceded. "Pray continue."

"I presume you have collaborators here, on whom you can rely. I do not propose to question you about them, but I will give you both ten minutes of privacy to discuss whatever arrangements you need to make with each other. Next, neither of you can leave this house either alone or together by the front door, that is clear. You will almost certainly be arrested. However, what I could do, Daniel, is walk with you as far as the Cross. That should get you past all the governor's men, but from there you are on your own."

I frowned. "Won't that look a little odd? I am dressed in workers' clothes."

"Not in the least," said Alice. "You could easily pass as a worker from the print shop, as they are regular visitors here."

"And Alexander?"

"I'm afraid Master Clowes will need to leave the way he came, but he is welcome to stay here and out of sight until it is dark. He can then escape through the trees as far as Wyle Cop, from where he can walk back up though the town. Once you are both gone, I will undertake not to betray you to the authorities while you are in Shrewsbury."

"And what about Lieutenant Saltonstall? He is not much more than a boy if the truth be told."

"I had not thought about him," admitted Alice. "He bears some degree of responsibility for the predicament he is in. He will also be more problematic, as he is imprisoned in the castle, but very well. I will put some thought to him too."

"And the quid pro quo?" I pressed. "What are we expected to do in return for this?"

Alice smiled. "As I have said before, there is no reason for you to remain in Shrewsbury. Bressy has the treasure he took from Nantwich, and the mint is set to be closed. So, you will remain here as long as it takes for you to discover who killed Jakob De Vries and the nature of the threat to Ben Collie, but then you will leave Shrewsbury, return to Nantwich, and leave me to my business. That is all I require, nothing more and nothing less. Are we agreed?"

I thought briefly about how I was going to explain to Sir William Brereton why we had returned to Cheshire empty-handed, but despite my misgivings I could see no alternative. I looked to Alexander for guidance, but he could only shrug, and so I sighed, looked Alice in the eye, and took her outstretched hand.

Chapter 11

It was past midnight before Alexander managed to find his way back to the Townsends' cottage, by which time I had spent several tense hours wondering whether my friend had succeeded in negotiating the woodland at the bottom of Alice's garden without being seen by anyone patrolling the town walls, and indeed whether he had subsequently understood my directions as to how to avoid the busy thoroughfare of Mardol by approaching our place of refuge from the rear.

In the event, he had been spotted by Gideon Townsend on his way back from The Sacristry and followed until he had reached the narrow path behind the house. From there, Gideon had shepherded him discreetly through the allotments towards the safety of his kitchen, where Faith and I had been waiting nervously.

Earlier in the day, Alice, true to her word, had helped me avoid the attention of the lookouts in front of Halton's house by making me carry an armful of newsletters as far as a bookseller's premises on Pride Hill. From there I had parted company with her and headed off down the hill towards Mardol. I made sure I was not being followed by doubling back several times through side streets, but the townsfolk of Shrewsbury, it seemed, were more interested in going about their daily business than people like me. I had therefore been able to reach the Townsends' house without incident.

I was truly grateful to Gideon and Faith Townsend, for they were risking much for Alexander and myself, and being able to take stock of our changed situation in relative safety was, I confess, a godsend. However, the next day seemed interminable. Unable to risk being seen, we were forced to stay in our chamber out of sight of the windows, so when the time came for me to visit Alice's print shop, I was champing at the bit for something to do.

The fact that Hugh Furnival had chosen to establish his printing business within the confines of Shrewsbury's grammar school had struck me as somewhat odd, and my initial impression had not been altered now that I was able to take in the grandeur of the place at my leisure.

Constructed in light grey stone, in contrast to the red sandstone walls of the castle, the school was an impressive building indeed. Consisting of three storeys and topped with a slate roof lined with crenellations fashioned in the shape of the cross, the school seemed to be made up of three separate parts constructed in phases. To the left stood the main body of the school, a solid structure with stone mullioned windows and an arched entrance. Next to it on the right was a clock tower, which rose above the rest of the school, whilst adjoining it, looking almost like an afterthought, stood the school's chapel, its large, Gothic style window standing sentinel over the roadway below.

It was a stiflingly hot summer afternoon, and the spacious yard in front of the school was teeming with scholars making the most of a break between lessons. As I approached the entrance, my attention was drawn towards two statues standing on pillars above the archway, one with his arms clasped across his chest and the other holding a hat. I was so taken in by the sight of the two figures that I did not notice the tall, black-robed individual who had approached me from the side.

"They are Philomathes and Polimathes," said the newcomer, forcing me to start slightly at the unexpected intrusion. "They make a most engaging pair, do they not? They represent the process one goes through in this institution. One is a student willing to learn, the other a learned scholar. The inscription below is from Isocrates. How is your Latin?"

"As good as non-existent," I admitted.

"Then let me enlighten you. It says, 'if you are a lover of learning, you will become learned'."

I nodded my thanks and surveyed the newcomer more closely. A young man in his mid-twenties, he cut an imposing figure, at least six feet tall with an immaculately groomed black beard and moustache. What I had taken for a robe, I noticed, was in fact the black gown of academia.

"I'm sorry," said the man, with a smile. "I did not introduce myself. My name is Maredudd Tewdwr. I teach divinity here."A Welshman then, not immediately apparent from his voice, for education had taken the edge off the man's accent, but armed with the knowledge of his name, I could now detect the slight lilt to his speech that marked out the welshness in him.

"Tewdwr?" I said. "An appropriate name for a teacher in a Royalist town."

"Indeed, so I am often told, although to my knowledge I cannot claim common ancestry with the royal line of the same name. And you are-?"

"Daniel Cheswis," I said, shaking his hand. Continuing to masquerade under the name of Humphrey Jakes, I realised, was completely out of the question, for the whole town would by now have been alerted to the presence of a fugitive with that name. Using my own identity, I considered, was no more dangerous than any other, unless of course, I happened to run into Sir Fulke Hunckes, and he would recognise me by sight anyway. "I have an appointment with Mistress Alice Furnival. I believe she operates a printing press here."

"Ah, the young widow," said Tewdwr. "Yes, indeed, but her workshop is not within the main body of the school. It is located within one of the older buildings towards the rear of the site. If you will permit me, I will take you to her."

Tewdwr led me through the main archway and along a corridor flanked by a series of classrooms, before reaching a door, which led out into a yard looking out towards the town walls and the arm of the river which flanked the town on its Welsh side. In the yard was a large timber-framed building, which looked nearly a hundred years old.

"This was the original school building," said Tewdwr. "It was founded by King Edward VI as a school based on Calvinist principles. Many fail to see the irony of its location in a town which now strongly supports a king whose religious principles have often been the very antithesis of that."

I smiled. "That is indeed a paradox," I agreed, "but tell me, Mr Tewdwr, you seem to know a lot about the school, and yet you do not seem old enough to have taught here for long."

"A matter of months, but I was a scholar here once. I take a personal interest in the history of the place."

"Then perhaps you will agree," I pressed, "for an educational establishment of such standing, is it not somewhat incongruous that it should be renting out space to a printing workshop?"

I thought perhaps I had gone too far, for Tewdwr stopped abruptly and gave me a level stare, but then, after stroking his beard thoughtfully for a moment, he burst out laughing.

"Yes, indeed," he affirmed. "You are most astute, Mr Cheswis, but it was not always so. The school has long had a reputation for academic excellence, but demand for places has been in decline of late, especially since the start of the war, and needs must, you know."

"So, the press has not been here that long?"

"A year at most, or so I'm told. Before that Mr Furnival operated from a benefactor's house elsewhere in town, but Mr Furnival prospered, and the school did not. What we now have here is a symbiotic relationship, if you like – of benefit to both parties. The press prints educational leaflets for the school's use from time to time."

"I see."

"But I talk too much," said Tewdwr. "I see Mistress Furnival has already registered our presence."

Indeed, Alice had emerged at the front of the building and was gesturing to me to walk over and join her. She looked as beautiful as always, but there was something about her demeanour that suggested that all was not quite right.

I turned to thank Tewdwr for his help, but to my surprise the schoolmaster had already disappeared. All I caught was the sight of the door closing softly behind him as he retreated back into the main school building.

I had no time to consider the curious nature of the Welshman's sudden disappearance, for Alice was already talking to me.

"You had better come in, Daniel," she said, a hint of urgency in her tone. "We have a crisis here. Ben Collie has gone missing."

"Missing?"

Alice indicated for me to be silent and ushered me quickly inside the building and into a functional office furnished with a couple of tables and half a dozen chairs. The tables were piled high with books, newsletters and loose sheets of print.

"Yes," she confirmed at length, after closing the door to assure our privacy, "Ben Collie has not been seen since yesterday evening. He should be here working today, but did not show up this morning."

This was a worrying turn of events. "When was he last seen?" I asked.

"Last night when I left the tavern, he and Charlie Hipkiss were drinking there. They are good friends, but last night the two of them seem to have had some kind of argument, and Hipkiss stormed off home without finishing his beer."

"And what does Hipkiss say about this?"

"Very little, so far," said Alice. "Maybe you can extract more from him than I was able to do. You wanted a discussion with him anyway."

I nodded in acquiescence. "Very good," I said, "lead me to him."

Alice's print workshop was located in a spacious but dimly lit room to the rear of the building. The smell of ink, turpentine and human sweat was almost overwhelming, but the overriding impression was one of quiet industry. I counted eight people in the workshop, two operating the press and handling the freshly printed sheets of paper, the remainder working with the lead type and placing it into blocks to create the next set of pages to be printed.

"The press can print just over two hundred sheets an hour," explained Alice, "so you can see, we can turn around a newssheet here relatively quickly. Any slack is taken up with work we carry out for the school or for booksellers."

"Your business is expanding, I understand," I said.

"Indeed, it is. The war has brought much work with it. People are hungry for news – for opinions. However, the limiting factor is the ability to acquire a second press, and I fear that only peace will allow us to do that. Come," said Alice, "Hipkiss is over there by the press."

My eyes fell on a broad, muscular fellow with a thick beard, who was using his left hand to hammer an ink ball onto the surface of the typeface, in order to coat it evenly. He shook my hand with his right, which fortunately was relatively free of ink.

"Who are you?" he asked, getting straight to the point. I opened my mouth to respond, but Alice answered for me.

"This is Mr Daniel Cheswis, a long-standing friend of mine. He is a merchant trading in cheese and salt, and he happens to have some business to conclude in Shrewsbury. I have asked for his help looking into Ben's disappearance and the attack on Jakob. I believe they may be connected."

I smiled inwardly, and caught a hint of amusement in Alice's expression too, for every word she had said was true.

"Connected?" echoed Hipkiss, immediately on the defensive. "What has brought you to that conclusion, mistress? And what does it have to do with me, or him for that matter?"

"I was in Oswestry last week," I said, "and came across a family called Davies, whose daughter was raped and murdered a few months ago. I am told you had some dealings with that family."

Hipkiss's eyes widened momentarily, and I thought I caught a look of uncertainty in his expression, but he recovered quickly and responded with anger.

"God's bones," he hissed. "I thought I had heard the last of this. My brother was accused of this murder, and he was killed fighting for the King before he had a chance to defend himself. Why is this being brought up again? Will this episode be forever a blight on my family?"

"I understand the effect this must have had," I began.

"You know nothing," insisted Hipkiss. "Who is this man, mistress? And why was he in Oswestry? Does this mean he is one of Mytton's men? A Roundhead? The place is full of them these days."

I glanced nervously at Alice, but she raised her hand almost imperceptibly to stop me from answering. "Charlie," she said, "with my background do you honestly think I would be inviting Parliamentary spies in to interview you? What do you think I am? Mr Cheswis simply has a few questions he wishes to ask. Perhaps we can do it in my office."

The irony of it! I was now being portrayed as a Royalist sympathiser, but it seemed to calm Hipkiss. He put down the ink ball, wiped his hands on a rag, and followed Alice meekly into the office. As soon as he was seated and the door was closed I came straight to the point.

"I am given to understand that you had some contact with the Davies family after their daughter's murder, so you will be aware that Millie's brother Ellis disappeared at the same time."

"He was assumed to be dead."

"Indeed. However, Evan and Hester Davies have recently received word from their son, who is alive and well in Shrewsbury, and a youngster meeting his description was seen running away from the scene of Jakob De Vries's murder on Wednesday."

This certainly gained Hipkiss's attention, and he swallowed nervously. "Are you saying the boy killed Jakob?" he asked.

"Not necessarily, but he did say he knew the identities of the other five murderers and has sworn revenge. I thought you may be able to help identify them too."

Hipkiss frowned and shook his head. "But Jack refused to reveal the identities of the other men who were with him that night. I don't think I can help."

"Of course you can," I insisted. "We already have a good idea of the identities of three of them. I do not consider it much of a stretch for you to at least have a guess at identifying the other two."

Hipkiss wiped a bead of sweat from his brow and stared in Alice's direction, but she was busy looking at her fingernails.

"Very well," conceded Hipkiss, his shoulders slumping. "Tell me what you know, and I will try and fill in the gaps."

"Thank you," I said. "Firstly, we know that two of the murderers were foreigners, probably Dutchmen. One of these answered to the name of Corni. We think these are Jakob De Vries and his friend Cornelis Smits, who presented himself briefly at the murder scene on Wednesday. Witnesses at The Bell Inn in Oswestry also mention someone called

Ben. We were wondering whether this might have been Ben Collie, but of course we cannot prove it. We were hoping you might be able to shed some light on this, especially as Collie seems to have vanished into thin air. As for the other two, we have no idea, other than the fact that there was a youth with an injured arm. We are looking to you for suggestions. If the remaining four men involved in this crime are in danger from a vengeful killer, then we need to identify and locate them as soon as possible, so they can be duly warned."

Hipkiss flexed his fingers and blinked. I could not understand why the man appeared so nervous. Evan Davies had described him as an honest and godly man, but he was not giving that impression. I soon found out why.

"You are right, Mr Cheswis," said Hipkiss. "Jack was my brother, and of course I know his friends well, but I am no snitch. When I started being stopped in the street, I realised Jack had been involved and confronted him. He admitted everything, but refused to give himself up, and I suppose I cannot blame him. Who would put his own neck into a noose? In the end, though, events caught up with him. Jack and his friends all fought with Marrow at Whittington, and whilst Jack lost his life, the other five managed to escape over the fields once it become clear that Marrow had been routed. They all made their way back here."

"And their names?" I pressed.

Hipkiss wiped the sweat from the back of his neck and rocked back on his chair. "You are right," he said. "Jakob De Vries and Corni Smits were both there. Two Dutch mercenaries. Tough as nails. You wouldn't want to get on the wrong side of either of them."

"And Ben Collie?"

"He was the most surprising. Ben has always been a gentle soul, but Jack said the war changed him. Exposed a mean streak in him that Jack hadn't thought was there."

"That sounds rich coming from your brother, from what I've heard," I said.

Hipkiss laughed for the first time. "Aye, you're in the right of it there. He were a proper bastard, our Jack, and that's the truth of it. Ben was different, though. When I questioned him about what had happened that night in Oswestry, he said he had not wanted to hurt the girl. It was as though an unseen force took control of him and forced him to defile her, as the others did."

I watched Alice wince out of the corner of my eye. It was clear that these revelations were new to her, but I felt obliged to continue my questions.

"So he regretted it?"

"Aye, so he said. Came over all religious. Spent more time in church, praying and the like. Said it was in penitence for his sins."

"I see. That leaves the two other men."

"Yes, Jack never said who they were, but I worked it out for myself. The young lad with the withered arm, that will be William Stubbs. Lost the use of his left arm as a child, but can wield a fair sword with the other. His family run a cook shop at the bottom of Fish Street, so you'll probably find him there. The other man is Joseph Finch. He runs a smallholding on the edge of town on the Abbey Foregate. Keeps a few pigs, grows some vegetables, that sort of thing. Not the most conspicuous of men is Joseph. Tends to disappear into a crowd, but he was there that night, I know it."

Alice, by this time, had taken one of the chairs and was applying a kerchief to her brow. From what I had seen of Alice since her return to my life in January, she was not a person who was easily shocked, but the revelation of Collie's role in Millie Davies's murder seemed to have shaken her to the core.

"If you knew all of this, Charlie, why did you not tell me?" she demanded.

Hipkiss shrugged apologetically. "I'm sorry, mistress. It did not seem relevant. This was something that happened in war in a town far from here."

"Millie Davies was an innocent serving girl. Her murder had nothing to do with the war," I pointed out. "However, facts are facts. We must deal with things as they are. The fact is we now have six names. Jack Hipkiss, Ben Collie, Jakob De Vries, Cornelis Smits, William Stubbs and Joseph Finch. Two of these men are dead, and one is missing. One thing that we do know is that only Hipkiss, Collie and De Vries worked here, so we must assume that the connection with your print works is merely coincidental."

"Perhaps," mused Alice, "but if that were the case, why have I received two coded letters? There is something odd about that. If Jakob De Vries's murderer merely visited me so I would report the murder in my newssheet, surely he would have sent me something more straightforward. Why the cryptic clues and the bible verses? There is a certain arrogance about these messages, as though the murderer is trying to make a moral point. Perhaps he even wants to be caught."

"Coded letters?" interjected Hipkiss, a look of puzzlement on his face. "What are you talking about?"

I glanced at Alice, and she nodded, so I told him about the two messages Alice had received and our fear that Collie had also been targeted by Jakob De Vries's killer. Hipkiss began to pale and, once I had finished speaking, he rose to his feet.

"Then we had better find Ben Collie," he said. "Come, I will take you to the house where he lives. It is not far from here. Hopefully that will cast some light on the matter."

Chapter 12

Ben Collie, it turned out, lived only a few yards away from the school, renting a chamber in one of the town houses that lined Castle Street.

"Ben is unmarried," explained Hipkiss, as we weaved our way through a throng of soldiers and passers-by as well as a line of tradesmen waiting to leave the town by the only exit that did not involve crossing a bridge. "He has always lived frugally, so he has no need for extensive rooms. His fellow tenants are mostly younger men – bachelors, but Ben doesn't mind. He has what he needs."

We were met at the door by a stern, sour-faced woman dressed in maroon bodice and plain grey skirts. She appeared to know Hipkiss well and led us up to Collie's room without complaint.

"I don't think you'll find him at home, Mr Hipkiss," she said. "I haven't seen him since yesterday evening, when he went out. Why do you seek him? Is something amiss?"

"We don't know, Meg," said Hipkiss. "It's just that he is missing from work. This is Mistress Furnival, our employer, and her friend Mr Cheswis. They would seek him out."

"Is there anything in particular which makes you think there might be something wrong, mistress?" I asked, noting the woman's troubled expression.

"I could not say for sure. It's just that he has seemed somewhat careworn this week, as though something were eating away at him. He said something about needing to go to the church, to set matters straight with God. He's always been a regular churchgoer has Mr Collie, but I did not expect him to show such a degree of dedication and zeal."

The woman knocked at the door of Collie's room, and when there was no response, she slipped a key into the lock and pushed the door open to reveal a surprising sight. In the middle of the room, which was well appointed with a fine wooden bed, an upholstered settle, a desk and chair and a large trunk, stood an artist's stool and easel on which hung a half-finished sketch of what looked like two soldiers standing facing each other.

Alice gasped. "I did not realise Ben had a talent as an artist," she said. "He seems to possess a gift for the work."

Hipkiss, however, was unmoved. "Oh aye, he's always drawing something or other," he said. "He just didn't shout about it, that's all. I expect you'll find plenty more where that came from. If you look under his bed, you'll see what I mean."

My eyes shifted to the floor underneath the bed and realised the space was stuffed with rolled-up parchments and sheets of paper. I pulled a few of them out and found a mix of sketches and paintings – portraits and landscapes in the main plus one or two battle scenes.

I got to my feet and took a closer look at the drawing on the easel. I realised that both figures in the picture, dressed in officers' uniforms with swords hanging prominently from their hips, bore a striking resemblance to Hipkiss, but both with longer hair and no beard. Underneath the two figures was a short inscription, 'Jack and Charlie – Feb 1644'. An older picture then.

"Aye, I remember him doing that one. Ben has been a good friend to Jack and I. Looks like he was making some finishing touches to it."

"So it seems," I said. "I wonder what made him do that?"

"I cannot say, sir," said Hipkiss.

"I would suggest that is irrelevant at the moment," opined Alice, somewhat impatiently. "More important is that we find him as quickly as we can."

I smiled indulgently and turned to the landlady. "Mistress, you say he wished to pay a visit to the church. The nearest church to here is St Mary's. I suggest we begin there."

But Hipkiss shook his head. "No. Ben, like William Stubbs, grew up on the Abbey Foregate. His local church is the Church of the Holy Cross – the abbey church on the other side of the river. If he has gone to pray, that is where he will be."

"It's getting too late to go over there now," said Alice, "and we still have work to do in the print shop. I will send someone over there to search for Ben, but in the meantime, Mr Cheswis, I suggest you return to your quarters, and we reconvene first thing in the morning. If Ben has not re-emerged by that time, then perhaps we can walk there together."

☙

In truth, I was somewhat relieved to avoid having to accompany Alice to the abbey, for I was wary of the need to arrive back in Mardol in good time to walk over to Bennett's Hall with Gideon Townsend and Alexander, in order to infiltrate the mint. Returning, as always, through the allotments, I arrived in time to find Gideon already back from a day's work at the mint and devouring a stew of bacon and potatoes. At his feet was a large roll of cloth wound around a long wooden staff.

"For authenticity," explained my host, as Faith ladled stew into a bowl for me. "Quickly, eat your food. We need to be on our way as soon as we can to avoid suspicion. We can rest once we are in place inside the workshop."

Twenty minutes later Alexander and I were walking in full sight along Mardol and back up Pride Hill, each with one end of the roll of fabric balanced on our left shoulders. Gideon walked a few paces ahead of us, tipping his hat at passers-by as he went. Once we reached Bennett's Hall he led us through a side gate into a cobbled yard at the rear of the property. From here the fire damage suffered by the original building was even more evident, for nobody had bothered tidying up the façade for the benefit of the public. The walls were streaked with black, and the stone around the window frames was crumbling badly, but the wooden structure inside the walls seemed functional enough.

Gideon led us through an arched doorway, which led to a second wooden door and a flight of stone steps on the right, which led down to the undercroft. Through the second door was a wooden staircase leading up to the workshops on the second floor. The second door was slightly ajar, which struck me as odd, considering the workshops were deserted, its occupants having returned home for the weekend, but I thought no more of it at the time.

Alexander and I hauled the roll of cloth up the staircase into a large room unlocked by Gideon, which contained more rolls of fabric, a wooden bench, and a collection of tools and equipment commensurate with that which one might find in a tailor's workshop. We laid the roll of cloth on the floor and sat down on it, using it as a makeshift chair, whilst Gideon locked the door behind us.

"What now?" asked Alexander.

"Now we bide our time," replied Gideon. "Make yourselves comfortable, for we have a wait in front of us. Get some sleep if you can. I'll take the first watch. I'll wake one of you up in a couple of hours."

Under normal circumstances I would not have contemplated trying to sleep at such an early hour, but I must confess the stress of the last few days had made me feel inordinately tired. Using a roll of cloth as a pillow, I curled up on the floor and within a few minutes I had fallen into a dreamless sleep. It was not until I was shaken awake by Alexander, just in time to hear the one o'clock bells, that I realised I had slept not only through Gideon's watch, but Alexander's too.

"Your turn," whispered my friend. "It's all quiet, but keep your eye out for anything unusual. Gideon says to wake us both at three."

I wiped my eyes with the back of my hand and forced myself to my feet, for I would have otherwise fallen back into my slumber. It was a bright, moonlit night, but quiet as a graveyard, the silence punctuated only by the rhythmic sway of Gideon's breathing and the occasional snore from Alexander. The moonlight cast eerie shadows across the floor of the workshop, and my mind began to play tricks on me, as though the shadows were the flickering flames of the inferno that had consumed this building so many years before.

"Take no notice of old ghosts," I told myself.

About an hour into my watch I almost fell asleep and was woken abruptly by what I thought were footsteps outside in the yard. I glanced outside over the cobbles but could see nothing, and realised the noise must have been no more than my own nightmares. I settled back against the rolls of fabric and watched until the bells of St Mary's gave notice that it was time to wake the others.

I touched Gideon lightly on the wrist, and he was immediately awake, lifting himself silently to his feet. Alexander took a little longer to rouse, but soon he too was fully alert. Outside I could hear the distant sound of cart wheels on cobbles getting steadily louder. I put my nose to the window and watched a horse and cart slowly pull into the yard below, coming to a halt in the shadows next to the archway leading to the undercroft. Once she was satisfied, Faith looked upwards and gave us a silent salute.

"Right, let's go," whispered Gideon, beckoning us to follow him back along the corridor and down the wooden stairs to the entrance.

Without the benefit of windows, the stairs were dark, and I lost my footing halfway down, causing Gideon to whisper an urgent curse in my direction. Once on the ground floor, we began to descend the stone steps to the undercroft.

"Now we can light a candle," said Gideon, stopping to extricate a set of flints from a pouch attached to his belt and lighting a small hand lantern he had brought with him.

He passed the lantern to me and descended the steps to the bottom, where a stout wooden door barred our way. Gideon reached once again into his pouch, and this time retrieved a set of keys, one of which unlocked the door. As it creaked open, I was met with a mix of aromas: tobacco, leather, spices and smoked meats.

"This place is used as a warehouse by some of the town's merchants," Gideon explained. "Come, follow me."

It was hard to see clearly in the flickering light of the lantern, but it seemed as though the undercroft had been split into several storage units, some open, but others protected by locked doors of their own. Along the far wall, one of the open units was empty, and Gideon led us directly to this. It was then that I saw the solid oak door set into the wall's brickwork. Fixed into the wall were several thick metal bolts, which Gideon slid back one by one before inserting another key into the lock.

"Why are the bolts on this side of the door?" I asked, curious.

"A good question," smiled Gideon. "Only the mint has a lock to this door, so Bushell knows that it cannot be opened from this side. If access is gained to the mint from here, it can only be an inside job. However, it seems the merchants who rent this storage space are more concerned about employees from the mint providing access to thieves who might wish to rob them of their goods. Rather ironic I always thought."

Gideon turned the key in the lock and pushed the door open to reveal a large space, the boundaries of which I could not see with a single lantern. However, shadows were cast from the corner of the workshop by several large items of machinery, which I took to be the mint's melting and casting equipment packed and ready for transportation.

Gideon made a beeline for a space between two of the pieces of equipment, but then stopped short and scratched his head, before casting his eyes around the workshop in consternation.

"Quick, give me the lantern," he breathed, before snatching it out of my hand and walking systematically around the workshop, removing sheets covering the machinery and searching in each corner of the space. As he worked he seemed to be becoming more and more agitated. Eventually he returned to me and Alexander, his demeanour now totally changed.

"We are undone," he said. I could not see his features clearly in the dim light offered by the lantern, but his eyes betrayed his panic. "We must leave here quickly, without delay."

"Wait!" I said. "Aren't you going to tell us what is going on?"

Gideon gripped me by the arm. "We have been betrayed," he whispered. "I left the boxes of piles and trussels in the space between the two machines over there, but they are gone and nowhere to be found. I left the workshop the same time as Bushell yesterday evening, so they can only have been removed since the mint closed for the night. There can only be one explanation. Someone knew we were coming and has removed them. We need to get out of here before we are arrested."

With a start, my mind cast itself back to the noises I had heard during my watch, and which I had taken to be my own dreams and hallucinations, and I realised that Gideon was right. The dies had already been removed and, in all probability, were no longer in Shrewsbury. The implications, I would eventually have to deal with, but for now my priority was to get out of the mint in one piece. Expecting an ambush at any moment, we retraced our steps as quickly as we could, taking care to bolt and lock the door behind us.

"No point in making it easier for them to track us down," said Gideon.

Once we reached the cobbled courtyard, one look from Gideon was enough for Faith to immediately realise what had happened. She had been standing by the cart horse, holding its reins and allowing it to nuzzle its nose into her shoulder, but now she straightened and clambered back into her seat. Gideon made to climb up alongside her, but I grabbed his arm.

"What do we do now?" I hissed.

Gideon clapped me on the shoulder and gave me a tight-lipped grimace. "One thing is certain. We cannot go back to our house in Mardol. The governor may have men already waiting for us there. We will have to take the cart and take our chances at the English Bridge, and hope that Bushell has not yet worked out which of his employees was helping you. God willing, we will get through before a hue and cry is raised. If we succeed, we will go back to Wem and offer ourselves for further service."

"But what about us?"

"There is another safe house for contingencies such as this. You must go there now. It is the house immediately next door to the row of alms houses in the old College of St Chad that adjoins the churchyard. To be sure you have the right house all you need to do is take a look at the wrought iron door knocker. It is in the shape of a two-headed eagle. It is the occupant's idea of a joke."

When I did not respond to this, Gideon looked me up and down and tutted.

"I forget, you are not from these parts," he said. "A double-headed eagle is the coat of arms of the Mytton family. The door knocker is far too small to be noticed by anyone, unless they were specifically looking for it, but it marks out the house well enough for those who would find it, and cocks a snook at the King at the same time. As for you, all you need to do is knock three times, wait ten seconds, knock three times again, and then the same thing a third time. That should be enough to identify you as a friend. But go there now before you attract suspicion. Whether it's day or night is of no matter. You will be let in regardless."

I thanked Gideon and embraced him, Alexander doing likewise.

"Godspeed," I said. "Make sure you reach Wem safely."

As Gideon climbed up alongside his sister and set the cart in motion, I had a thought. Why, I wondered, if Bushell knew we were about to steal the dies, was there no reception party waiting for us in the mint? It would have been the simplest thing to do. The only explanation, I realised, was that the removal of the dies had been arranged by someone who had an interest in making sure Bushell managed to relocate the mint to Bristol successfully, but who also wanted to make sure Alexander and I were not arrested.

There was, I realised, only one person who fitted that description. I did not know whether to laugh with gratitude or throw my hat to the floor in frustration. One thing was certain, though. Once again, I had been played for a fool.

Chapter 13

Sir Fulke Hunckes stood at the cell door and curled his lip in disdain at the stinking, dirt-streaked bundle of humanity huddled in the corner.

"Good Lord, Colonel," he breathed, addressing the tall, immaculately dressed officer who had accompanied him to Shrewsbury Castle's small but secure gaol house, "what in the name of Jesus have you done to him? He's only been here three nights, yet he smells like he's spent a month locked in a cowshed."

The castle turnkey, who had led the two officers to the cells, shuffled uneasily in his boots at Hunckes' words, but Colonel Robert Broughton, Hunckes' successor as governor of Shrewsbury, merely raised an eyebrow and cast an amused expression in his colleague's direction.

"It is not my fault that the fellow has soiled himself, Sir Fulke. I merely thought three days chained to the wall of this place with nothing to eat or drink other than a hunk of mouldy bread and a jug of water might focus his mind and make him more likely to tell us what we need to know."

"And?"

"Nothing so far. He's a stubborn bastard, I'll give him that, but he'll talk eventually. They always do. I'm just curious to know of what interest he is to you."

Hunckes said nothing but stepped over to the prisoner and gave him a gentle kick with his boot. Philip Saltonstall stirred slightly, grunted and returned Hunckes' stare through swollen eyelids.

"Good morrow, Lieutenant, I see I have your attention at least," said Hunckes.

"And who the devil are you?" retorted Saltonstall, wriggling his body into an upright position.

Hunckes could feel Broughton bristling with anger behind him, but he put a hand in the air to quieten his colleague and smiled patiently at his captive.

"You have spirit, young man, and for that I will give you an answer. My name is Sir Fulke Hunckes, one time governor of this town, and this is Colonel Robert Broughton, who is the current incumbent of that office. You need not introduce yourself, for your old school friend, who you were unfortunate enough to run into in The Sacristy on Wednesday evening, has told us everything we need to know about you. However, you will be pleased to know that you are not our main concern. I'm more interested in the two people who accompanied you to Shrewsbury, for I have a notion as to who they might be."

Saltonstall snorted with contempt. "You have me wrong, sir, if you think I would betray my colleagues."

"I would not dream of it," replied Hunckes. "All I require is that you lend me your ears and confirm what I already suspect to be true."

In truth, Hunckes had initially been as nonplussed as everybody else as to the identity of the two men who had accompanied Saltonstall to Shrewsbury, more so their purpose. All he had managed to ascertain was that the young lieutenant was related to Thomas Mytton and had most recently been serving under Sir William Brereton in Northwich. The fact that Brereton had managed to develop a wide network of informants who had infiltrated deep within the Royalist ranks was well known, but Prince Rupert had his own informants, and Saltonstall was an unknown name to him. What on earth was the young officer up to?

For a whole day, Hunckes had racked his brains to no avail, but when Alice Furnival had contacted him on the Thursday evening and told him to warn Thomas Bushell to remove the dies from the mint as a matter of urgency, bells had started to ring, and things had started to fall into place.

One thing that had bothered him about the curious events at Combermere two weeks previously had been the unexplained role of the cheese merchant from Nantwich, who had somehow become embroiled in the whole affair. Why, he wondered, had Daniel Cheswis been accompanied by someone as prominent as Richard Wilbraham to talk to George Cotton about unspecified inheritance matters, and was it not perhaps more than a coincidence that it turned out to be Cheswis' housekeeper's daughter that had been kidnapped and incarcerated in Cotton's summerhouse? Why, he wanted to know, had he turned up at the Cotton residence with a view to finalising arrangements to ship the contents of Lord Herbert's valuable library to Combermere, only to find the house in turmoil and Cheswis at the centre of everything?

Hunckes had only been told the very basics of how Jem Bressy had come into possession of a hoard of valuables dug up in a Nantwich field, but he could not help wondering what Cheswis had to do with the whole thing.

He then remembered the conversation at George Cotton's dinner table when it was revealed that Alice Furnival had known Cheswis since her youth. And did the description given of the two men who had teamed up with Saltonstall at Richard Halton's house not match that of Cheswis and his friend, the large sandy-haired fellow who had been present at Combermere the night the young girl had been rescued? What was his name? Alexander Clowes, that was it. A common chandler and bellman, if he recalled correctly.

Armed with these thoughts, Hunckes had spoken to his commanding officer, Sir Michael Ernle, who had confirmed that Cheswis was a known intelligencer working for Sir William Brereton. That he was in Shrewsbury was, in itself, no surprise, for it was inconceivable that Brereton, having had Massey's treasure lifted from under his nose, would not try to recover it, but how had Alice Furnival known about it? And more to the point, how had she managed to deduce that the dies to Bushell's mint were at risk? It was something he meant to ask her as soon as the opportunity arose. In the meantime though, he had to be sure he was right, and the person who could confirm it was Lieutenant Philip Saltonstall.

"It is quite simple," said Hunckes, fixing his eyes on the young lieutenant. "Your mission here in Shrewsbury was to destroy the mint, and you had two accomplices when you arrived in Shrewsbury. Their names are Daniel Cheswis and Alexander Clowes, are they not?"

Saltonstall's eyes widened momentarily, but then he exhaled and slumped back against the wall. "If you know this much, then why are you asking me?"

Hunckes looked at Saltonstall and gave a smile of satisfaction. "Thank you, Lieutenant," he said. "That is all I needed to know." He then turned to the gaol keeper and tossed him a shilling. "Make sure this man gets fed properly and is given a clean pair of breeches."

Chapter 14

Alexander and I waited in the cobbled courtyard of Bennett's Hall until the echoing sound of Gideon and Faith's cart wheels had faded into the distance. On reflection, and considering the likelihood that a search party would already be out looking for us, we came to the conclusion that trying to negotiate the empty streets of Shrewsbury in the middle of the night would be asking for trouble, so instead of leaving by the front gate and heading off down Pride Hill, we clambered over a fence at the far end of the courtyard and emerged into the large meadow which ran behind the hall. To the left we could make out the silhouettes of the houses on Mardol a few hundred yards away, but flickering torches across the field indicated that a search was indeed being carried out among the allotments behind the Townsends' house.

It was a quiet, cloudless night, but the fact that the moon had sunk below the horizon offered us some protection against those who would seek us out. Nonetheless, we felt it prudent to manoeuvre our way down the edge of the meadow and wedge ourselves between two hawthorn trees, which backed onto one of the properties a little further down Pride Hill, and there we remained until the first vestiges of dawn began to appear over the rooftops to the east.

Once it began to get light enough to risk betraying our position, we crawled through the trees before emerging into the back yard of one of the houses. Several yards away a dog started barking, but we were not for waiting around. We quickly skirted around the side of the building and emerged onto Pride Hill, where we were able to mingle with the first of the day's traders preparing for work.

Fortunately, we managed to reach the safe house in the college precinct at St Chad's without incident. No longer used for its original purpose, the college, which adjoined the south-western corner of St Chad's Church, consisted primarily of almshouses and other private residences, but was spread over a considerable area. The main building, a large, red stone structure, was separated from the street by a wall perhaps twelve feet high but connected to the church itself by a gallery, which ran along a raised area inside the churchyard. To the north lay a terraced area bordered by a low wall lined with sycamore trees.

We entered the precinct via a gateway set into the wall, which we followed down the hill in the direction of the town walls, until we reached the row of almshouses described by Gideon. On identifying the correct house immediately adjoining them, we were relieved when the pre-arranged knocking procedure resulted in the door being opened abruptly by a severe-looking woman of middle years dressed entirely in black, who ushered us quickly inside.

"You will find Mr Greaves waiting for you in the parlour," she said without ceremony, before disappearing upstairs into one of the chambers.

Greaves, it turned out, was the landlord of The Sacristy, and we found him sitting patiently on a simple wooden chair, chewing a hunk of bread and holding a tankard of ale in his spare hand.

"Good morrow," I said in surprise. "How did you know where to find us?"

"A signal from Gideon Townsend," said Greaves, with a grimace. "I knew that if Gideon and Faith passed by The Sacristry this morning in their cart, that would mean they were on their way to the English Bridge, a sure indication that they had failed in their task. Had they succeeded, they would have left Shrewsbury by the Welsh Bridge. When I saw them ride by I knew I had better prepare this place for you."

I nodded gratefully. "And for that I thank you heartily," I said, "but tell me, what do we do now?"

"I would advise you to remain here and stay out of sight for a couple of days, after which you may be able to get out of town via the English Bridge without being noticed. In the meantime, I have retrieved your belongings from Richard Halton's house, and your horses are out the back."

This was indeed good news, for I had begun to wonder whether I would ever see Demeter again. I thanked Greaves again for his attentions, but realised that laying low for several days was going to be out of the question, for one thing was certain. I needed to talk to Alice.

ଓ

Having sent Alexander forth to trawl the taverns, market stalls, and side streets in search of Ellis Davies, I had fully intended to take Alice to task over the previous night's events at the mint, even though, on reflection, she could not really be blamed for having Bushell remove the dies out of our reach. In all honesty, I had to admit I probably owed her a debt of gratitude, for she had most likely somehow persuaded Thomas Bushell not to have us arrested on the spot. What puzzled me was how quickly the governor's men had worked out that Gideon and Faith were involved and had been able to mount a watch at their house, for I was certain Alice had not known where I was staying. I could only assume that Bushell had already had his suspicions about Gideon, or that he had found out about his rental of the workshop space above the undercroft. Of course, it was also possible that someone had seen us carrying the roll of cloth to Bennett's Hall the previous evening and reported it to Bushell, who had then put two and two together.

However, any thought I might have had of addressing this issue were swiftly sidelined when I presented myself at Alice's print workshop that morning around eleven, for the grim expression on her face immediately betrayed the fact that the very worst had happened.

"Ben Collie is dead," she stated, simply.

I noticed a smudge on Alice's cheek and realised she must have been crying. I had not considered Alice to be of a particularly emotional disposition, even less so as I got to know her more, but Collie had been employed in the Furnivals' print works for some time, and his sudden demise had obviously shaken her.

"Dead? Where?" I asked.

"In the Church of the Holy Cross. It seems Ben had gone there to pray. It may have been just as we suspected. Something was troubling him. Whatever his motives for being there, he was taken violently ill as he sat in one of the pews. It was the minister himself who found him, but it seems there was nothing to be done for him. He died within minutes of being discovered."

"And when did this happen?"

"No more than an hour ago. A messenger was sent over here to inform me almost immediately."

"And where is Collie now?"

"Still in the church, I believe. The nave has been closed until the coroner can be found."

I nodded. "Then we must make haste," I said. "If we are to find out what killed Ben Collie, we must get there before the coroner does. There is just one thing, though."

"What is that?"

"Do you know a good apothecary in this part of town? If so, we should bring him with us. He may prove to be of some use, for it sounds very much as though Ben Collie was poisoned."

⊗

The Abbey Church of St Peter and St Paul, otherwise known as the Church of the Holy Cross, had once been the richest and most prestigious place of worship in the area. The riches of the Benedictine monastery situated on the banks of the Severn had for centuries stood in juxtaposition and rivalry to the town and castle on the opposite side of the English Bridge. Now, however, with no monks to sustain it, the whole area looked rather forlorn. Although the church itself was still in one piece, many of the monastic buildings had fallen into disrepair and decay, the lead having been stripped from their roofs and stone removed for building houses elsewhere in and around the town.

The main advantage from my point of view was that the church was outside the town walls, and for a brief few minutes I considered the possibility of striking out up the road and heading for Wem, where I could secure the services of a messenger to ride to Oswestry and alert Colonel Mytton to Saltonstall's predicament as well as to secure Alexander's escape from the town, but I knew that such action would have been folly. I had no way of knowing what the colonel would say when he found out that not only had his nephew been arrested and incarcerated in Shrewsbury castle and the identity of three of his agents compromised, but the dies for the mint had been removed from Shrewsbury along with Massey's treasure. However, whatever comments recent events elicited, they were unlikely to contain anything complimentary about me. No – I had got myself into this mess, and it was now incumbent upon me to get myself out of it.

As Alice and I approached the church along the Abbey Foregate together with an ageing and bespectacled, white-haired apothecary called Leach, I could see that a small crowd had gathered by the roadside, from where the vicar was manfully trying to keep a number of curious onlookers at bay. A crowd, I noticed, was jostling him and pressing on the gate to try and gain access to the churchyard.

"It seems as though the minister may need some help," I ventured, but Alice waved me away with a smile.

"There is no need for concern," she said. "Looks can be deceptive. James Logan can take care of himself." And as if to prove a point, the minister, who was of slight frame and little more than five feet in height, grabbed the shirt of a young farm boy, who had squeezed past him and was heading for the church door, swivelled him around and propelled him with force back through the gate towards his friends, who jeered in derision.

"Very impressive," I said to Alice. "Logan, you say? An Irishman perchance?"

"His grandfather," said Alice, "and no, it's not what you're thinking. He is no papist, not even a Laudian or Armenian. He did not inherit his faith from his forefathers. Only his ability to fight."

"Well, he can certainly do that," I said, as I watched the minister slam the gate shut on the trespassers, before turning his attention to Alice and the apothecary with a relieved smile.

"Mistress Furnival, Master Leach," he said, "won't you join me in the nave? There is something you ought to see."

"Certainly," replied Alice, "but I would have Mr Cheswis join me too. He is a long-standing friend from my home village, who is skilled in investigative work. He is helping me look into the unfortunate event which took place at St Alkmund's on Wednesday. As you will be aware, Mr De Vries was also an employee of mine. I fear the two events may be connected."

I could have sworn it was impossible for a five-foot man to look down his nose at me, but somehow Logan managed it. "Very well," he sniffed, "you had better follow me."

Once inside the church, Logan led us down the nave towards a set of pews at the front, facing the altar, where a man was sat silently praying, but as we got closer I began to perceive an unpleasant aroma and realised that the man was, in fact, not praying at all. He was stone dead. Now I noticed that his head was lolling slightly to one side, and a pile of vomit lay at his feet. It was all I could do to keep the contents of my own stomach in check.

"This is Collie?" I asked.

Alice, who was looking a little green around the gills herself, nodded and held a kerchief over her mouth before backing off to a safe distance. Leach, however, stepped forward and grasped the corpse's chin with a bony hand, moving the head from side to side and looking closely into the man's eyes. As he did so, Collie's mouth dropped open, and I gasped, for wedged inside his cheek was a small silver chain with a crucifix attached. I stepped forward and slowly pulled the item out, dangling it for Alice, Logan and Leach to see.

"Can you explain how this got here, Mr Logan?" I asked.

The minister, who looked genuinely dumbstruck, stared wide-eyed firstly at me and then at Alice.

"I-I cannot say," he stammered. "What manner of devilry is this? He died with me beside him, and he did not leave my sight until ten minutes ago, when I went outside to deal with the restless crowd."

"So, someone must have gained entry to the church while you were outside, which also suggests the murderer cannot be far away."

"Murderer?" said Logan. "Who said anything about murder?"

"Oh, he was murdered right enough," cut in the apothecary. "Poisoned, without a doubt, although with what I cannot say at this stage."

I stared grimly at Collie's body before addressing Logan. "I think we'd better start by you giving an account of what happened, what you saw, and what you did."

The minister gave me an indignant look. "I hope you don't think I had anything to do with this," he protested. "I am a man of God. I should be most offended if—"

"I did not say that," I interjected, although it had indeed occurred to me that the minister could not be discounted as a suspect. "Perhaps you could begin by telling me what Collie was doing here."

"I had been busy preparing tomorrow's service when he arrived. Said he wanted to discuss a matter of conscience with me, although I am not prepared to betray his confidence by divulging the exact nature of the matter."

"That is of little import," I said. "We know what was troubling him. The man was guilty of murder."

Logan gave me a thin smile. "Then you know the story. He seemed somewhat distressed and agitated, and I took this to be down to his guilty conscience, but he had been with me no longer than a few minutes when he started to feel unwell."

"Can you describe the symptoms?" asked Leach, who had been listening intently.

"He said he had a burning sensation in his mouth and a numbness in his limbs. He then vomited, as is evident from the mess on my pews, and he seemed to be gasping for breath. I was just about to go for help when he suddenly grasped his chest and groaned. After that he didn't move anymore."

Leach squinted at the minister over the top of his spectacles. "You are describing the symptoms of monkshood poisoning," he asserted, "and a fairly substantial dose too by the sound of it. It can easily be imbibed with food. Do you know what he ate today?"

"Of course not," said Logan. "I am his vicar, not his housekeeper, but the evidence is there before you, as it were."

The apothecary stared at the reddish pool of vomit on the floor and curled his lip in distaste. "Looks like bread of some description," he said, "and eaten very recently too."

"And wine also," added the minister. "It's almost as if he were given the sacrament before he died. Who in the name of God would commit such a crime?"

"That," I said drily, "is the very crux of the matter."

Logan offered a single raised eyebrow in response. "An unfortunate choice of words given what we have just found in the man's mouth," he said.

At this point I became aware of Alice opening her purse and retrieving one of the notes that had been delivered to her house. "Perhaps you can tell me what you make of this," she said, offering the paper to Logan. "We believe it was written by the murderer and may offer some clue as to why Ben Collie was killed."

Logan took the scrap of paper from Alice and read it out loud. "BC Luke Twelve Forty-four."

"Indeed," said Alice. "We were hoping you might be able to tell us what it signifies."

Logan looked at Alice as though she were stupid. "Well, that's quite obvious, is it not? It refers to this place, of course."

"What? To the church?"

"Yes, naturally. Luke Twelve Forty-four refers to ravens, does it not?"

"Yes, but I don't see—"

"The church used to be part of a Benedictine monastery," explained Logan. "Surely, you must know this. I think the person who wrote this note may be referring to a famous story involving St Benedict, after whom the holy order was named. Benedict, it is told, was once given poisoned bread by a priest who was jealous of him, but Benedict, who knew the bread had been tampered with, elicited the help of a raven, which often came to feed from his hand, and the bird took the poisoned bread away so nobody could eat it."

"But the raven did not come to help Collie, it seems."

"Precisely."

Whilst Logan and Alice were talking, my brain began to turn over. I was beginning to get an idea of how the murderer's mind worked. And then I thought of something.

"Alice," I said, "Ben Collie. His name."

Alice looked at me blankly at first, but then realisation began to dawn. "Yes," she said, "Ben is short for Benedict. So, the murderer killed him here at the Holy Cross because he saw a connection between Ben's name and that of the saint associated with the order of monks, who once resided here."

"And also committed murder in a manner that has a direct relevance to that particular saint," I added. "It's as though the saint were sitting in judgement on Collie."

"That is sacrilege indeed," said Logan, "but tell me, you said there was a connection with the murder at St Alkmund's earlier this week."

Of course, if Logan could solve the riddle set for us by Collie's death, perhaps he could shed some light on the message relating to De Vries too.

"Mistress Furnival received a letter prior to Jakob De Vries's death at St Alkmund's with a similar cryptic clue, this time referring to Matthew's Chapter Twenty-six, Verse Fifty-two. It is the passage which basically says that he who lives by the sword, shall die by the sword. On the face of it, this was directly relevant to De Vries, for he was indeed killed with a sword. But why St Alkmund's?"

Logan smiled. "I think I can answer that," he said. "St Alkmund was the son of a king of Northumberland, who lived about eight hundred years ago. He was killed in battle."

"So, he too died by the sword," I mused. "There seems to be a pattern emerging. The person who did this appears to be attacking and killing the perpetrators of the crime against Millie Davies in a manner which suggests that the saints are sitting in judgement on them."

"But why would someone do that?" asked Alice.

"I haven't the slightest idea," I admitted, "but what I do know is this. There are three other churches in Shrewsbury, are there not? St Mary's, St Julian's and St Chad's. And there are three of Millie Davies's murderers still alive – Joseph Finch, William Stubbs and Cornelis Smits. In the absence of any other clues I recommend we try to locate these people before our murderer does."

ജ

I suggested to the apothecary, Leach, that he might wish to remain at the church with Logan for the inevitable arrival of the coroner and the local constable, so that both men might have the benefit of his expertise. For my part, I considered it would be prudent to avoid coming into contact with either man, so I suggested to Alice that we go in search of Finch, Stubbs and Smits.

As we left the church, however, I was surprised to see that the crowd that had gathered by the churchyard gate had not yet dispersed. Indeed, it appeared to have grown somewhat larger, and if I was not mistaken, the young farm boy who had been manhandled by Logan, together with his group of rowdy friends, was still at the centre of it.

When they saw us emerge from the church, one of the group, a craggy-faced man, slightly older than the rest, stepped forward and called over to Alice.

"Is it true, Mistress Furnival, that Ben Collie is dead? The killer that stalks this town has struck again, we hear."

Alice looked across, startled, to where the voice was coming from, but then her face adopted a more puzzled expression.

"Do I know you?" she asked, surveying the man with a mixture of curiosity and suspicion.

"My name is Edwin Hodgson," came the response, "a humble farmer of this town. You don't know me, mistress, but I know your newssheet, as do many in these parts, and you can only be here for one reason. There has been another killing."

Alice seemed to hesitate for a moment, so I stepped up alongside her. "It is true that Collie is dead, Mr Hodgson," I said, "but I am curious to know why you talk of murder. Why is that so? I don't believe Mr Logan ever suggested foul play was at hand here."

"But it is common knowledge, sir," replied Hodgson, backed by numerous murmurs of assent from the crowd. "Collie was poisoned, the whole town knows it."

"Aye, and the young street urchin was here too," shouted the young farm hand. "Why has he not been arrested?"

"Street urchin?"

"Aye, the young lad who ran away from St Alkmund's on Wednesday. He is the killer, of that there can be no doubt."

"Where is he now?" shouted someone else. "He must be caught and made to face justice."

This was a new turn of events, and one which threatened to spill over into violence. If Ellis Davies had been present that morning, could it be that I had got things wrong – that Ellis was the murderer of De Vries and Collie after all? I shuddered to think.

"Who saw the boy," I asked, "and did anybody see where he went? What about you, Mr Hodgson?"

Hodgson shrugged and looked to his friends for support. "I didn't see him myself, sir, but it was common knowledge. Everyone knew he was here."

I repeated the question to the whole crowd, but all I received in response were a few murmurings and shuffled feet. What, I wondered, if Ellis had not been here at all, if details of Collie's death and false reports of his presence at the scene had been spread by the murderer himself?

"Does anybody here at all know who first announced that Collie was dead?" I asked. Again, all I received in response were shrugs and blank faces.

"It's time we went, Daniel," said Alice. "This is becoming nothing better than a lynch mob. We are wasting our time. I suggest we focus on the job in hand."

❦

In the event, Joseph Finch was the easiest of the three men to find, as it turned out that he farmed a small strip of land adjoining the river that had once belonged to the abbey. Given the time of year, it took little more than an intelligent guess to ascertain that he was likely to be knee deep in vegetables, and we were not disappointed. We found him wheeling a barrow full of potatoes along a path that ran alongside his smallholding, to a cart, which stood ready on a stony track running through the old abbey grounds towards the main road.

A tall, spindly man with a thatch of thick, corn-coloured hair, Finch showed due deference to us at first and tipped his hat to Alice, who he evidently recognised, but when we told him the reason for seeking him out, his attitude changed immediately, and he became cold and distant.

"Oswestry? Millie Davies? I haven't the faintest idea what you're talking about."

"But you were there in March, were you not?" I pressed.

"Of course, as were many others. Now, if you don't mind, it is harvest time, and I have work to do."

I tried to explain the potential danger he was in, considering the deaths of De Vries and Collie, but he did not seem in the slightest bit interested. Instead he dragged his wheelbarrow up towards his cart, which he then started loading, pretending not to hear a word I was saying. After a few moments, I gave up and hastened after Alice, who had already begun to make her way back towards the English Bridge.

As we crossed the Severn, Alice slowed and stopped. I stood beside her for a moment, taking in the view downstream to the meadow known as the Gaye on the right hand bank, and the steep escarpment protecting the town on the left. In the background stood the imposing red sandstone bulk of Shrewsbury Castle.

"That is where your friend the young officer is currently being held," said Alice.

"Will they hang him, do you think?" I asked.

Alice turned to me and shrugged. "I have no idea," she admitted. "It depends on his value to the governor, I imagine."

"He is a great-nephew to Sir Thomas Myddelton."

"Then that will almost certainly guarantee his safety. He will be of considerable worth in a prisoner exchange. He will be going nowhere for the foreseeable future, though. The dungeon in the castle is well-nigh impregnable."

We stood quietly for a few moments, watching a pair of ducks swimming towards the bridge against the current. It was I who eventually broke the silence.

"Why do our paths keep crossing in this manner. Alice?" I said. "Is there still unfinished business between us, do you think, or is fate merely continuing to remind us of the mistakes we made in the past, I for leaving Barthomley to seek work in Nantwich, and you for eloping with Hugh Furnival?"

Alice put her hand on mine, and it felt as though a bolt of lightning had shot through my arm. I let it stay there for a few moments and then withdrew my hand gently.

"I do not think I am being punished," said Alice, "for I loved Hugh, and I have three children by him, who surely have a purpose in this world. No, I believe our paths are already written. So long as this war continues, our relationship could never be any different to what it is, apart from which, you now have a wife of your own."

"Who I love dearly," I added, "and who now expects our first child."

Alice's eyes widened at this, but then she smiled. "Then there you have it," she said, turning away from me and continuing across the bridge. "In that case, we both know where our respective roads must lead."

Alice was right, of course, but as I followed her onto Wyle Cop, I could not help but feel this was not how things would eventually play out, that fate had something entirely different in mind for me.

The search for Cornelis Smits concluded even less successfully than our discussion with Finch. Enquiries made at the Dutchman's workshop on Wyle Cop revealed that he had left to go to work on a job earlier that morning and had not yet returned. Smits had not left word as to where he was working. I made a mental note to call back on the Monday to see if I could find him.

I was beginning to feel frustrated at the lack of progress on the case, but there was still one more address to visit, so we made our way up the broad curve of Wyle Cop until we reached St Julian's Church at the bottom of Fish Street, where my mind was distracted by the enticing smell of roast meat coming from a building a couple of doors up the narrow street on the opposite side to the church.

"Stubbs's chophouse," explained Alice. "There are many who say it's the best in town."

The cookshop was clearly popular, for it was brimming with customers. Indeed, it was so full that the owners had placed a couple of tables out on the street, which was teeming with people going about their daily business. Most of the other properties on Fish Street appeared, ironically, to be butchers' shops, a whole row of houses fronted by clapboard tables, on which the shop owners could display their produce. The proprietors of each shop appeared to be competing with each other by shouting as loud as they could to attract the passing goodwives, who had come out to buy meat for the following day's dinner. On the opposite side of the street the sound of banging and the occasional metallic clang emanated from the bell tower of St Julian's, where some kind of construction work seemed to be being carried out. It was a chaotic scene.

As we approached the cookhouse, a young man of no more than eighteen or nineteen years emerged from the building carrying two trenchers of food balanced on one arm. His other arm, I noticed, hung thin and useless by his side. Indeed, when he approached the table he was serving, one of the customers had to take the trenchers from the young man's arm so he could serve the other plate without spilling anything. When he saw me watching, the youngster coloured slightly and then addressed me and Alice together.

"Sir, madam, I'm terribly sorry. I'm afraid we cannot accommodate you today. As you can see, we are full to the brim."

"It's not food that we seek," I said. "It is information that concerns us. You are William Stubbs, I presume?"

At the mention of his name the youth eyed me curiously. "Aye, what of it?"

"It concerns an incident in Oswestry in March this year," I said. "Does the name Millie Davies mean anything to you?"

Stubbs froze, and the colour drained from his face. "Who are you, sir, and why do you want to know about Millie Davies?" he asked, hesitantly.

"My name is Cheswis," I said, "and this is Mistress Furnival, who you may recognise, as she is of this town. You have nothing to fear from us. We simply seek the whereabouts of one Ellis Davies, who we believe to be in Shrewsbury."

"The brother? He lives?" exclaimed Stubbs with incredulity.

"So we believe, but we also suspect that all those associated with the unfortunate event in March may be in danger."

"Danger?"

"We believe so," I confirmed, trying to look as serious and official as I could.

At this I could see Stubbs mulling over whether he should co-operate with us or not, but it was Alice who prompted him to do the right thing.

"We just need to talk to you, William," she said. "It won't take long. Is there somewhere more private we could go?"

Stubbs took a long look at Alice, but then his shoulders slumped in submission, and he gestured for a serving maid to come over.

"Mary, I have some business to attend to. Would you please take care of my customers for a short while? I won't be long."

The young girl gave Stubbs an irritated look, but agreed nevertheless, and Stubbs led us through the chophouse and up some stairs to a neatly kept room, which I took to be the Stubbs's private living space.

"It was not of my doing, what happened to the girl," said Stubbs, as soon as the door was closed. "I wasn't even supposed to be there."

"Tell me about it," I said. "If what you say is true, then this is your opportunity to make amends, at least in so far as that may be possible."

"We had been on sentry duty at the Black Gate," said Stubbs, hesitantly. "I normally didn't associate myself with Sergeant Hipkiss and his crowd, but on this occasion the sergeant invited me to join them. I know not what his purpose was, but you didn't turn down an invite from Sergeant Hipkiss, not if you knew what was good for you, so I followed them to The Bell Inn, where we drank our fill. The sergeant and the two Dutchmen, De Vries and Smits, started having some fun with one of the serving wenches, and by that time, we were all the worse for drink."

"There was a fight, I believe."

"If you know that, sir, then you will know the reason," said Stubbs, casting an anxious glance in Alice's direction.

"There is no need to temper your description for Mistress Furnival's benefit," I reassured him. "She is broadminded enough. But no matter, I know why you were thrown out of the tavern. What I want to know is what happened after you left."

"Hipkiss was proper angry, spitting feathers like, so he made us wait outside the smithy. The sergeant knew where the girl lived, see. We were there for ages. I was cold and needed to piss, but the sergeant made us wait."

"And when she finally arrived, you all followed her into the workshop, and that's when things really started to go wrong."

"I didn't think they would do that to her, truly I didn't," said Stubbs. The youngster's voice was shaking now, and I could tell he was close to tears. "They wanted me to have a go too, but I refused, I couldn't bring myself to assault the girl like that. It was evil what they did to her, sir. Evil."

"I can tell that you did not violate her," interjected Alice, softly. "Your tone is not that of a liar, but how many of them did rape her?"

"Nearly all of them, mistress. Hipkiss, De Vries, Finch and Collie. All except for Smits."

"And why was that?" I asked.

"We discovered the brother lurking behind a cart in the corner of the workshop. He cracked Joe Finch on the knees with a pair of clinch cutters and then ran for it. Corni charged after him like a man possessed, but even if he'd stayed, he would not have joined in."

"How can you be so sure?" I asked, curious.

"You mean you haven't found out yet? Smits is more interested in boys than girls. It is a well-known fact."

"You mean Smits is a sodomite?"

"If you want to put it like that. De Vries just used to say he lived on the other side of the Severn, but we all knew what he meant. I would have pitied the boy if Smits had managed to catch him."

"But he didn't."

"I don't think so," said Stubbs. "Corni would have said if he had. That is good news, surely?"

"Perhaps," I acknowledged, "but you should know that the lad has written to his parents saying he has identified all six of those who were in the smithy that night and has sworn to enact vengeance on his sister's murderers. We have just come from the Church of the Holy Cross, where Ben Collie lies murdered, poisoned by an unknown hand. Add that to the untimely death of De Vries earlier this week, and that gives us grounds for concern, don't you think?"

This at last produced the required response, and Stubbs blanched noticeably. "Collie, dead?" he exclaimed. "How can that be? And you think the young lad is responsible?"

"We doubt it, to be honest," I admitted. "We feel another force is at play, but we urgently need to locate Ellis, as he is also in danger from those who would blame him for those deeds. Have you seen him, perchance?"

"I would not recognise him," said Stubbs. "It was dark in the smithy, but now you mention it, there has been a young lad hanging round here recently, watching our customers, begging for food, that sort of thing. The strange thing is, he was here only half an hour ago, but he left with a man I've never seen before, a large broad-shouldered fellow with sandy hair, dressed like a servant. Strange areally, because the man bought him a meal. Why would someone do that, do you suppose?"

Alice raised an eyebrow at this, for she recognised the significance of what was being said. Things were beginning to look up.

I smiled as I stood to leave and emitted a soft chuckle. "I can think of a good reason."

I expected Alice to attempt to join me in search of Alexander and Ellis Davies, which would have created its own problems – I would have needed to dream up a plan to maintain the integrity of our safe house near St Chad's. However, as we emerged from the chophouse back onto Fish Street, this particular problem was solved when Alice's attention was drawn to the sight of a young man weaving his way through the crowds, waving an envelope in the air. I recognised the newcomer as one of the apprentices from Alice's print workshop.

"What is it, Matthew?" asked Alice.

"I've been looking for you everywhere, mistress," replied the youth, breathlessly. "You have another letter. I thought you should know."

Alice took the letter from the young apprentice and began to break the seal. "Who delivered this?" she asked.

"I don't know. We didn't see. We were all too busy with the press. It was about an hour ago, and I heard a banging on the workshop door, so I went to investigate. There was no one there, but this letter had been nailed to the door."

I peered over Alice's shoulder as she opened up the contents of the envelope, but what I read made my heart sink, for it made the identity of the murderer's next victim all too clear.

CS 1 Corinthians 69

Chapter 15

Shrewsbury – Saturday August 31ˢᵗ, 1644

In retrospect, I have to concede that I displayed a remarkable amount of naivety during my stay in Shrewsbury. Granted, it had crossed my mind as being a little odd that Alice had not sought to ensure that Alexander, Gideon and I were arrested at Bennett's Hall, but at the time I had simply put it down to a desire to make sure I was available to help her identify Jakob De Vries's killer. And yes, perhaps I flattered myself to believe that she may still have held a modicum of affection for me, and at least enough loyalty to have prevented her from betraying me and guaranteeing me an appointment with the hangman. However, it did not occur to me that Alice's mind might harbour some altogether darker motives, which would re-emerge with a vengeance in the months to come.

To be honest, I should have guessed something was afoot when Alice made no attempt to come with me or to follow me to ascertain the location of the safe house in which Alexander and I were staying. Had she done so, of course, she would have been able to burst wide open Mytton's network of informers in Shrewsbury.

Instead, I arranged to meet her that evening in the seclusion of St Chad's churchyard, chosen so that I could watch her approach from the safety of The Sacristy, where I could mingle unnoticed among the crowds of drinkers, whilst also remaining under the watchful eye of my protector, Greaves.

Why I carried on in blissful ignorance of Alice's scheming, I cannot say. Perhaps it was the speed at which events were unfolding, but more likely it was the effect that my first love was having on me. Over the previous few days I had spent more time in Alice's company than at any time since the heady days of our betrothal, and I was beginning to feel that having her close to me, working and interacting with her as though nothing had happened in the intervening years, seemed almost to be a natural state.

As I walked back alone towards St Chad's, I realised with a pang of guilt that during the course of the day I had not thought once about Elizabeth and the fact that she was carrying our child. Looking back, I feel nothing but shame.

ભ

I waited until the coast was clear before approaching the safe house, but as I did so I was relieved to see Mistress Eliza, for such was the name given to me by the owner of the house, open the door slightly, allowing me to slip noiselessly inside.

"They're in the kitchen," she said, casting her eyes up and down the street to check I had not been followed, "eating me out of house and home."

I found Alexander sat at the table, thoughtfully watching the young boy devouring a bowl of pottage.

"I was told you had already fed him," I said.

Alexander nodded as the boy ladled spoon after spoon into his mouth. "I did," he said, "but the lad hasn't eaten properly for weeks. He's taking advantage whilst he can. He needs the food."

I looked closely at the boy, who had barely registered my presence when I entered the room. He was certainly somewhat emaciated, dressed in clothes that were beginning to fall from his back. I was also becoming aware of an unpleasant odour, which I realised was several months' worth of dirt and sweat.

"He needs a bath too," I added, "and some clean clothes would not go amiss. How did you find him?"

"I didn't," replied my friend, flashing the boy a conspiratorial grin. "He found me. He's a resourceful lad is Ellis. Seems he was outside The Sacristry the night Saltonstall was arrested. He had gone to hide in the churchyard after escaping from St Alkmund's earlier that evening. Of course, he recognised us as having been present immediately after the murder, and having seen the disturbance at The Sacristry, realised that we must be fugitives of some sort. He figured that he might be able to profit from us in some way, so he's spent the last few days following me around. He didn't realise we were looking for him at the same time, though. I saw him this morning down by the Holy Cross, but I believe one or two of the locals had heard he was being sought after in connection with Wednesday's murder, so, with events unfolding as they did this morning, he had to make himself scarce."

"So, you knew about Collie, then?"

"Yes, as soon as I realised what had happened I followed Ellis back across the English Bridge and intercepted him before he could disappear among the alleyways. He has a nerve – I'll grant him that. Offered not to betray me to the authorities if I bought him breakfast, so we went to the chophouse on Fish Street."

At this point the youngster finished his pottage, belched loudly, and looked up, giving me the broadest grin I'd ever seen. "And very grateful I am too," he said, pushing his bowl across the table.

"That may well be so," I riposted, attempting with mixed success to keep a straight face, "but I would lay odds that Mr Clowes does not know that the young man who served you was one of those who assaulted your sister."

Alexander opened his eyes wide. "No, I did not know that," he admitted, and then to Ellis, "You are a proper piece of work, young man, and no mistake."

"How have you managed to survive all these months, Ellis?" I asked, getting straight to the point.

The boy gave me a puzzled look. "Survive?" he said. "How does anyone survive in my position? A good turn here, a bit of begging there. Some honest work from time to time too. I've slept rough at times, in barns if I was lucky, but I've managed to get by. Most recently I've been sleeping in a blacksmith's workshop down Grope Lane. If you have spoken to my parents as Mr Clowes says, then you will know I am comfortable with such surroundings. When the blacksmith discovered I could do his work passably well, he let me help from time to time and gave me the odd meal and a few coins in return. It was he who helped me get a letter out to my parents."

"And you're still sleeping there?"

"No, as soon as the blacksmith discovered I was being sought for the death of the Dutchman, he got nervous and cast me out onto the street. At first, I slept in a street by the allotments behind the house on Mardol in which you were staying, but last night the place was crawling with soldiers –

searching for you, I've since been told – so I made my way over to St Chad's church and slept among the gravestones."

"In the churchyard?"

"Aye. It's a good place to sleep rough. The headstones offer shelter from the wind, no-one bothers you at night, and I'm not frightened of any spirits that might lurk there."

I scratched my head in wonderment. Ellis was little more than a boy, but he had displayed a degree of self-sufficiency well beyond his years.

"But tell me," I enjoined, "your parents have been worried about you. Why did you run, and why did you not leave word with your family?"

"I wish I could have," came the response, "but I was scared. Terrified. When they discovered where I was hiding, the younger Dutchman, Smits, chased me down an alleyway, but I managed to vault over a garden wall and take refuge in some bushes. I could hear him searching for me, becoming more and more frustrated, but I was well hidden. In the end he gave up, but not before announcing he would have me on the end of a pitchfork if I ever showed my face back in town or said anything to implicate him and his friends."

"And you believed him?"

"Why would I not? He was a part of the garrison. If I'd betrayed Hipkiss and his men, they would have only denied it. Who would believe a boy like me against the word of an officer like Hipkiss? I tried to get back home the next day, but I found out that Millie was dead, so I ran for it, survived off the charity of others and eventually made my way here.

"I was doing alright too, the blacksmith who befriended me was giving me more work, bit by bit. I figured if I played my cards right, he would eventually give me more regular work and permanent shelter, but then one day I was down the bottom of Fish Street, and I saw William Stubbs outside his family's chophouse. I couldn't fail to recognise him with his withered arm, but fortunately he was not able to identify me. I asked him some questions and found out that Oswestry had fallen to Parliament, and that his regiment had been defeated at Whittington. I asked after the sergeant responsible for killing my sister, pretended my family had known him before the war, and from that I learned the bastard was dead.

"After that it was easy enough to track the others down. Stubbs told me that Collie was working with the sergeant's brother in the print works. It was there that I found De Vries, and through him I was able to track down Smits. Finch was more difficult. He and I have much in common, as we both like to keep ourselves hidden, but I came upon him by chance in the market one day, selling his vegetables, so I followed him back across the river and discovered he was farming a smallholding down by the Meole Brook."

"So, you spent your days watching these men, plotting your revenge, and when you found all Millie's killers you wrote to your parents to let them know you were alive and that Millie's death would be avenged."

"That was my idea. I monitored all as closely as I could, all except Smits, for I was afraid he would recognise me. I was going to kill Finch first, as his plot of land is quite secluded among the old abbey grounds. I was going to kill him with his own spade, but things rather caught up with me. Last Wednesday I was walking up Grope Lane towards the Smithy when I saw De Vries come out of one of the brothels down that street."

"De Vries was a frequenter of whorehouses?"

"I don't know. Yes, maybe. I had not seen him there before, but such information is always useful, and I was curious, so I followed him, and to my surprise he went directly to St Alkmund's. When he arrived, he entered the church and walked straight down the nave towards the altar. I managed to sneak in behind him and secrete myself between two rows of pews. After a few seconds, I heard voices and it became clear that De Vries was talking to someone else, but whoever it was had concealed himself in the north transept out of sight of where I was hiding. The voice was oddly familiar, but I couldn't quite place it. I then heard a brief scuffle and a heavy thud. I dared to look over the pews and saw that De Vries was propped up against the door clutching his chest. His hands were covered in blood, and he was gasping for breath. The Dutchman saw me and tried to call for help, but there was something caught in his throat that seemed to be choking him, and after a moment or so he fell back motionless against the door.

"I got up and went over to him, but at that moment the minister burst into the church from the vestry and saw me. I wasn't going to wait for anyone, so I tried to move the body out of the way and open the door, but the corpse was too heavy and the minister too quick. It was then that you arrived on the scene."

It was Alexander who noticed the implication of this. "So that means the murderer was still in the church when we were there?"

"I suppose so," said Ellis.

"Either that," added my friend, "or he escaped out through the door to the vestry."

I considered this for a moment. The murderer's actions were, I had to admit, most curious. I understood why the killer would not have wanted to leave the church by the front door, given that the street outside was full of people, but to hide in the shadows in wait for Jakob De Vries and escape through the vestry suggested three things – firstly that De Vries was lured to his death and probably knew his killer, secondly that the killer knew the church well enough not to be worried about being discovered should the minister have happened to walk through the vestry door, and thirdly, he must have been aware of the escape route through the vestry and been confident enough to rely on being able to use it. So, who could that have possibly been?

"Alice has received another message," I said to Alexander. "It reads 'CS One Corinthians Sixty-nine. The good news is that thanks to the minister at the Holy Cross, we now understand the significance of the first two messages. The first message was a direct reference to St Alkmund and the manner in which he died, the second referred to a legend about how St Benedict avoided eating poisoned bread. So, the clues suggest three things – the identity of the next victim, where he will die, and the manner of his death. It seems as though the clues draw reference to the saints to whom the churches of Shrewsbury are dedicated. What we know is that there are three more churches in Shrewsbury and three more potential victims. It seems as though the murderer is deliberately trying to test us, challenging us to work out where the next murder will take place and how. The next victim – CS – is clearly intended to be Cornelis Smits. What is worrying is that he appears to have vanished, but what do you make of the rest of it?"

"I cannot say," admitted Alexander, but then he turned to Mistress Eliza. "Do you have a bible, mistress?" he asked.

"Of course," came the reply, "but I do not need to refer to the good book to remind myself of the contents of one Corinthians Chapter Six, Verse Nine. It refers to unnatural sin, to the kind of relationship that should only exist between a man and a woman."

"You know the verse?"

"By rote. 'Know ye not that the unrighteous shall not inherit the kingdom of God? Be not deceived: neither fornicators, nor idolaters, nor adulterers, nor effeminate, nor abusers of themselves with mankind.'" Eliza spat out the words as though they tasted of bile. I suppose I should not have been surprised that such a dour, straight-laced woman should possess the kind of strict puritan values that would elicit such a reaction.

"The quote refers to the sin of sodomy," I said. "I understand that Smits is this way inclined."

"But it doesn't explain how the murderer plans to dispose of him or where," pointed out Alexander.

"It must do," I said. Fortunately, there was a pot of ink and a quill on the table Alexander and Ellis were sitting at, so I asked Mistress Eliza for a sheet of paper and made her repeat the quote word for word until I could read it all, but I still could not make any sense of it.

"There are three more churches, St Chad's, St Julian's, and St Mary's," I said. "There must be a clue in here that points towards which church the killer has in mind."

Alexander leaned forward on his chair and reached for another piece of bread. "Perhaps," he said, "but we are hardly in a position to mount a watch on all three places just in case Smits shows up."

"That is true," I agreed. "I have arranged to meet with Alice later, perhaps she has been able to locate where Smits is hiding."

"I should like to accompany you," cut in Ellis, with a smile. "Perhaps I can be of some help."

Alexander looked at me aghast, but I had already formulated my response.

"You will stay here where you can be watched," I said. "I want to be able to deliver you back to your parents in one piece. It has taken long enough for us to track you down. The governor's men are searching the town for all three of us. There is no reason to make things easier for them."

Ellis gave me a sullen stare, but he acquiesced, especially at the promise of a bath and some fresh clothes. For my part I suddenly realised how hungry I was, having not eaten since the previous evening, so I helped myself to a bowl of Mistress Eliza's pottage and a hunk of bread, and ate until I was full.

The food and the delayed effects of the previous night's exertions slowly began to make me feel sleepy, so I returned to the spare chamber that had been designated for our use, curled up on the pile of rushes that had been laid out for me, and fell into a restless sleep, punctuated by a vivid dream in which I wandered aimlessly around Shrewsbury with Lieutenant Saltonstall, Gideon Townsend and Alexander, searching for some elusive entity, a black shadow which always remained frustratingly just out of reach. One by one my companions slowly disappeared, Saltonstall in the castle, Gideon in Bennett's Hall and Alexander in The Sacristry, until I found myself quite alone in St Chad's churchyard. It was then that I realised I was not searching for anything at all. In fact, it was I who was being hunted. I felt a sudden sense of foreboding and turned around to see a smiling Alice approaching me from behind holding a crucifix.

I awoke suddenly to find Alexander clutching my arm.

"You were dreaming," he said, simply.

I ran my hand through my sweat-sodden hair and wiped it on my shirt. "You are right, my friend," I said. "Bad dreams."

It was then that Alexander showed his true worth as a friend, for he was able to disassociate himself from his cares and treat problems with a levity and a freedom from worry that I could never manage.

"You are concerned about how we get ourselves out of this maelstrom of events in which we find ourselves," he said. "You must free yourself of negative thoughts, and then the solution will present itself."

"Your optimism is commendable," I replied, "but maelstrom is the right word. I feel as though we are being slowly pulled under. We must work out how to get Massey's treasure back from Jem Bressy, or at least locate and destroy the dies from the mint, we must secure Saltonstall's release, solve a murder, and get Ellis back to Oswestry, all the time making sure that we don't end up on a gibbet somewhere, having been convicted of spying."

My friend smiled and clapped me on the shoulder. "But we will do this, Daniel, we always do." And then as an afterthought he added, "We must have faith, and if all else fails, we must pray to the saints, for it seems they have a stake in this too."

☙

That evening I sat alone in St Chad's churchyard, waiting for Alice. I was having trouble shaking off the air of melancholia that had settled over my shoulders, so I left the house early, leaving Alexander in the company of Mistress Eliza, who it seemed had taken something of a shine to him. I wandered down the hill to the town walls, from where I could see across the area of common ground south of the walls, which ran down to the broad sweep of the Severn as it circumvented the town. From there I followed the walls back round to Mardol, and was able to stroll unnoticed past the Townsends' house, now guarded by a couple of sentries. I returned to St Chad's along Market Street, passing in front of The Sacristry, from where Greaves gave me a nod of recognition as I passed.

Despite my suspicions about her motives, I found myself looking forward to seeing Alice again, and so it was with a pang of disappointment that at the appointed hour, it was not Alice's blonde curls that I saw approaching me through the churchyard gate, but the auburn thatch of the young apprentice from Alice's print shop. When he saw me, the young lad raised a hand in recognition and hurried over to where I was sitting.

"You are alone?" I asked, rather more brusquely I suspect than was necessary.

"Yes sir. Mistress Furnival has been called away and has had to leave Shrewsbury at short notice. She asked that I give you this."

The youth handed me an envelope, and I immediately realised that my dream, albeit figuratively, had come true. I tore open the envelope, dreading the words I was about to read.

My dearest Daniel,

It seems as though events have once again conspired to keep us apart. I have been called away urgently. You may hazard a guess as to where.

In my absence, I have asked Charlie Hipkiss to help you with your investigations. He may prove to be of some help as he knows all those involved with the case. I have also asked James Logan to assist you in any way he can. You may call on him after church tomorrow.

The disturbing news is that Cornelis Smits is still missing. There is no sign of him at his lodgings, and his housekeeper knows not where he can be. Despite what he has done, we must pray he has not fallen into the hands of the murderer.

I wish you good fortune in your quest to identify the murderer, Daniel, and I have not forgotten my promise to you to do all that I can to help facilitate the release of Lieutenant Saltonstall.

Yours as ever,

Alice

I exhaled wearily and stuffed the letter inside my shirt.

"Is everything alright, sir?" asked the apprentice. "Can I be of assistance in some way?"

I reached inside my purse and gave the lad a couple of coins.

"Tomorrow is Sunday," I said. "I believe you must know where Mr Hipkiss lives. Please tell him to meet me outside the school at nine in the morning. If we are to be better acquainted, we can start tomorrow at church."

Chapter 16

Shrewsbury – Sunday September 1ˢᵗ, 1644

I spent much of the night wondering what had made Alice depart Shrewsbury so suddenly. Given the importance she had attributed to finding whoever had murdered De Vries and Collie, it could only have been King's business that had taken her away, and it probably had something to do with Jem Bressy and Abbott Massey's treasure.

As I approached Charlie Hipkiss, who I found smoking a pipe on the school steps, I could tell that her employee was just as nonplussed.

"Not sure what this is about Mr Cheswis," he grumbled, "but I've not seen Mistress Furnival move so fast in years as she did last night. It was as though someone had shoved a halberd up her arse."

"So, she left in some haste?" I probed.

"I should say so. She had me accompany her as far as the Welsh Bridge. Said she had no time to lose and needed to give me instructions on the way. I've no idea what your relationship with her is, but it can't be anything good. I've never seen her like this before. She was not her normal self."

I stared at Hipkiss with curiosity. "What do you mean?"

"I don't know. She was behaving differently and sort of scared."

I scrutinised Hipkiss's face, but could detect no sign of insincerity in his expression. Alice did not seem the type of person who was easily cowed, so what had frightened her so much that she needed to leave at a moment's notice? And where was she headed? If she had left town by the Welsh Bridge, then it seemed likely she was travelling towards the area that Sir Thomas Myddelton's forces were looking to occupy. The fact had not escaped me that there was one person who had been present during the unfortunate events at Combermere, who was from those parts, and who might still be a target for Alice's attentions. Could it be, I wondered, that Alice was on her way to meet Bressy, in Montgomery? If I was to have any chance at all of recovering the treasure for Sir William Brereton, I would need to find a way of getting out of Shrewsbury sooner rather than later.

"So, what is the plan?" asked Hipkiss, shaking me from my thoughts. "Mistress Furnival said I was required to help you in your quest to find out who killed Ben and Jakob."

"Indeed," I said. "Come with me. I have some questions I need to ask Reverend Logan at the Church of the Holy Cross, but first we have a church service to attend."

ରେ

Logan's congregation was largely made up of farmers and labourers from the houses along the Abbey Foregate. Much different, I mused, to how the place must have looked not much more than a hundred years previously, before the great abbey was dissolved and destroyed by King Henry. For centuries, the Benedictine abbey of St Peter and St Paul and the town of Shrewsbury had co-existed in a kind of symbiotic rivalry. Town against church. But although the rivalry still existed to a degree, with the wealth of the abbey long since gone, Holy Cross was now very much the poor relation to the town inside the walls.

In truth, knowing the history of the place, and seeing the ruins all around me, I felt a pang of sadness that the area had been brought so low. That is not to suggest that the people of Holy Cross were anything other than assiduous in their devotions, for the church was full of people come to listen to the sermons offered by Logan and Maredudd Tewdwr, the schoolteacher. Even the group of boisterous young men who had almost come to blows with Logan were present, their voices put to better use than the day before.

Joseph Finch was there also, although it took me a while to notice him sat inconspicuously in a corner at the back of the nave. My eyes were fully on him though when Logan began to talk about Ben Collie's untimely death the day before. I could have sworn I saw Finch shuffle uncomfortably in his pew and look anxiously in the direction of Hipkiss and myself. Like the rest of the congregation I closed my eyes at Logan's behest to pray for Collie's soul, but when I opened them again Finch's pew was empty.

After the service was over I spent a few minutes in quiet reflection to give the church time to empty, but I could see Hipkiss was getting impatient, so I eventually got to my feet and went in search of Logan. We found him deep in conversation with Tewdwr by the church gate where I had first seen him the day before. Both men saw us coming simultaneously and greeted us cordially.

"Thank you for attending our service," said Logan, pleasantly. "Mistress Furnival intimated you might be here. She has left on her travels already?"

"So I believe," I said, "although I expect I am no better informed than you."

"King's business," said Logan, confirming my suspicions, "although I know not where. She informed me you would be continuing to investigate the deaths of Mr Collie and Mr De Vries in her absence. If there's anything I can do to help—"

"You must be well acquainted with Mistress Furnival," interjected Tewdwr, stroking his beard thoughtfully. "I did not realise she had left town, but it explains why Mr Hipkiss is here, I suppose."

Under the circumstances, I felt it incumbent on me to give a brief account of how I, a stranger in Shrewsbury, knew Alice, so I explained to Tewdwr that Alice was a childhood friend, without revealing the true nature of that friendship, and I explained that I had some experience as a constable in Nantwich, during which time I had enjoyed some limited success in solving a series of murders while the town had been under siege, without, of course, going too deeply into the intricacies of that particular episode.

Tewdwr appeared delighted at this. "Then you are truly qualified to make this investigation on her behalf," he exclaimed. "Like Mr Logan, I am at your service."

With two such willing volunteers at my disposal, it would have been remiss of me not to take advantage of their undoubted knowledge of the scriptures, so I reached inside my doublet and retrieved the piece of paper on which I had written the verse from 1 Corinthians that Alice had seen the previous day.

"Another note?" probed Logan, his eyes twinkling with curiosity. "I presume you would like us to decipher it for you?"

"I believe we are some way along that route already," I began, not sure how much I should confide in Tewdwr. "We are concerned for the safety of the Dutchman, Cornelis Smits, who has been missing since yesterday morning. The latest note includes his initials and includes a reference to One Corinthians, Chapter Six, Verse Nine."

"Ah, the verse relating to the sins of fornication, idolatry and adultery," said Logan.

"Indeed, but not those sins alone."

"Mr Smits is a sodomist?" cut in Tewdwr, a smile playing at the corner of his lips. "And someone wants to murder him? Forgive me if I sound flippant, but is that really such a surprise?"

"It is not a matter of motive that concerns me," I said, "more one of location. So far, the killer has struck at St Alkmund's and here at the church of the Holy Cross. My belief is that he intends that Cornelis Smits die at one of the other churches in Shrewsbury. The biblical verse is intended as a clue to how and where the killer plans to carry out this act. We must assume Smits will die in a manner in keeping with his perceived sin – but where? Will he strike at St Julian's, St Mary's or St Chad's?"

Hipkiss, Logan and Tewdwr stood in silence for a few moments as they considered the question, but neither was able to come up with an answer.

"Perhaps it would be helpful if you consulted the Bible and studied the verse in detail," suggested Tewdwr. "Maybe there's something in the specific wording that is important."

He then disappeared back inside the church to fetch a copy. When he emerged a few moments later, he handed the book to Logan, who flicked through the pages until he found the relevant verse.

"'Know ye not that the unrighteous shall not inherit the kingdom of God', that is fairly straightforward," he said, "but the next section lists a variety of people who God denounces as sinners: 'Be not deceived: neither fornicators, nor idolaters, nor adulterers, nor effeminate, nor abusers of themselves with mankind.'"

"But there is nothing that helps us to identify in which church the killer intends to strike next," I pointed out.

"Oh, but I think it does," said Logan, with a smile of triumph on his face. "The clue is not in the comment denouncing 'abusers of themselves with mankind' – the phrase which has most in common with the sin Smits is accused of, but in the word 'effeminate'. What does that suggest to you, Mr Cheswis?"

I shrugged. "I don't know, an ambiguity in sexual orientation, perhaps?"

"Yes, of course, but the clue is more abstract than that, and refers to the identity of the saint himself, or rather herself. You see, the church at the bottom of Fish Street may well be known as St Julian's but it was originally named after a female saint – a young woman from Bithynia who died as a martyr for the Christian faith over a thousand years ago for refusing to marry a young man of noble birth on account of the fact that he was a pagan. Her name was Juliana."

ca

On reflection, I should have known it. Cornelis Smits was a carpenter, and when I was outside Stubbs's chophouse with Alice the day before, I had heard the sound of construction work coming from the church belfry at St Julian's. That must, I reasoned, have been where Smits was working.

Given that the church was no more than a stone's throw from Smits' lodging, the fact that the Dutchman was still missing did not bode well for what we would find, but in truth, nothing could have prepared me for the depravity that awaited us in the bell tower at St Julian's.

Hipkiss and I were accompanied to the church at the bottom of Fish Street by Logan and Tewdwr, for both knew the minister, Andrew Harding, a slim and sprightly fellow of my own age, who we found talking to one of his parishioners at the top of the steps leading down from the porch to the corner of Fish Street and Wyle Cop.

"Yes," he said, once we had explained the reason for or presence. "Smits was here yesterday repairing some of the wooden beams in the belfry. Some of the wood up there is centuries old and has been showing signs of being affected by woodworm."

"At what time did he leave?" I asked.

"I can't be sure," replied the minister. "I went out after lunch and returned about five in the afternoon. By that time, he was gone."

"But you didn't actually see him leave?"

"No, there was no sound from the belfry, so I assumed he had returned home."

"And you didn't check the belfry to make sure?"

"No, why would I? He had told me he would cease work around four and return on Monday to complete the job."

A dark feeling of unease began to take hold of me at this news. A quick glance at Hipkiss, who was biting his bottom lip nervously, confirmed that he too was sharing the same sense of disquiet.

"May we take a look, Mr Harding?" I asked. "Just to make sure."

"Be my guest," said the minister. "Just let me get a lantern, for the stairs to the belfry are dark."

Harding led us inside the church and up a dingy spiral staircase, which ran around the inside of the square bell tower. This eventually emerged onto a wooden platform illuminated by four short, pointed bell windows, one on each wall.

As he emerged onto the wooden platform ahead of me, Harding swung his lantern around him so he could see all four corners of the bell tower. He then suddenly emitted a loud gasp and staggered backwards slightly, almost causing him to fall back down the stairs towards me.

"What is it?" I breathed, putting my arms out in front of me to catch him, but Harding appeared dumbstruck.

I pushed myself up past the minister onto the wooden platform and took the lantern from him. I followed Harding's eyes, which were fixed on an area underneath one of the bell windows, and as my eyes grew accustomed to the light, my feeling of disquiet gradually changed to one of horror, for tied in a sitting position to a wooden post directly under one of the bells was the dead body of Cornelis Smits. The Dutchman, I noticed, had been stripped completely naked, and a bloodied white shirt stuffed between his legs. He had also been gagged using his own hose, but this could not hide the wide-eyed expression of pain and terror that lined the man's face. Cornelis Smits, I realised, had died in agony.

Hipkiss, Logan and Tewdwr clambered into the belfry beside me and stared at the corpse in disbelief.

"What the fuck is that?" breathed Hipkiss, pointing to a wooden trencher beside the body. I had been too consumed by the expression on Smits' face to notice it, but now I looked closer.

On the trencher was what looked like a human finger, wrapped around which was the now familiar sight of a chain and crucifix. At first, I thought the murderer had tortured Smits by hacking off one of his fingers, but then I took another look at the shirt jammed between the Dutchman's legs, and the horrible truth began to dawn on me. On the trencher by his body sat the remains of Cornelis Smits' genitals.

The truth had clearly also hit Harding, for the minister had staggered towards the opposite wall of the belfry and vomited onto the floorboards. Tewdwr gave me a quick glance of concern and stepped over the body towards where Harding was crouching, to make sure the latter did not pass out. Logan, seemingly made of sterner stuff, was simply staring at the cadaver, scratching his head.

"So, the murderer crept in here yesterday afternoon and killed this man in this foul way, simply to make a religious point?"

"That is possible," I said, "but wait a moment. Something is not quite right here." I grabbed hold of Smits' leg and found that I was still able to bend it fully. I then untied the gag that bound the Dutchman's mouth and studied his head more closely. I was surprised to see little spots of blood inside his ears.

"This is strange," I said. "Smits must have been attacked yesterday afternoon, but he did not die yesterday. If he had, his corpse would be as stiff as one of these floorboards by now. As you can see, his leg is still fully flexible. My guess is he died within the last couple of hours."

"But how can that be?" asked Logan. "There was a church service here this morning."

I contemplated this for a brief moment, and felt a knot tighten around my stomach as the full nature of Smits's death began to dawn on me.

"I have a good idea," I said. "Mr Harding, can you confirm whether you rang the church bells this morning?"

"Of course," replied the minister, "we rang a fifteen-minute peal as we usually do."

I nodded. "Then that explains it. Smits was tied up here, deliberately directly below the bells. He was tortured and gagged yesterday. He must have lost plenty of blood and was probably very weak. However, this morning when you rang the church bells he would have been absolutely deafened. Fifteen minutes would have been far longer than he could have withstood. As you can see, the noise perforated his ears. He probably died of heart failure in the worst pain imaginable."

"It has been engineered to look as though St Juliana herself were carrying out both judgement and punishment on him," said Logan, thoughtfully.

"What a sick bastard," exclaimed Hipkiss, his face devoid of colour. "Who would do such a thing?"

Harding said nothing, but simply headed back to the other side of the belfry and finished emptying his stomach.

"I do not know," I conceded, "but one thing is for certain, we must find some answers soon, for we are running out of people and churches."

Chapter 17

Montgomery – Sunday September 1st, 1644

*S*he found Bressy wearing a face like thunder and nursing a *tankard of ale in a quiet corner of The Old Bell, the compact yet homely inn that nestled at the foot of the craggy escarpment at the top of which sat Montgomery Castle. The landlord recognised her as she announced her presence in the taproom and welcomed her effusively, for it was here that Alice had secured accommodation on her previous visit to the town. The inn, she knew, was not the type of place that usually attracted the patronage of ladies of her standing, but she was an adaptable woman and she was comfortable enough in such an environment. She smiled and nodded indulgently in recognition of the welcome and sat down opposite the man she had come to see.*

"Remind me again," said Bressy in a world-weary tone, "why is it we are preparing to bribe this eccentric old fool with such a large proportion of the hoard of valuables I risked my life to secure? He is as confused as the inside of a beehive and as stubborn as a mule."

Alice sucked her teeth in irritation, but kept her voice low and even. "You are perfectly well aware of why this course of action is necessary. We must secure a repository for the silver until it can be transported to Bristol, and, if we can use the opportunity to secure Montgomery for the King, we will have killed two birds with one stone."

"Well we had better hurry up about it, for I hear Sir Thomas Myddelton is planning a move on Montgomery, and he is currently no more than a couple of days' march away. He will be banging on Herbert's door at the first opportunity, you can be sure of that. Do you realise I've now spent four wasted days here trying to get Herbert to receive me? I have explained my connection to you several times, but the old goat has steadfastly refused to open his gates. He suspects trickery on my part, I am convinced. Meanwhile, Hunckes' name has ceased to cut any ice now that he has lost his position as governor."

"If the situation is so hopeless, then why have you summoned me?"

"I would have thought that was patently obvious," said Bressy. "You are our one remaining iron in the fire. Herbert is a fool for a pretty face, this is common knowledge, so perhaps you will have more success in making him see sense than I have had. Let us pray that I had the foresight to summon you in time."

As it happened, the rider bearing Jem Bressy's request for help had delivered his message to Alice's house the previous lunchtime whilst she was otherwise engaged with Daniel Cheswis in Stubbs's Chophouse. Had she returned home immediately afterwards instead of going in search of Cornelis Smits, she might conceivably have managed to leave for Montgomery a little earlier, in which case she might have avoided having to deal with Sir Fulke Hunckes.

Until the former governor had turned up in forthright mood at her door, Alice's overriding emotion had been one of irritation that Bressy had been unable to deal with Herbert on his own. She had plenty to cope with in Shrewsbury without the inconvenience of having to set off at such short notice, and at such a late hour – but getting to Montgomery with the utmost *haste was vital. Considering the likelihood that she would have to ride at least part of the way in the dark, she had realised she would need an armed bodyguard to guarantee her safety. Charlie Hipkiss would have been the ideal choice, being an ex-soldier and of substantial build. However, realising that her employee would be of invaluable help in the search for De Vries and Collie's murderer, she had decided to make do with one of her domestic footmen, who, somewhat reluctantly, had been dispatched to saddle up two horses, with a view to making at least some progress before nightfall.*

However, barely two minutes had passed when the footman returned with a determined-looking Sir Fulke Hunckes in tow, the latter having accosted the servant on the way to the stables.

Hunckes had been brief and to the point. "I would like to know everything you can tell me about Daniel Cheswis."

"Is that so?" Alice had replied, trying her best to feign an air of nonchalance. "I do believe there's not much to tell beyond that which you already know."

"Do not presume to dissemble with me, mistress," Hunckes had snapped. "This is a man who you freely admit you have known since your youth and who was right at the centre of the disastrous chain of events which resulted in us failing to find a suitable repository for Lord Herbert's library, therefore ruining our chance of securing Montgomery for the King. It has now been confirmed by the young lieutenant captured last week that Cheswis and his friend Clowes are both in Shrewsbury and have been seen masquerading as servants to a bogus merchant in the very next house to your own. You cannot expect me to believe you knew nothing of this."

Alice had fought hard to maintain her smile and evenness of speech. "You do me a disservice, Sir Fulke. I saw Daniel Cheswis at Mr Halton's house the night before your lieutenant was arrested. Mr Halton himself will confirm that. It was, in fact, I who informed Colonel Broughton of his presence in Shrewsbury and warned him to arrange the premature removal of the dies from the mint. I understand this was successfully done."

"Indeed, it was, although the opportunity to arrest Cheswis and his conspirators was lost, as the governor, it seems, was somehow persuaded to mount a watch at the property of one Gideon Townsend instead, thereby allowing everyone to get away scot free. Can you explain why that was?"

"Of course. Townsend was already suspected by Thomas Bushell of being a traitor, but on that night Townsend left his wife at home when he went to the mint in search of the dies. The governor suspected Townsend's wife was also a collaborator but needed proof, so he decided to wait until all four could be captured together trying to flee."

"But it was you who suggested that?"

Alice had shrugged. "An unfortunate miscalculation, Sir Fulke."

Hunckes had snorted in derision. "Then tell me," he had demanded, "why have several witnesses seen you in the company of someone who matches the description of Cheswis, asking questions about the three murders that have taken place here these past days. What say you to that?"

"It is true that I have been concerned about these strange killings," Alice had replied after a moment's hesitation, "but I would have hoped you would have considered that to be understandable, given the circumstances. Two of my employees have been murdered. I have asked my employee Charles Hipkiss to help me investigate, as I believe these unfortunate events have something to do with an attack on a young girl that took place in Oswestry earlier this year, and Hipkiss knows all those who were involved. I can only assume it was Hipkiss your witnesses saw me with."

Hunckes had narrowed his eyes and fixed Alice with a penetrating stare. "That, unfortunately, is something I cannot disprove," he had conceded. "However, I have to say, the unlikely set of coincidences that seem to link you, the town of Nantwich, Daniel Cheswis and Abbott Massey's treasure, are indeed a strange kettle of fish. The more I look into them, the more interesting they become. Firstly, it would appear you spent some time in Nantwich during the siege of that town, trying to launch a Parliamentarian newssheet called The Parliament Scout. Why would you do such a thing? You purport to be a Royalist."

"A business venture, Sir Fulke, and a means of gaining privileged information that may have been of use to the Royalist cause, and not an indication of my political loyalties, or indeed that of my late husband. In any case, only one edition of that particular newssheet was ever published."

"Hmm, perhaps so, but then there is the issue of how you escaped from that town. I have it on good authority that you were kept prisoner in Nantwich Church after the battle, dressed as a camp follower, and yet you managed to escape back to Shrewsbury. How? And that is not all. I made some further enquiries and discovered that Daniel Cheswis was a prisoner at Dorfold House in the lead-up to the battle. You, I discovered, were also there that day. Strangely, it seems the soldiers guarding Cheswis were drugged, and the prisoner and his accomplice both escaped. How could that have happened, I asked myself. And then, of course, there is everything that happened at Combermere."

Alice had stared back at Hunckes, unmoved. "Are you accusing me of being a traitor, Sir Fulke?"

Hunckes had curled his lip and laughed sardonically. "I am accusing you of nothing yet," he had replied, acidly. "However, if you are as loyal to the crown as you say you are, I'm sure you will be happy to report the whereabouts of Mr Cheswis, should he put in another appearance. After all, you know the man, but I have only seen him the once and would struggle to recognise him in a crowd."

Faced with such an ultimatum, Alice had been left with little choice. Hunckes would never understand the complicated nature of her relationship with Daniel Cheswis, and so the only way of convincing him of her loyalty to the King was to ride to Montgomery and meet with Bressy with a view to securing the castle for the King.

But now, as she sat with Jem Bressy in a Montgomery tavern, plotting how the two of them would gain access to the castle, her thoughts kept drifting back to Shrewsbury and to the man whose fate seemed somehow inextricably entwined with her own. Daniel Cheswis, she knew, was on his own, but at least, she reasoned, as long as she herself was in Wales, she would not be forced to betray him.

Chapter 18

Shrewsbury – Monday September 2nd, 1644

Following the horrors I had witnessed in the belfry of St Julian's Church, I had spent much of Sunday night tossing and turning on my pallet, mulling over in my mind what it was about the killings, other than the cryptic notes, that bound them together. Why was the murderer systematically carrying out the attacks on different church premises in a ritualistic manner, and in a way that made it look as though the individual saints to whom the churches were dedicated were passing judgement on Millie's killers?

"Why do such a thing?" I wondered. What was it that connected Millie Davies and the Shrewsbury killer to make him carry out these murderous acts in such a bizarre manner? It did not make sense.

The thing I found most difficult to comprehend was the degree of control which the murderer was exhibiting over those who would unmask him. Not only was he clearly teasing us with his cryptic clues, but he also seemed to be acutely aware of our every step. It was as though he was willing us to solve his clues and to understand his motives for slaughtering his victims, which, he seemed to be telling us, lay beyond simple retribution and more in the realm of divine judgement. He also seemed to be anticipating our every move in solving the clues, and so far, he had always managed to make sure he had killed his victim in the time between delivering his letter to Alice and us arriving on the scene.

The killer, I noted, was also accelerating in his quest to complete the execution, for that was what these acts were, of the remaining participants in Millie's murder, and I wondered whether the perpetrator was becoming nervous that he might be apprehended before he was able to complete his murderous spree. It came as no surprise, therefore, to discover that a fourth letter had been nailed to the front door of Alice's print workshop sometime in the early hours of Monday morning.

Hipkiss brought it with him to our agreed meeting place in the graveyard at St Chad's. With Alice now gone and the governor's men still on the lookout for Alexander and me, I had realised that I could not continue to show my face at the school on a regular basis, for fear that someone would recognise me and betray me to the authorities. Hipkiss had looked at me a little strangely when I had suggested the meeting place, but he had acquiesced nonetheless, and so I waited for him in a secluded spot by an old oak tree in the corner of the churchyard, from where I was partially hidden by a large marble tomb and a row of weathered gravestones of people long since dead and unlikely to be of interest to anyone currently living.

I saw him before he saw me, weaving his way between the headstones and clutching a letter. With him, I was surprised to note, was Reverend Logan.

"A fourth communication from the murderer, I presume," I said. "I see our man is not wasting any time."

Hipkiss looked at me gravely and handed me the envelope. "Pinned to our door when I arrived at the workshop this morning," he explained. "I asked, but nobody saw who it was. I took the liberty of calling on Reverend Logan before I brought the latest letter to you. I considered he might be helpful in deciphering it."

I took the letter from Hipkiss and noticed that the envelope had already been opened. I briefly wondered why the messenger had taken the trouble to deliver the message at such a ridiculously early hour, and how he had managed to gain access to the school's back yard without a key.

The letter was in the style of all the others, but this time, I noted with shock, the message consisted of two lines;

JF Matthew 1:19

ER Proverbs 31:29

"So," I exclaimed, somewhat nonplussed, "two verses – two victims. Is that what we are supposed to believe?"

"So it appears," replied Logan.

"You know the passages in question?" I asked.

"Yes, indeed." The minister reached inside his cassock, extracted a copy of the bible, and flicked through a few pages before beginning to read: "'Then Joseph, her husband, being a just man, and not willing to make her a publick example, was minded to put her away privily'. I believe your murderer may have a strong sense of irony," he added.

"Irony?"

"The message is quite clear," continued Logan. "The clue refers to JF, obviously Joseph Finch. It does not take a genius to work that out, but the passage also refers to Joseph and his wife, who, of course, was Mary."

"So, the murderer intends to kill Joseph Finch at St. Mary's."

"Of course, or at least that is what he is insinuating."

"But why the irony?"

Logan sighed impatiently. "Because the bible refers to not wanting to make a public example of Mary, and yet the act of killing Finch in St Mary's Church would have done precisely that.

I nodded my understanding. "I would say that qualifies him as having a particularly dark sense of humour," I commented, wryly. "So, if the first victim is Finch, who on earth is the second, ER? The only other person on our list of potential victims is William Stubbs."

Logan shrugged. "That I cannot say," he said.

"Perhaps the content of the bible quote will shed some light on that," suggested Hipkiss.

Logan nodded thoughtfully and once again leafed through the pages of his bible.

"Proverbs, Chapter Thirty-one, Verse Twenty-nine. The verse in question refers to the virtue of a young woman; 'Many daughters have done virtuously, but thou excellest them all.'"

"A reference to the young victim, Millie Davies, perhaps," I mused.

"Perhaps," agreed Logan, "but there is something about this quote that is familiar, I've seen it before somewhere, but I can't quite place it."

"Well, we have little time to waste on something we cannot yet decipher," I pointed out. "Surely we must now head for St Mary's to see if we can save the life of the person we know is in danger."

Hipkiss and Logan glanced at each other momentarily as though they knew something they were not telling me, but then suddenly the precise meaning of what Logan had said earlier struck me.

"He's already dead, isn't he?" I said. "You said killing Finch in St Mary's *would* have made a public example of St Mary's, but it didn't, because he was murdered elsewhere, wasn't he?"

"I'm afraid so," admitted Logan, "a corpse was found this morning in the Meole Brook, the stream which borders the original grounds of the abbey – and before you suggest it, there is no point going there. The cadaver will already have been removed by the coroner."

"I don't understand," I said, "the land alongside the brook which runs into the Severn south of the abbey is where Finch's smallholding is, but why kill him there rather than in the church as the clue suggests?"

Logan smiled patiently. "That is not yet known," he said. "Indeed, neither will the coroner have been able as yet to identify the body definitely as being that of Joseph Finch."

I stared at Logan, uncomprehending. "And why was that?"

"For a very good reason," said the minister. "The corpse was headless."

I gaped at Logan in disbelief, speechless, but only for a moment, for the full horror of the murderer's latest debauched act was beginning to dawn on me.

"Wait a minute, if the victim's head was not with the body, that means it must be somewhere else."

Logan blanched, and I suppose he must have also uttered some kind of response, but I failed to notice, for I was already halfway across the graveyard, marching in the direction of St Mary's.

The curate of St Mary's Church, whose name was Nicholas Prowd, had, as I later found out, been the incumbent minister at Shrewsbury's oldest church for less than a week when Logan, Hipkiss and I descended upon him that morning in a state of panic. A Royalist through and through, Prowd had arrived in Shrewsbury from Ireland, having been driven from there by the rebellion. He had been recruited to replace the previous minister, a Parliamentarian, who had left Shrewsbury in 1642 to avoid taking the royal oath. Prowd was a corpulent man of jovial demeanour, with greying, curly hair and a reddish nose, which made me suspect the communion wine in the churches under his care had not always been used for its designated purpose.

Prowd had been taking a peaceful morning stroll across the large open space in front of the church when we came careering into view from the direction of St Alkmund's. Until it was suppressed in the 1540s, St Mary's had been known as a collegiate church, and now, a hundred years on, its grounds still bore the air of a college precinct, which meant Prowd saw us coming from some distance away, but this did not stop him from reacting like a startled rabbit at the sight of us charging towards him.

We were led by Logan, who had shown a remarkable turn of speed and overhauled me by the time I had reached the top of Fish Street. The man demonstrated a level of fitness I had not been expecting. Hipkiss, being of much bulkier build than Logan or I, lagged some fifty yards behind and lumbered in our wake, breathing like an old horse.

"Mr Logan," said Prowd, warily, "you appear to be in something of a hurry."

Logan, it emerged, having connections of his own in Ireland, had been one of the first people to welcome Prowd to his new seat, and so was already known to him. He briefly introduced Hipkiss and myself and explained what we were looking for – perhaps in retrospect, not the best of ideas, for it made Prowd look at us even more as though we had lost our minds.

"A severed head?" he said, doubtfully. "What in God's name makes you think someone would have been able to smuggle such a thing into my church?"

"That is what we are trying to ascertain," I pointed out. "Tell me, have there been any visitors in church this morning?"

"Yes, of course. The church is always open to individual worshippers. There were two elderly women, who I recognised as being from my congregation, a local baker come to see about a christening, and a tall, portly man, who I didn't recognise."

"I see." I thought about this for a moment before asking the obvious question; "This last person, the one that you didn't recognise. What did he look like?"

"Well, tall obviously, dark hair, beard, not too old, but definitely overweight. Looked like he enjoyed his ale a little too much. He was also wearing a cloak, which struck me as odd, considering the fact that it is a warm day."

"And he was in view the whole time he was in the church?"

"Most of it, but not all of it. As I recall, I disappeared round the back at one point to use the privy."

I gave Logan a look, and he asked Prowd a question of his own. "Did you see the man leave?"

"Yes."

"And was he as portly when he left as when he came in?"

"Yes, of course," gasped Prowd, irritated now. "What do you take me for? Look, if you don't believe me, you are welcome to look inside the church to see what you can find."

To be honest, there was no reason not to take Prowd up on his offer, so we followed the minister through the porch and into the nave.

I was immediately struck by the light, spacious feel of the interior of the church. The lofty nave was separated from the steeple by a pointed arch, whilst the side aisles were visible through four semi-circular arches on each side of the nave. The ceiling of the nave, I noticed, was oak-panelled, with a centre beam carrying various pendants such as flowers, pelicans, and angels playing musical instruments.

Logan, Hipkiss and I split up and searched everywhere within the main body of the church – in the aisles, by the pews, in the font, by the altar, and even in the pulpit, but we found nothing.

"Where did this man sit while he was in the church?" I asked, eventually.

"Over there," replied Prowd, "close to the entrance to the Trinity Aisle."

"The Trinity Aisle?"

"Yes." Prowd gestured towards a circular arch on the eastern side of the south transept. "The Trinity Aisle is a large chantry chapel funded by the Guild of Drapers. You may take a look inside, if you wish."

"Aye, you may want to do that," said Hipkiss, who had wandered over to the arch and was looking intently at an inscription carved over the top of the door. "Come and have a look at this."

Logan and I strode over to the door, and I gasped as I took in what Hipkiss was showing me. Above the door was a coat of arms and a plaque showing three quotes from the bible. It was the middle one which caught my attention

Prov 31:29

"Many daughters have done virtuously but thou excellest them all"

"I knew I had seen this somewhere," exclaimed Logan. "The coat of arms is that of Queen Elizabeth. ER refers to her – Elizabeth Regina. The murderer was not announcing yet another victim. He was simply pointing us in the direction of where he has secreted Joseph Finch's head."

I stared at Logan in fear and disbelief. Surely not, I thought. Surely the murderer had already reached the limits of his depravity. My senses were screaming at me to turn around, get out of the church and leave Shrewsbury for good, but something in my nature forced me on and refused to allow me to yield to my inner weaknesses. I tentatively pushed at the door to the chapel, and it creaked open to reveal a spacious but dimly lit room.

In front of the altar were several rows of benches with finely embroidered pillows to kneel upon. As my eyes grew accustomed to the dark, I noticed that one of the pillows was missing from the front bench. I groaned as I realised how the 'portly' worshipper had managed to get into church with a severed head and out again without appearing different.

I barely dared look, but when Logan gasped and reached over towards the altar, I could do little else but watch transfixed as the minister grabbed a hessian sack lying next to the cross and reached inside, extricating Joseph Finch's gore-covered head by the hair. As he did so, the dead man's mouth fell open, and a crucifix fell to the floor with a metallic clink. Behind me, I heard a sharp intake of breath, a crash, and a dull thud as Nicholas Prowd collapsed senseless on the floor.

Chapter 19

"*I* will give you your due, sir, today you have come up with something a little different from your usual bluster, not that it cuts any ice with me, of course."

Bressy stared sourly at the smirking guard. "Just go and fetch his Lordship, would you? You are wasting our time. We have urgent business to discuss with him."

"As you have explained on numerous occasions these five days past. However, Lord Herbert has made it clear he knows not who you are and refuses to receive you. Behaving like an impertinent jackanapes will make not a jot of difference, nor I suspect, will the tactic of hanging a lady from your arm."

Knowing Lord Herbert's reputation, Bressy rather doubted that, but it was Alice who spoke next.

"He will see me," *she said, with a hint of authority.* "Tell me, soldier, what is your name?"

"Thomas Lloyd, my lady, but–"

"Well, Thomas Lloyd, you can inform his Lordship that Alice Furnival awaits his attention and that she has news arising from the events at Combermere that may be of interest to him."

Lloyd opened his mouth to say something, but thought better of it and marched off grumbling across the drawbridge into the middle ward of the castle where Herbert's newly built brick mansion was located, leaving another soldier to keep an eye on Alice and Bressy.

Five minutes later, Lloyd reappeared with Herbert. Alice noted with shock that the old aristocrat's health seemed to have deteriorated somewhat since the last time she had seen him less than a month ago. He walked hesitantly across the drawbridge with the aid of a stick and was shielding his eyes from the sun as though he had some kind of eye condition. The one thing that remained undimmed was his smile.

The last thing to desert an incorrigible ladies' man is his charm, thought Alice, as Herbert welcomed her.

"Mistress Furnival," he said, "what a pleasant surprise. How good of you to visit me here again, how fare you?"

"Passably well, my Lord, and yourself?"

"As you can see, I could be better. This affliction of the eyes, which threatens to blind me, is of some concern. To be honest, it is in my plans to move to London, where more professional care for my condition might be available."

This was not good news, and Bressy shifted uncomfortably at his Lordship's words. The last thing Alice wanted was for Herbert to be removed out of reach of the King's influence.

"I am sad to hear that," she said, "but perhaps we may persuade you otherwise, as we have a proposal you may find to your liking."

Herbert raised an eyebrow and smiled. "A proposal?" he said. "And related to the strange events at Combermere too, I am told. You have piqued my interest, but first perhaps you would be so kind as to introduce the gentleman who accompanies you. I know him not."

Bressy stepped forward and removed his hat. "Jeremiah Bressy, my Lord. I am an intelligencer in the service of his Excellency Prince Rupert."

"A spy, eh?" said Herbert, with a chuckle. "You wouldn't have anything to do with the strange events at Combermere these past weeks, would you?"

"Not with the kidnapping of the young girl, my Lord, but I was there, certainly, and on King's business too."

Herbert shifted the weight on his feet and stared Bressy in the eye. "What kind of business?"

"I was there to recover a hoard of silver, gold and other valuables hidden in a field in Nantwich. The kidnapper of the girl, and the girl's adopted father, himself an intelligencer for Sir William Brereton, had an interest in this matter too. I'm pleased to report that we managed to recover the treasure."

"I see, and where is that treasure now?"

"It is in a safe location not far from here, but it can be retrieved within the hour."

"And what does this have to do with me?"

"My Lord, I know you operate this place as a de facto garrison for the King."

"I am a loyal subject of His Majesty."

"Indeed, but we are well aware of Parliament's designs on this place, and Prince Rupert wishes to be assured of your ongoing loyalty. After all, you have already refused to allow the Prince to garrison the place himself, according to his policy."

"Well that's not strictly true."

"You consented to the Prince sending sixty soldiers to Montgomery, but you insisted on nominating the officers, wanted them to be under your command, and agreed only to allow a guard camp in the outer ward of the castle. You argued that you and your son, Richard, were quite capable of garrisoning the place on your own."

"Which was true, but the Prince decided to post my son to Aberystwyth, a move designed to force my hand, perhaps?"

Bressy smiled, but said nothing.

"But the stick did not work, did it?" continued Herbert. "So now the Prince wishes to bribe me with a carrot. You are offering me this treasure in exchange for my loyalty to the King?"

"Not all of it," said Bressy. "The silver is destined for Bristol. As we speak, the mint is being relocated from Shrewsbury by Thomas Bushell. The Prince, meanwhile, is already on his way from Chester and expected to arrive in Bristol any day. Once he is there and the mint is once again operational, the silver is to be shipped down the Severn to produce coin. However, until it is ready to be shipped it must be kept somewhere secure. As for the rest of the hoard, that consists of gold, plate, jewellery and other valuables. I am sure that some of this could be negotiated as due payment for your services."

There were a few moments' silence whilst Lord Herbert considered Bressy's words, but then he smiled and turned to the guard, Lloyd.

"Thomas," he said, "please show Mr Bressy and Mistress Furnival to the library, and make sure they are comfortable. I will join them presently, when I think we will have some things to discuss, which may impact on the course of this war in Wales."

Chapter 20

"So, what now?" puffed Logan, as we transported the semi-conscious Prowd out of the chantry chapel and sat him down on one of the aldermen's pews near the front of the church, his head between his knees. As he lurched forward and started to heave, I noticed a sizeable lump on the back of his skull, caused, no doubt, by cracking his head on the stone floor.

"First things first," I said, unbuckling a ring of keys from Prowd's belt and securing the door to the chapel. "It's best to keep Finch's head locked away from prying eyes until the coroner and constable are in a position to attend. In the meantime, I suggest we make ourselves scarce." It was becoming patently obvious that I could not keep turning up at every crime scene in Shrewsbury without eventually being arrested, and with Millie Davies's killers being dispatched on a daily basis, it was clear that I would fairly soon need to get out of town regardless of whether the killer was found.

"But you can't just leave him here," said Logan, a look of concern spreading across his face.

I took a closer look at Prowd and realised Logan spoke the truth. The curate had turned a pale shade of green and was drawing in air in deep, rasping breaths. The last thing I wanted was another corpse on my hands, so I bade Hipkiss remain with Prowd until he was fully recovered.

"Once he is in a fit state to be left on his own, you can alert the coroner," I said. "You may then return to the print workshop. I imagine it will not be long before another letter turns up there."

We left Hipkiss gamely attempting to get Prowd to drink a cup of water and headed for the street. I looked grimly into Logan's eyes. There was no need to explain where we were going. We paced our way purposefully back towards St Alkmund's and down the steps to Fish Street, before making a beeline for Stubbs's Chophouse.

It was still too early for lunch, but Stubbs's kitchen was a hive of activity. A plump woman with short curly hair, who I took to be William Stubbs's mother, was busy stuffing pastry with pie filling, whilst two young girls, one of whom I recognised as the young servant girl who was present on my previous visit, were working their way through a mountain of vegetables on the worktop, peeling, chopping, and putting them into two large cookpots. Steam rose from a further cookpot bubbling away with a stew of some kind, and freshly baked bread gave off a yeasty aroma as it lay in a basket on a side table. The air was thick with the smell of roast meat, and I suddenly became aware that I had skipped breakfast that morning.

Recognising Logan's presence and paying due respect to his position as a man of the cloth, the older woman cut off a few slices from a leg of lamb that was roasting on a spit and put them onto a serving tray with a hunk of bread. Logan and I dug in hungrily.

The older woman said something to the young servant girl, who looked me up and down with curiosity before grabbing her friend by the arm and scuttling away into an adjoining room. Stubbs, meanwhile, was sat on a stool overlooking a rear window, through which he was staring blankly. He must have been expecting me, for he had barely reacted when Logan and I walked through the door.

"Finch is dead," I announced, simply. "You are the only surviving witness to Millie Davies's murder, save her brother, of course. Your life is in danger, I am sure of it."

Stubbs turned around on his stool, but avoided my gaze, looking instead at his boots with a resigned expression on his face.

"What will be, will be," he said. "Whatever happens to me, I will surely have deserved it."

"You committed a grave sin," I conceded, "there is no escaping it, but you are young, and you were intimidated by your peers. At the end of it, however, you did not rape Millie, nor did you play an active role in the decision to end her life. That, in my book, means you are not beyond salvation."

"Mr Cheswis speaks the truth," agreed Logan. "If you ask the Lord for forgiveness, there is always hope."

"But first we must get you somewhere safe," I added, "somewhere as far away from St Chad's as possible."

Stubbs gave me a puzzled look. "Why St Chad's?"

"Well, that is quite obvious," I said. "So far the murderer has claimed a victim at each of Shrewsbury's main churches. De Vries died at St Alkmund's, Collie at the Holy Cross, Smits at St Julian's and Finch's severed head currently lies on the altar at St Mary's. That only leaves you and St Chad's. My advice is that you return with Reverend Logan to the Holy Cross and stay there until the murderer is caught. If you stay the other side of the river, then there is little risk of you being lured to St Chad's."

"I have a spare chamber at the vicarage," added Logan, "you can remain concealed there for the time being. You will be safe enough for a while, but time is of the essence. We must leave now."

Stubbs hesitated for a moment, as though unwilling to leave the familiarity of the chophouse, but eventually he gave a resigned sigh and smiled gratefully.

"I cannot thank you enough for your kindness," he said. "I will rue that day in March as long as I live."

Logan gave Stubbs a relieved look, but then he stopped still and scratched his chin thoughtfully.

"Just a moment," he said. "May I ask, when exactly in March did this unfortunate incident occur?"

"It was a Saturday evening, the second of March, if I recall correctly."

To my surprise, Logan clenched his fist in triumph and emitted a strange sound, which I realised was a barely suppressed whoop of exhilaration.

"I knew it," he said. "The second of March is the feast day of St Chad. All the way through this affair, the murderer has the saints passing judgement in turn on each of Millie Davies's attackers."

"Of course," I said. "In his warped mind, the killer must have assumed that St Chad would have been mortally offended for his feast day to have been marked by such an evil act. He had all the other saints pass judgement on Millie's attackers, one by one, but St Chad's was always going to be the scene of the final murder – the ultimate act of judgement."

Logan nodded in agreement. "Then there is but one course of action open to us," he said.

It needed little discussion. Once we had finished our meal, Logan departed with Stubbs down Wyle Cop in the direction of the English Bridge, but not before I had promised to meet him together with Alexander and Hipkiss the following day in the churchyard at St Chad's.

My main concern was that Stubbs and the minister would be unable to complete the stroll back to the abbey church without being spotted by the murderer, for as far as I knew, the killer could be anywhere. That said, my own walk back to the safe house, where Alexander, Ellis and Mistress Eliza were waiting, was not without worries either. I had begun to realise that I could not keep on walking to-and-fro past St Chad's without somebody eventually realising who I was and informing the authorities. This was not helped by the fact that I had the strangest feeling that I was being watched. I kept turning around and looking over my shoulder, but I saw nothing. I decided I must have been imagining things, but nonetheless, I was relieved when the front door to my place of refuge was opened for me and I was able to slip inside.

My relief was short-lived, however, for within ten minutes of my return there was a sharp rap at the door and a scraping sound as something was pushed underneath it. I could have sworn I saw a shadow pass in front of the window, but I could not be sure.

It was Alexander who was quickest to his feet. Leaping across the room with an agility that defied his bulk, he lifted the envelope off the floor almost before it had stopped moving. He made to open the door to see if there was any sign of the messenger, but Mistress Eliza stopped him.

"Have a care, Mr Clowes," she warned. "It may be a trap to make us expose ourselves. It is always better to be cautious."

I groaned inwardly as my friend handed the letter to me, for the paper and handwriting were entirely familiar. With a sinking heart, I realised I now knew three things for certain: the murderer knew where Alexander and I were staying, his means of communication had shifted from Alice to me, and finally, unequivocally, the killer's end game had now begun.

Chapter 21

*Wem and Shrewsbury – Saturday August 31 to Monday
September 2ⁿᵈ, 1644*

*G*ideon Townsend was not a man to accept defeat easily.
He hadn't spent two years cultivating relationships in
Shrewsbury for nothing, and so once he was certain that he
and Faith had safely negotiated the checkpoint by the English
Bridge, he began to put his mind to what his next move
should be.

Mytton would not thank him for leaving his brother-in-law's
foppish great-nephew languishing in the castle dungeon, nor
did he feel inclined to leave Sir William Brereton's two agents
to their fate, for he had found the two Nantwich men to possess
levels of integrity and determination of which he wholeheartedly
approved. And so by the time the last straggling farmhouses on
the edge of Shrewsbury had disappeared behind the trees and
hedgerows of the Shropshire countryside, he had already begun
to formulate a plan.

The road was quiet, devoid of Royalist scouts, and with the
parliamentary garrison at Wem lying only a matter of eleven
miles from Shrewsbury, it was no surprise to Gideon that his
cart was able to trundle its way up Mill Street well before the
sun had reached its zenith.

Loath to waste any time, he delivered Faith into the hands
of his brother-in-law's family, who ran a cordwainer's workshop

on the High Street. Leaving the horse and cart with them, he then presented himself to the garrison commander, who agreed to send word to Mytton in Oswestry regarding Saltonstall's arrest, the whereabouts of his two colleagues, and the loss of the dies from the mint. He then borrowed a horse, a buff coat, and some coin, and was back on the road by mid-afternoon.

Gideon's role as one of Mytton's agents in Shrewsbury was to develop relationships with anyone who might conceivably be of help in undermining the Royalist war effort, men such as Abel Hook. A short, weasely man with crooked teeth and a questionable approach to personal hygiene, Hook was the kind of person Gideon would normally have wished to avoid. Abel Hook, however, had one thing going for him. He also happened to be the turnkey responsible for the dungeon at Shrewsbury Castle.

Hook was in his mid-forties and had been married twice, the second time to a young woman twenty years his junior, who having quickly bored of the novelty of having an older husband with access to all manner of bribes and other illicit money-making opportunities, had seen fit to use the regular nature of her husband's work shifts to commence a relationship with a young tanner called Richard Wollascott, who had taken the habit of swiving the young wife in Hook's own front room on a Monday evening, while the latter was busy watching over prisoners in the castle dungeon.

Having developed a friendship of sorts with Hook, and having suspected a certain lasciviousness on the part of the turnkey's young wife, Gideon, one Monday evening, had had his interest piqued by a chance sighting of Martha, for that was her name, conversing in a flirtatious manner with Wollascott outside *The Sacristy*, where Gideon was a regular.

Having followed the pair at a safe distance back to Hook's house on Butcher's Row, Gideon had hardly been able to believe his luck when he pressed his face to Hook's front window to catch the sight of Martha bent over a table and Wollascott grunting like a hog with his breeches around his ankles.

Keeping himself in the shadows and taking care not to be discovered, Gideon had mentally filed this information for future use at an opportune moment. That moment, Gideon decided, had now arrived.

Wary of being present in Shrewsbury any longer than he needed to be, Gideon had spent the Saturday evening in the village of Albrighton, four miles north of the town, before slipping across the bridge during Sunday morning, whilst the majority of people were at church.

He knew that Hook was in the habit of dropping by the castle briefly on a Sunday afternoon to feed his prisoners, and so Gideon waited in the shadow of the motte, before accosting Hook and getting him royally drunk in one of the taverns on Pride Hill. In doing so, he was able to ascertain not only that Saltonstall was alive and well, or at least as well as could be expected given the circumstances, but also that Hook would, indeed, be on guard duty as usual the following night.

Satisfied his plans were in place, Gideon then retired to Albrighton for the night and did not return until the following evening, when he took up a position outside a tavern on Butcher's Row, lit a pipe, and waited for Richard Wollascott to show up.

He did not have to wait long. Barely fifteen minutes after arriving, he watched the young tanner walk nervously up the street and stop outside the Hooks' house, before looking hesitantly in both directions and letting himself in.

Gideon waited ten minutes before gently tapping his pipe against the wall and striding through a gate that led to the rear of Hook's house, from where he was able to let himself into the kitchen by forcing the lock on the door.

The kitchen was dark, but he could see Wollascott's shirt and breeches slung untidily on the table. Suppressing a chuckle, he picked up both items and shoved them inside a cooking pot, replacing the lid so they could not be seen.

From the next room, the sound of Martha and Wollascott's passion gave way to a brief silence, followed by anxious whisperings of alarm, as the young lovers began to realise something was amiss. Gideon felt no remorse for what he was about to do, for both were sinners in the eyes of the Lord. Grabbing a rolling pin from the worktop, he positioned himself by the door and watched as Wollascott, totally naked, burst through the door, his erect manhood waving around as though its owner were brandishing a sword.

Gideon waited just long enough to register the look of panic on Wollascott's face as he realised his breeches were missing before swinging the rolling pin violently between the man's legs, sending him crashing to the ground in a rolling, groaning ball of agony.

"Sit back down, mistress," commanded Gideon, as Martha appeared in the doorway clutching a blanket across her breasts.

"I thought you said your husband was at work tonight," gasped Wollascott.

"He is," Martha squeaked, as she retreated back into the hall.

"Then who the fuck are you, sir?" groaned Wollascott.

"That," said Martha, "is Gideon Townsend, Abel's friend, the one that the governor is on the lookout for."

"*The traitor from the mint? What is he doing here?*"

"*Be quiet and sit still,*" said Gideon, calmly. "*There is no need for me to hurt you any more than I already have, so long as you hold your peace and listen. But first,*" he said, addressing Wollascott, "*cover your member from view, sir, it is offending me.*"

Gideon stepped back into the kitchen, retrieved the tanner's breeches from the cooking pot, and tossed then towards him. Wollascott, still clutching his testicles in agony, did not make to get dressed, but at least made some attempt to cover himself with his shirt.

"*What is this about, Mr Townsend?*" asked Martha, eventually. "*Is my husband paying you for this?*"

"*Your husband knows not that I am here, and he will not find out he is being cuckolded, so long as you do as I say.*"

"*You would blackmail us, sir?*" put in Wollascott.

"*Call it what you will,*" said Gideon. "*I do not care, but listen well and you will soon understand my motives. Your husband, mistress, currently holds in captivity a young man whose freedom I would very much like to secure.*"

"*The crophead spy?*" spat Martha. "*Abel has told me about him. An arrogant young fop by all accounts.*"

"*His name, madam, is Philip Saltonstall, and he is a brave young officer. I would see him released, and you are going to help me.*"

"*Pish,*" said Martha, curling her lip is disdain. "*And what if we refuse?*"

"*Then we stay here until your husband returns from the castle, at which point you may make your peace with him.*"

That wiped the supercilious expression from her face. Glancing nervously at Wollascott, she opened her mouth to speak, *but the young tanner shook his head. Grimacing, he pulled his breeches back on and struggled to his feet.*

"So, what do you want us to do?" he asked.

ભ

Twenty minutes later, Richard Wollascott was walking up Pride Hill clad in one of Martha's skirts, a plain bodice, and a coif, his arm linked somewhat self-consciously through Gideon's. The clothes were a little tight, admittedly, but Wollascott was not a large man, and, so long as he did not stare anyone directly in the face, his clean-shaven features and shoulder length locks made him a passable woman, at least in the dark.

"This is madness," *hissed the young tanner through gritted teeth.* "What makes you think Martha will not raise the alarm?"

"Because she is not stupid," *said Gideon.* "Whilst you were busy squeezing yourself into her clothes, I paid her two guineas to keep her silence, with the promise of two more if we are successful. I suppose the threat of telling her husband about her infidelity may have helped somewhat too."

"Martha would not betray me, Mr Townsend," *said Wollascott, trying to feign a measure of confidence which he was not feeling at that moment.*

Gideon laughed. "Do not fool yourself, sir. You are nought but a pretty bauble to her. She values her house and her reputation more. She would not risk being labelled as a whore and cast into the street by her husband."

Wollascott knew Gideon spoke the truth, so he kept his counsel and continued his walk as far as the castle gates, where Gideon rang the bell and waited for Hook to appear.

"Are you mad?" said the turnkey with incredulity when he saw who was at the gate. "I cannot be seen with you here. You are a wanted man. Get yourself back to Wem, while you still can." He then inspected the figure standing at Gideon's side and hesitated. "And who's this?" he asked.

"This," said Gideon, pressing a crown into Hook's fist, "is Lady Jane Saltonstall, your prisoner's sister. She knows her brother will hang as a spy. All she desires is ten minutes with her brother to say her farewells. Surely you can grant her that?" Gideon reached into his purse and dangled another coin into the gaoler's face.

Abel Hook hesitated, but only for a moment. Snatching the coin from Gideon's grasp, he unlocked the gate. "Only ten minutes, mind," he said, "and not a moment longer."

○

Ironically, this was almost exactly the amount of time that had elapsed when Gideon and Saltonstall, now dressed in Martha's clothes, slid down the grassy and overgrown slope that fell away towards the river bank, having let themselves out via a postern gate, out of sight of the guards patrolling the castle walls.

Abel Hook, meanwhile, sat in his prison cell, bound, gagged and cursing his luck, wondering who the hell the naked man was who had been locked in the dungeon with him.

Chapter 22

Shrewsbury – Tuesday September 3rd, 1644

Knowing that the killer had already determined that St Chad's would be the scene of his final act of depravity and murder, there seemed little point in opening the final letter, and so it remained untouched overnight on top of Mistress Eliza's bible box. However, when I got up the next morning, I approached the matter with renewed vigour and tore open the envelope with anticipation. What I read was, at first sight, predictable.

WS Numbers 5:2

That William Stubbs was the intended victim was patently obvious, but what biblical reason had the murderer given? I opened the Bible at the relevant verse and began to read out aloud, just as Alexander and Mistress Eliza entered the room.

"Command the children of Israel that they put out of the camp every leper and everyone that hath an issue, and whosoever is defiled by the dead."

"What do you make of that?" asked Alexander, "William Stubbs has a withered arm, just like a leper."

"You are right," I agreed, "so the verse is not an allegorical reference relating to the morality of a murderer. It is simply a physical description of Stubbs."

"We are talking about providence," interjected Mistress Eliza in a voice which reflected the zealous puritan that she was. "Those who are unclean must be cast out." In truth, it was no surprise to me to hear Eliza's interpretation, for in my experience, the overtly godly always had something to say on such issues.

"You mean unclean morally?" I said. "That those who have committed a sin as vile as murder, like Stubbs, should pay for their sins?"

Mistress Eliza nodded the affirmative, but it was Alexander who got to the nub of the matter.

"That may well be so," said my friend, "but why St Chad's? All the other clues we have received contain some reference, however obtuse, which points to the proposed murder site. What has St Chad's got to do with leprosy?"

This, of course, was something I could not answer.

"Logan will know," I said. "I will make a point of consulting him, but there is little point in speculating. If we are to catch the murderer, we must mount a watch at St Chad's and be quick about it."

It was agreed that we would work in five-hour shifts with Alexander taking the first until three in the afternoon, during which time Mistress Eliza would be sent to seek out Hipkiss and alert him to our plan. I would take the second shift, followed by Hipkiss, who would come to relieve me at eight in the evening.

"What if he doesn't come?" asked Alexander, not unreasonably.

"He must come," I riposted, "he has been killing people at the rate of one per day. I'll wager he knows exactly where Stubbs has been secreted and that some effort will be made to lure him over to St Chad's during the course of the day. Logan will need to be alerted to what is afoot, but we must be ready, and if the murderer has not shown himself by the time Hipkiss has finished his shift, we must be ready and willing to relieve him."

It all seemed straightforward enough, so long as Alexander and I could remain out of the reach of the governor's men. Something told me, however, that our time was running out, and that we would soon have to be on our way, regardless of whether we were successful in our quest to reel in the killer.

The morning and early afternoon were interminable. Alexander was the first to go out, followed by Mistress Eliza, leaving Ellis and I to pace around the house like a couple of captive animals.

It came as little surprise, therefore, that shortly before three, my young companion announced that he intended to accompany me to St Chad's and help me in my reconnaissance duties. I objected, of course, but relented when Ellis made it clear that he intended to come anyway, and that there was little I could do to stop him. The last thing I needed was for the youngster to get himself arrested and thrown into the castle with Saltonstall, so at three o'clock I led him quietly through the old college precinct and into the churchyard.

I had expected to find Alexander hiding among the gravestones in a quiet corner of the churchyard, from where he could keep an eye on the main entrance to the church. Instead, I found him actually inside the main body of the church, engaged in conversation with the minister, who was introduced to me as Mr Lendall. With them, I was surprised to note, was Maredudd Tewdwr, the schoolteacher.

"I did not expect to find you here," I said to Alexander, more in surprise than anything.

"It is my fault, I'm afraid," said Lendall, apologetically. "I make a point of holding a prayer meeting every day. Today Mr Tewdwr was conducting the prayers, and when he saw your friend sat over by the gravestones at the back of the churchyard, I invited him in to join our congregation."

Lendall, it turned out, had not been in his post at St Chad's much longer that the unfortunate Nicholas Prowd at St Mary's, but, like Prowd, he had the air of having been appointed by the crown. A well-built man of middling years, Lendall was wearing vestments more elaborate than the puritan clergy I was used to seeing in Nantwich, and he held himself with an air of ceremony that smacked of Laudianism. A glance over his shoulder at the altar rail and the communion table set at the east end of the chancel was enough to confirm my suspicions.

"Alexander and Mr Tewdwr will no doubt have explained our purpose in Shrewsbury and the reason why we are keeping watch on your churchyard. Assuming that is so, they have presumably also explained our interest in knowing more about the saints to whom the churches of Shrewsbury are dedicated," I said. "If you don't mind, Mr Lendall, what can you tell me about St Chad?"

"There is really very little to tell about our patron saint other than that he was a prominent and revered churchman, who lived in the seventh century, and had a considerable hand in the conversion of the East Saxons to the Christian faith. He was from Northumberland, but exercised most of his ministry in Mercia, and finished his career as Bishop of Lichfield. That is all there is to tell."

"He was not ill at any time, or subjected to any afflictions of the skin?"

Lendall gave me a strange look, but shook his head. "No, I don't think so. As far as we know Chad lived a peaceful life and died a peaceful death."

There was a momentary silence as I took in Lendall's words, but then I noticed Tewdwr blinking at me with interest. "That is a curious question, Mr Cheswis," he interjected. "What makes you think St Chad may have suffered from some kind of skin disease?"

I hesitated for a moment, uncertain as to whether I should be confiding in any more people than was necessary, but, as the schoolteacher already knew about the murderer's cryptic clues, I decided it could do no harm, so I extracted the latest note from the lining of my doublet and handed it to him.

"Numbers, Chapter Five, Verse Two?" said Tewdwr, raising an eyebrow. "You are correct in so far as this verse relates to the treatment of lepers, but what makes you think it refers to St Chad?"

"You will be aware that Ben Collie's killer has struck twice more since we last spoke," I said. "We believe there is just one more person who he aims to kill. We would protect this man, and to that end he is safe in our care. However, we believe the killer intends to strike here at St Chad's. We are simply attempting to decipher the message to see if it might offer some clue as to the murderer's identity.

Tewdwr smiled and handed the message back to me. "I see," he said, "that is most interesting. I wish you luck in your endeavours, but I'm afraid I can see no connection between this verse and St Chad."

"So, what does the message mean?" I asked, frowning.

"I cannot say for certain, but is it not possible that the message is nought but a smokescreen? That the murderer knows you are getting close to him and is making an attempt to persuade you that the next killing will take place somewhere other than you think?"

With that, Tewdwr made his excuses and left, saying he had a late afternoon lesson to conduct at the school. Alexander, meanwhile, was despatched back to the safe house to get some food and an afternoon nap, so I thanked Lendall and left him to his business. Ellis and I settled down on a pew towards the back of the nave to wait to see whether the church would receive any visitors, but after an hour or so, Ellis's eyes began to droop, so I dragged him back outside to get some fresh air. Like Alexander, we positioned ourselves at the back of the graveyard, where we were at least partly concealed by trees, but from where we could observe all the comings and goings from the church itself.

Lendall left around six in the evening to get some food but returned again about seven to conduct evening prayers. By eight o'clock, both Ellis and I were struggling to keep awake. Dusk was approaching, and it was beginning to get cold sat in the shadows, with only the occasional bat to keep us company. It was something of a relief, therefore, when, within a couple of minutes of the appointed hour, Hipkiss strode into the churchyard bearing a lantern. I was surprised to see James Logan with him.

"I was told you had received another letter," said the minister. "I thought you might need some assistance with it."

I had to smile. The manner in which Logan was reacting to the nature of the cryptic clues being set by the murderer was indeed helpful, but faith, I was beginning to wonder whether the man might be more cut out to be an intelligencer than a man of the cloth.

I was about to show Logan the letter, when Hipkiss noted the presence of Ellis.

"Who is the boy?" he asked, "I did not realise you had availed yourself of an apprentice since your arrival here."

"Such a thing would indeed have been a stroke of luck," I admitted, "but Ellis is no apprentice. He is the brother of the unfortunate girl around whom this whole sorry state of affairs revolves."

In retrospect, Hipkiss's response to this was curious, in that he stiffened slightly and maintained his silence. I would have thought nothing more of it, had it not been for the reaction of the youth when he saw the hand proffered by Hipkiss, for he took one look at the printer's palm and recoiled to a position behind me in a manner most disconcerting.

There followed a somewhat uncomfortable silence. I am certain I would have chided Ellis for his lack of manners were it not for the fact that the tension of the moment was broken by Logan demanding a look at the letter. I retrieved the envelope from my doublet and gave it to the minister to inspect.

Logan opened the note and began to study it, but as he did so, he began to scratch his head, and his features took on a worried expression.

"Is something amiss, Mr Logan? I asked. "The clue obviously refers to William Stubbs. It could not be clearer, surely?"

Logan folded the note in two and handed it back to me. "That is true," he said, "but I'm afraid it has nothing to do whatsoever with St Chad's. To a Shrewsbury clergyman such as I, the biblical reference points to but one place, the Church of St Giles."

"St Giles?"

"Yes, St Giles is a small church on the very edge of town, half a mile further along the Abbey Foregate from the Church of the Holy Cross. It is an integral part of my own parish. You may ask why a church was constructed in such a location, but there was a very good reason for it. In centuries past, St Giles was known as a hospital for lepers and the infirm. There can be no mistake that the verse from Numbers has been used to refer to it."

I stood rooted to the spot, trying hard to persuade myself not to panic.

"Then surely all is not lost," I said, "all we need to do is to hurry back across the English Bridge and reinstate our vigil at St Giles."

Logan smiled thinly and stroked his chin. "That may be so," he said, "but I fear we may be too late. Not thirty minutes ago, as I left the vicarage to come here, Stubbs announced he was going to take a stroll to the village of Upton Magna. I believe he has cousins who farm the land thereabouts, and he received a message this morning to say one of his cousins had become dangerously ill with a fever. The problem is that to reach Upton Magna from the vicarage, you have to walk directly past St Giles."

Chapter 23

"Why, in the name of Satan, did you not tell me there was another church in your parish?" I asked Logan, as he, Ellis, and I stumbled our way along the dimly lit Abbey Foregate.

The three of us had left Hipkiss to maintain a watch at St Chad's, but had sprinted down Wyle Cop as though our lives depended on it, attracting strange looks from passers-by, returning only to a more leisurely pace once, in the case of Logan and myself, our age and fitness began to catch up with us. By the time we had reached the abbey ruins, only Ellis did not look as though he was badly in need of a rest.

"I did not see the need, for you did not ask," puffed Logan, his lantern clanking against the ring of keys attached to his belt. This much was true, of course.

"But did you not consider that this might have had some relevance, given the nature of the clues?" I pressed.

Logan grimaced, accepting the point, but then changed the subject. "To be honest, I would have thought it more important to consider the implications of what this means in terms of your investigation," he said, pointedly. "If the murderer intends to attack William Stubbs at St Giles and not St Chad's, then what conclusions must be drawn from that, do you think?"

I gave Logan a sideways glance. The minister was right. In my haste and concern for Stubbs's safety I had completely ignored the fact that I had misunderstood something that had been staring me in the face all along. If the murderer's design was to complete his act of judgement on Millie's attackers at St Chad's, and if William Stubbs was meant to die at St Giles, then that could mean but one thing.

"Oh, Sweet Jesus," I exclaimed, as the horrible truth began to dawn on me. I ground to a halt in the middle of the street and clasped my hand to my forehead, only to feel the pull of Ellis tugging at my sleeve.

"Master Cheswis," said the boy. "There is something you should know."

I pulled myself together and gave Ellis my full attention. "Yes, tell me."

"Well…" Ellis hesitated, "the man you just introduced me to purports to be Charlie Hipkiss, the brother of the sergeant who killed my sister, but I can tell you that cannot be so."

"How do you mean?"

"That night, in Oswestry, whilst I was hiding in our workshop, I watched as that sergeant sat astride my sister and held her down on the floor, but Millie was brave; she had a knife concealed within her skirts and she stabbed the bastard in the right hand. The wound must have been significant, for he yelled like a stuck pig. The man to whom I was just introduced had a livid scar on his right palm. Don't ask me how, but I would swear that the man who currently sits in St Chad's churchyard is not the innocent brother, it is Jack Hipkiss himself."

I stared at Ellis for a moment, and then everything seemed to fall into place.

"Wait a minute," I said, "you are right. I knew I had seen something of significance in Ben Collie's chamber, but I was too blind to realise what it was. Collie was an avid painter, and his room was full of his work, but he must have been so racked with guilt at what he'd done to Millie that he tried to leave us a clue in the only way he knew how, by leaving a message in one of his paintings.

"On an easel in Collie's room was an unfinished portrait of Jack and Charlie Hipkiss facing each other in their uniforms, but their swords were both visible in the portrait, indicating that one of the brothers was left-handed, and the other right-handed. The person on the left of the portrait, identified as Jack, is clearly left-handed, as is the man currently working in Mistress Furnival's workshop, for I watched him coat the typeface with an inkball in his left hand. That can mean only one thing."

"Jack Hipkiss is alive," said Logan.

"Yes. The sad thing is that Ben Collie was Jack Hipkiss's best friend, so he must have known that it was Charlie who died at Whittington – not Jack – and was implicit in that deception."

"No wonder he wanted an audience with me to confess his sins," said Logan. "The guilt must have been eating away inside him."

I suddenly felt sorry for Collie. Alice had found his involvement in Millie's death hard to believe, and I was beginning to understand why. Collie, it was becoming clear, was a fundamentally good man, who had the misfortune of befriending an evildoer and who had made one monumental error fuelled by drink, which had haunted his life until it had been brought to its end.

"There is little point dwelling on the past, though," said Logan, dragging me from my reverie. "We now have two potential murder victims to consider, both of whom are currently in exactly the place where the murderer intends that they will die."

"Then we must hurry," I agreed. "Perhaps we will still be in time."

We recommenced our walk along the Abbey Foregate, passing first the abbey ruins, which rose like ghostly shadows out of the gloom, and then rows of farm workers' cottages interspersed with fields. It was an overcast evening, and a soft rain had begun to fall, although the road was still relatively busy with empty carts returning to outlying farms and labourers returning to their homes within the town. Amongst the pedestrians I was surprised to see the tall figure of the teacher Maredudd Tewdwr walking towards us.

"Good evening, Master Tewdwr," said Ellis, doffing his cap.

The schoolmaster looked a little surprised at the greeting from who, to all intents and purposes, was nothing more than a street urchin, but he gave a courteous nod in response and hurried on his way.

We had gone fully fifty yards before the significance of the exchange occurred to me, and a deep sense of dread hit me in the stomach. I wheeled around and scoured the street for Tewdwr, but the schoolmaster had already disappeared into the darkness.

"Ellis," I said, "how is it that you know Maredudd Tewdwr?"

"Oh, didn't you know?" said the boy, as though it were nothing at all. "Mr Tewdwr used to be the rector at

St Oswald's Church in Oswestry. I was surprised when I first saw him in Shrewsbury a few months ago, but it was comforting to see a friendly face." I must have been gaping at Ellis like a simpleton, for his speech drained away into nothingness. "Is something the matter, Mr Cheswis?" he asked, eventually.

I placed my hand gently on Ellis's shoulder and looked despairingly up the road towards St Giles's Church, from where, I realised, Tewdwr must have come. Logan, meanwhile, had turned pale, for he too had realised the significance of Ellis's words.

"I fear so," began the minister, but he got no further, for in truth neither Logan nor I could bring ourselves to elucidate the realisation that had hit us both simultaneously, the fact that for William Stubbs, we had arrived five minutes too late.

◌

I felt an overwhelming sense of foreboding as I entered St Giles's churchyard. The wooden door to the ancient chapel, I noticed, was slightly ajar, but as I pushed it open, I could feel an eerie sense of malevolence pervading the atmosphere, and a sharp metallic smell that was wholly incongruous in the house of God. I could tell Logan felt it too, for he shivered involuntarily, as he squeezed past me and began to light candles so we could see.

"I unlocked the door first thing this morning," he said, "but I did not leave it ajar."

We found Stubbs lying face down by the font. A pool of blood had spread out across the stone floor, seemingly from his face, although it was difficult to see in the dim light of the church. He was clearly dead, but I grabbed hold of him by his coat and turned his corpse over. What I saw made me recoil in disgust, for Stubbs's face was barely recognisable. Both eyeballs were missing, his whole face was red raw, masked with blood, and his lips had shrunken back as though they had melted, exposing the roots of his teeth. It was like looking at a skull.

I had to fight to stop myself retching, but once I had regained control of my stomach, I reached out for the inevitable crucifix that protruded from between the youth's teeth – but then I dropped it suddenly, for my fingers had inexplicably started to burn. I made for the font to rinse my hands, but Logan stopped me with a curt warning.

"Not in there, Cheswis," he said, "not if you value your hands. Take a look. The font has been contaminated with quicklime."

I stood there dumbfounded as Logan fetched a jug of water which I could pour over my hands.

Ellis, meanwhile, strangely unaffected by the gore, was bent over Stubbs's corpse, inspecting it closely. Gently, he pushed Stubbs's arms away from his body with his feet and pointed to what was left of the corpse's hands.

"God's Blood," I exclaimed, as I began to take in what Ellis was showing me. "What unspeakable evil has taken place here?"

"He has been hit on the head," said Ellis, pointing to a mark next to Stubbs's temple. I held the lantern to the injury and nodded. Ellis was right.

"Then thank God for small mercies," I said. "Hopefully he was not conscious when he died, for he has had his face thrust into a pool of caustic lime until he drowned and his eyes melted." But that was not all, I realised. Tewdwr had also soaked Stubbs's hands in lime in order to recreate the ruined hands and face of a leper.

I sat down on a pew and immersed my hands one at a time in the jug of water that Logan had brought. Were it not for the fact that they were still stinging I would have buried my head in them. Fortunately, I had only touched the crucifix lightly, and I was able to feel the relief of cold water against my skin.

"You are lucky," said Logan. "They will be red and itchy for a day or two, but there will be no lasting damage."

It was then that something caught my eye. Protruding from between two buttons on Stubbs's coat was a rolled-up piece of paper. I reached over to the corpse and extracted it from where it had been placed, taking care to touch nothing else. Unrolling the paper, I recognised a familiar script;

JH Proverbs 6:17

"JH – Jack Hipkiss," I said to Logan, who had already found a copy of the bible and was leafing through the book to locate the relevant passage.

"A proud look, a lying tongue, and hands that shed innocent blood."

"It is a passage about evil," I said, "and in killing Millie, Hipkiss is certainly guilty of shedding innocent blood."

"Of course," agreed Logan, "but it is more than that. You have to take the verse in context. Here, I will read verses sixteen to nineteen."

So, I listened whilst Logan read out God's judgement on Jack Hipkiss;

These six things doth the Lord hate, yea seven are an abomination unto him.

A proud look, a lying tongue, and hands that shed innocent blood.

An heart that deviseth wicked imagination, feet that be swift in running to mischief.

A false witness that speaketh lies that soweth discord among brethren

"It is like an amalgamation of all the sins that Hipkiss has been guilty of in this sorry affair," I said. "It represents the culmination of all the saints' judgements on Hipkiss's five accomplices and a final judgement by St Chad, on whose day this evil act of murder was committed."

"You are right," said Logan, "but it seems Satan is not yet done for the day. Jack Hipkiss sits right now at St Chad's, and Maredudd Tewdwr heads there with murder in his heart. If we are to prevent the perpetration of more evil today, we must lock up the church for the night and head to St Chad's forthwith."

"You are most certainly in the right of it," I agreed, "but first there is one thing that we must do."

And so it was that James Logan, Ellis Davies and I approached the altar of St Giles Church, knelt, and prayed for the soul of William Stubbs.

Chapter 24

*R*aindrops *dripped gently from the brim of Sir Fulke Hunckes's hat as he concealed himself in the narrow passage which ran along the side of The Sacristry. Pulling his cloak around him, he shivered in the unseasonably cool late summer air and settled down for the wait.*

Under normal circumstances, skulking in the gloom of a wet September night was not the erstwhile governor of Shrewsbury's wont, but tonight was different. Tonight, he was going to get to the bottom of the maddening imbroglio of information and misinformation that had begun to make him question his sanity. The more he delved into the perplexing issue of the hoard of treasure that had been recovered following the strange events at Combermere, the more people emerged from the murky depths and rose to the surface, all tainted, it seemed, with the distinct reek of the midden.

Now, as he loitered in the alleyway, watching Alice Furnival's typesetter, Charlie Hipkiss, pacing up and down in St Chad's churchyard, Sir Fulke Hunckes realised one thing above all. The more he looked, and the more he cogitated on the matter, the more everything seemed to come back to two people: Daniel Cheswis and Alice Furnival.

Following his impromptu appearance at Alice's on the previous Saturday evening, Hunckes had wondered whether the harshness of his approach had been warranted, and he had made up his mind to apologise, but when the widow had not turned up at church the following day, he had made a number of enquiries and discovered she had immediately departed for Montgomery. To see whom, he wondered. Lord Herbert? Bressy? One of Prince Rupert's spymasters, perchance? Or perhaps, worst of all, fearing betrayal, she had ridden there to await the arrival of Sir Thomas Myddelton? Nothing could be discounted.

He had tried to discuss the matter with Colonel Broughton, but the new governor had not wanted to know. Hunckes had been reminded about Alice Furnival's credentials as a prominent supporter of the King, of the fact that it was she who had alerted Broughton to the need to ship the dies down to Bristol before Gideon Townsend and his collaborators could get their hands on them. Why do that if her design was the destruction of the mint?

Stung by the lack of support from his successor, Hunckes had already made the decision to do some investigations of his own, when news began to emerge of a third murder in the town. This time the victim had been a young carpenter by the name of Smits, who had been killed in bizarre fashion in the belfry of St Julian's Church. Smits, it turned out, was a Dutchman, and a friend of the first victim, Jakob De Vries. Both of the first two victims, Hunckes recalled, had been employees of Alice Furnival, who herself had been seen around town, making enquiries with someone matching the description of the spy Daniel Cheswis. Furnival had denied this and claimed she had been with her typesetter Charlie Hipkiss, who, it emerged, had been privy to certain information regarding the perpetrators of a seemingly unconnected crime carried out at Oswestry earlier in the year, when that town had been a Royalist garrison under the command of Colonel Lloyd.

Hunckes had racked his brains trying to remember the details of that event, but it had seemed so inconsequential at the time. What he did recall, however, was that a sergeant bearing the name of Hipkiss had been rumoured to be the main perpetrator of that particular crime, but had died at Whittington. Charlie Hipkiss, he had discovered, was the man's brother.

Given the fact that he had no other leads to go on, Hunckes decided that he could do worse than find out more about Alice Furnival's typesetter, so on the Monday morning he found himself a suitable vantage point near to the castle and waited for Hipkiss to arrive at work.

He observed several people come and go, including the schoolteacher Maredudd Tewdwr, who had an empty snapsack slung over his back, but, just as the eight o'clock bells were ringing, Hipkiss arrived and disappeared into the school, from where he had presumably walked through the building into the rear yard and into Mistress Furnival's print workshop. Barely ten minutes later, he had re-emerged bearing a worried demeanour and clutching a letter.

Taking care to hang back far enough to ensure he would not be seen, Hunckes followed Hipkiss past St Mary's, along Dogpole to the bottom of Wyle Cop, and across the English Bridge. To his surprise, when the typesetter reached the abbey precinct, he turned towards the Church of the Holy Cross and hammered on the church door. After a few moments, the door opened, and Hipkiss was ushered inside by the minister.

Hunckes sat himself on one of the ruined walls of the abbey cloisters and waited. What, he wondered, did James Logan have to do with all of this? The number of people associated with this murky business was growing by the minute, but he swore he was going to get to the bottom of it.

As he waited for Hipkiss to emerge from the church, he was surprised to catch sight of Maredudd Tewdwr again, this time walking along a path behind the cloisters. Tewdwr's snapsack, he noted, was now full, although at the time he had no inkling of the significance of this fact. Tewdwr spotted Hunckes from behind the ruined wall, but he hurried on by, avoiding eye contact.

It was fully half an hour before the church door opened and Hipkiss emerged with Logan. The two men initially started making for the bridge, but before Hunckes could follow them across the river and back into town, his attention was drawn to the sight of a young farm worker gesticulating wildly and running through the abbey ruins from the direction of the fields by the Meole Brook.

"Come quickly! Murder!" the farmhand shouted. "There is a body in Joe Finch's field."

Hunckes gestured for the boy to come over and grabbed him by the shoulders. "Murder? Where?" he said. "Show me."

"Ah, Colonel Hunckes, sir," said the youth, recognising the ex-governor. "There is a cadaver, sir, and a lot of blood. 'Tis a gruesome sight. I fear it may be Joe Finch, the smallholder who works the land there."

"You fear so?" said Hunckes with surprise. "You mean you cannot tell from looking at his face?"

"No sir, I mean I cannot see his face, for the dead man's head is missing."

Hunckes followed the boy back through the abbey ruins and into the fields beyond, where he found himself being accompanied by several curious passers-by, who had overheard the boy's shouting. Hipkiss and Logan, he noticed, had also joined the group.

They found the headless corpse slumped on its side by a boundary fence. A bloody scythe lay a few feet away.

"Killed by his own tools," said one of the passers-by. "The reaper himself could not have done a better job."

Somebody went to fetch the coroner, and the constable responsible for the Parish of the Holy Cross and St Giles. Meanwhile, the crowd of onlookers come to see the macabre sight began to grow. Logan and Hipkiss, however, did not tarry long. After saying a prayer for the victim, Logan eventually nudged Hipkiss, and the two men sloped off back towards the main road and the English`Bridge. Again, making sure he was not seen, Hunckes followed them, and this time he was rewarded with what he had been hoping for.

To his surprise, Hunckes was led to St Chad's church, but instead of seeking out the minister inside the church, Logan and Hipkiss headed for a secluded and overgrown part of the graveyard, where they were met by a third man.

Hunckes crouched behind a large family tomb. He did not recognise the newcomer at first, for it was a few weeks since he had seen him, but then it suddenly hit him. Who could it be but the one man he had been searching for above all others – the Roundhead spy Daniel Cheswis?

Hunckes smiled to himself, for now was the opportunity he had been waiting for. He would arrest Cheswis and deliver him to Colonel Broughton, allowing him to get to the bottom of Cheswis's relationship with Alice Furnival.

But as he prepared to step out from behind the gravestones, two things stopped him. Firstly, despite the fact that Hunckes was armed with sword and carbine, he was unsure about the wisdom of trying to capture three men. Cheswis he could handle, but Hipkiss was a burly fellow, and Logan, he knew, had a reputation for being able to look after himself. Most crucially, though, before Hunckes could act, Cheswis had suddenly and without warning charged out of the churchyard as though he had been stung by a hornet and along Milk Street in the direction of St Julian's, closely followed by the other two men.

Hunckes had very little idea what was going on, but he spent the rest of the day in the shadows following Cheswis and his co-conspirators around town. Firstly, he followed them rather quicker than he would have liked to St Mary's. He then followed Cheswis and Logan to Stubbs's Chophouse on the corner of Fish Street, where they picked up the son of the owner, a young lad with a withered arm.

At this point, Logan headed off down Wyle Cop with the boy, leaving Hunckes to follow Cheswis past St Chad's to a house on the far side of the old college precinct close to the town walls. Cheswis knocked at the door and was let inside by a well-built, sandy-haired man, who Hunckes recognised as Cheswis's friend from Nantwich, Clowes.

Once he was sure Cheswis was not coming straight back out again, Hunckes walked up to the house and caught a glimpse through the window. Sitting in the main room together with Cheswis and Clowes was an austere-looking woman in plain black garb – the house owner, he guessed – and a teenage boy, who, he presumed, must be the young vagrant being sought for the murder of Jakob De Vries. As he walked past the house, Hunckes caught sight of the door knocker and smiled. How many times had he walked past here and not noticed the Mytton family coat of arms?

Sir Fulke Hunckes made a decision. Once he had explained his findings to Colonel Broughton, he would have Cheswis and his group of spies and conspirators arrested, and he would have the house ransacked for incriminating evidence. As he walked back up the hill towards St Chad's, though, Hunckes once again caught sight of the schoolteacher, Maredudd Tewdwr, this time walking towards the almshouses from the direction of the town walls. Slipping into an alleyway so he could not be seen, Hunckes watched as the schoolteacher approached the house in which Cheswis was hiding and post a piece of paper underneath the door. It was the third time he had seen Tewdwr close to Cheswis and his associates in the space of a day, and this time Sir Fulke Hunckes began to wonder.

ෙ

Now, twenty-four hours later, Hunckes stood in the shadows by The Sacristry, knowing that on this night there would be a reckoning, and that this reckoning would be centred around St Chad's.

He had gone to see Colonel Broughton that morning to convey what he had learned, only to discover that Cheswis's collaborator Saltonstall had somehow broken out of the castle dungeon. The gaoler, Abel Hook, had been rather vague about how the young spy had managed to break free, leaving himself and a naked man called Wollascott locked in his cell.

Broughton had been in no mood to listen to stories about Cheswis, and so Hunckes had simply told him to come to St Chad's with his men when he was ready, and as likely as not, he would be able to make multiple arrests. He then went through his own journal and realised that the date of the murder of the girl in Oswestry, around which the series of murders in Shrewsbury seemed to revolve, had actually taken place on March 2nd, St Chad's day. An interesting coincidence, Hunckes had thought, but then he walked over to the school and made some enquiries about Maredudd Tewdwr and discovered he too had been in Oswestry at the start of March.

Having by now also heard about the gruesome discovery in the Trinity Aisle Chapel in St Mary's, Hunckes had put two and two together and realised what the schoolteacher had been carrying in his snapsack when he had seen him among the ruins of the abbey cloisters the previous day.

Returning to St Chad's, he had seen first Clowes, then Cheswis and the boy, and finally Hipkiss mounting a watch there, and had realised that here was where the end game was going to play out.

Maredudd Tewdwr, he realised, was a murderer and would want to finish his killing spree at St Chad's. Cheswis, Logan and Clowes knew this, he surmised, and all three would eventually turn up, probably with the young boy who was staying with them in tow. Hipkiss was already there, and Saltonstall would, no doubt, also put in an appearance at some point.

Sir Fulke Hunckes suppressed a quiet chuckle and began to think about the plaudits he would get for solving this. Not only would he have identified a savage murderer, he would have been able to arrest several parliamentary spies, thereby protecting Shrewsbury from Roundhead infiltration. Indeed, with Broughton succeeding only in losing a key prisoner from the castle dungeon, was it not distinctly possible that he would be in prime position to benefit? Perhaps he would even be able to reclaim his position as governor.

Hunckes nodded to himself with satisfaction and settled back down to wait, but then he took a deep breath and smiled with anticipation, as he recognised the tall, bearded figure entering the churchyard and heading straight for Hipkiss.

Chapter 25

Shrewsbury – Tuesday September 3rd, 1644

We walked back to St Chad's in silence, Ellis and I, leaving Logan to secure St Giles from unwanted intruders until the scene of horror could be attended by the various town officials the following morning. I had begun to feel sorry for the coroner and the constable.

Our mood was not helped by the fact that the soft spots of rain that had begun as we approached St Giles had now developed into a solid and persistent drizzle, the kind of rain that feels light enough but soaks you to the very core and darkens your soul.

We had almost reached the top of Wyle Cop before either of us could bring ourselves to break the morose mood that had settled over us, and I admit to my shame that it was not I who was first to break the silence.

"He wasn't such a bad lad, Stubbs, you know," said Ellis. "He was the only one who refused to join in with Hipkiss when he was ravishing our Millie, but he could not bring himself to stand up against what he knew was wrong. I cannot swear I would have behaved any differently in his shoes."

I clapped Ellis on the shoulder in sympathy. "There is little sense in dwelling on what cannot be changed," I said, "but now we have an opportunity to make sure justice is done."

We approached St Chad's along Milk Street before skirting in front of The Sacristy and entering the churchyard at the north-western corner. As we passed the tavern I thought I saw a movement in the alleyway through which I had escaped with Gideon Townsend the previous Wednesday, but I was past caring about who might be waiting in the shadows.

It was a dark night, the moon being obscured by cloud, but we dared not light our lanterns in the churchyard for fear of them betraying our position. I could just make out the vast bulk of the church to my left and a line of trees to my right, but that was about all. The taller headstones loomed out of the dark at me like silent sentinels as we picked our way across the uneven terrain, but that did not stop me tripping over several smaller stones as I fumbled my way through the dark. I realised that anyone lying in wait for me would have heard me coming a mile off.

"Did you hear that?" whispered Ellis, suddenly. "Over to the left."

I stopped and listened intently, but could make nothing out. I was just about to move on when I caught a flash of light out of the corner of my eye, but before I could react, I felt a hand over my mouth and a knee in my back. I fell onto my knees and tried to swivel round, swinging my arms in an attempt to strike my assailant, but I was too slow and too weak. Before I could react any further, I heard a gasp, before feeling a blinding pain in the back of my head. I found myself staring into the dark eyes of Maredudd Tewdwr and realised that the gasp had been my own. It was then that I lost my grip on consciousness and passed out.

When I awoke, I found myself propped up against a headstone with my arms tied behind my back. Next to me, similarly bound, but also gagged, was a terrified-looking Hipkiss. Ellis, however, was nowhere to be seen.

"Do not worry about the boy," said a voice to my left, as though reading my mind. "He will not get far, and, after all, he seeks the same revenge as I."

I peered through the dark and was just able to make out the cassocked figure of Maredudd Tewdwr perched on a gravestone, a few feet away.

"I am sorry for the lump you will have on your head tomorrow," said Tewdwr. "I had no desire to hurt you beyond what was necessary to make sure I complete the judgements and sentences the saints have commanded me to execute on their behalf. Indeed, I have enjoyed our intellectual games these past days. I am gratified to see you worked it out in the end."

I stared at Tewdwr, not knowing how to react. The man was clearly deranged, but I knew I had to engage him in conversation and play for time.

"With the help of Mr Logan and Ellis, yes," I said, "but is that all it is to you, an intellectual challenge? You have murdered five people, and you would seek to reduce these acts to a game?"

Tewdwr's face darkened. "Do not presume to understand why these men had to die, and why Jack Hipkiss will now also be judged for his sins. They destroyed my faith in God and murdered the woman I loved, before fleeing back to Shrewsbury. For that they had to face the judgement of all the saints, and Hipkiss, the most evil of them all, will face the judgement of St Chad, on whose day he committed this atrocity."

I turned around to look at Hipkiss, who had managed to work his gag loose with his tongue.

"Do not listen to this madman," he said, coughing and spluttering as the gag came free. "This is nought but complete insanity. I am Charles Hipkiss, as you well know, my brother died at Whittington."

"I think that ship has long since sailed, Hipkiss," I said. "Pray be quiet. I would listen to what Mr Tewdwr has to say, particularly about what happened the night you killed Millie Davies."

Hipkiss scowled at me, but Tewdwr emitted a low chuckle.

"Tell me about your relationship with Millie," I said, "if you are prepared to kill in her name, then I suspect there must be more to this than meets the eye."

Tewdwr gave a sigh and got to his feet. "Millie was lovely," he said. "I had not been rector at St Oswald's for very long, and I knew few people outside our own congregation, but Millie always had a smile for me and would often stop to talk on her way home from work. I fell in love with her. It's as simple as that."

"And this love was reciprocated?"

"I do not know. I hoped so, and I had planned to talk to her of it, but I never took that opportunity. Now, of course, I never will."

"So how did you know Hipkiss and his friends were the ones who killed Millie?"

"I saw them, crude, leering soldiers, flush with drink, waiting for her outside her house. I was on my way home. I knew not why they picked on her at the time. I only found out about that later, but I saw them follow her into her father's workshop. I feared the worst, and it is to my eternal shame that I did nothing about it."

"If you had tried, I'd have killed you," said Hipkiss, simply.

Tewdwr smiled. "Well, the boot is now firmly on the other foot, is it not?"

Hipkiss growled and spat into the earth by his side, but I ignored him.

"So, what happened next, and what made you decide to carry out retribution in this way?"

"I did not find out what had happened until early the following morning," said Tewdwr. "I was woken from my sleep by a banging on the rectory door. I opened it up to find Ellis standing there shivering. He had been hiding in the graveyard all night, hiding from Cornelis Smits. I took him in, gave him some food and let him warm himself by the fire. I listened to his account of what had happened and offered to take him back to his home, but he said no, and very wise that was too, for when I walked over there myself later, I was told of the heinous act that had been committed in the smithy and experienced the shock and devastation of the Davies family for myself. I swore then that I would avenge Millie's death.

"It was clear that Ellis could not be seen in Oswestry until those responsible for the murder had been arrested and punished, so I gave Ellis some food and money and told him to go to Shrewsbury. I even gave him the name of a blacksmith on Grope Lane, where he might seek some work. I told him I would send word once it was safe for him to return."

"But that never happened, did it?"

"No, it very quickly became obvious that Colonel Lloyd, the officer in charge of the garrison, had no intention of seeking out the perpetrators of the crime, and that the evildoers who took Millie's life and her honour would get away with it, unless—"

"Unless you did something about it." I finished the sentence for him.

"Of course. So, before Ellis departed for Shrewsbury, I took descriptions of the six men involved. I also discussed the matter with Jack Morgan, the landlord of The Bell, so I was able to build up more of a picture of the men I was seeking. Smits and De Vries were the easiest to find, there were not that many Dutchmen serving the Royalist cause in Oswestry at that time – Stubbs too, his withered arm made him easy to identify.

"I did not find out about Hipkiss, though, until his brother, Charlie, was recognised by Jack Morgan, erroneously, as it turned out. But Morgan told me, and then I found out Charlie Hipkiss had been to see Evan and Hester Davies and had identified his twin brother, Jack, as the ringleader. This, of course, led me to Ben Collie and eventually also to Joseph Finch. I had identified all six of the killers, and, originally, I was planning to avenge Millie's death in Oswestry, so that the Davies family could see for themselves who the animals were who had killed their daughter. I then planned to send for Ellis and unite him with his family, but, unfortunately, fate intervened."

"Of course," I said. "Jack Hipkiss, or the person you thought was Jack Hipkiss, was killed at Whittington, and his accomplices fled back to Shrewsbury, so you followed them here."

"There you have it," said Tewdwr. "That is the nub of it."

"So, tell me," I asked, "I am curious. How did you work out that the person claiming to be Charlie Hipkiss was, in fact, his brother, Jack?"

"I was not sure at first, but I had my suspicions. I could not believe my luck when I presented myself at my old school, looking for work, and discovered Hipkiss and Collie working in Mistress Furnival's print workshop. I made some enquiries and discovered that the Hipkiss brothers and Ben Collie had been long-time friends and that both Charlie Hipkiss and Collie had worked for the Furnivals before the war. It also occurred to me that Charlie Hipkiss had seen fit to change his appearance dramatically on his return to Shrewsbury by cutting his hair and growing a beard, and I began to ask myself why this might be so."

"So, how did you find out for certain?"

"Collie told me. As you worked out, he was racked with guilt for allowing himself to become involved in Millie's rape and murder, but also for being persuaded to help his friend cover up the fact that he had murdered his own brother."

In retrospect, I do not recall what was louder, Hipkiss's snort of derision or my gasp of surprise.

"Yes, I thought that would make you sit up," said Tewdwr, his eyes wide and glinting in the darkness. "Collie told me that, although I own I did not believe it at first. Charlie had told Jack he must hand himself in or he would betray him to the authorities. Knowing that would have meant the rope for all six of them, it was enough for Jack to persuade Ben Collie to help him stage his own death. So, Jack waited until the battle at Whittington was at its height before shooting Charlie in the back. It was Ben Collie who was instrumental in retrieving Charlie's body after the battle and swearing it was Jack who had died."

"He bloody deserved it," snarled Hipkiss. "He was a traitor, who would have seen his own brother go to the gallows."

I slumped back against the gravestone, unable to find the words to express my feelings. In truth, sat in the presence of these two murderers, I could no longer work out which of the two was worse, the man who had killed an innocent girl in the heat of the moment for lust and then murdered his own brother as Cain did Abel, or the insane killer who had planned out a series of increasingly bizarre and bloodthirsty attacks in the belief that the retribution being carried out by his hands was sanctioned by the saints.

What disappointed me most was that it had taken me so long to work out that Maredudd Tewdwr was guilty of the murders of De Vries, Collie, Smits, Finch, and Stubbs. Of course, if I'd known that Tewdwr had been the rector at Oswestry, I would have worked it out much quicker, but with hindsight, I had received clues enough. The killer had to be educated and knowledgeable in the scriptures as well as familiar with all the churches in Shrewsbury and their ministers. He also needed to know where Alice Furnival lived as well as having ready access to the print workshop, in order to be able to deliver his messages.

The biggest clue of all, however, had been given to me by James Logan on the day of Collie's death. He had revealed that he had been preparing the sermons for the following day when Collie arrived at the church, which, given that Tewdwr was also scheduled to be giving a sermon on that day, meant the schoolmaster must have been on the premises at the time.

Collie had died in the ten minutes Logan had spent dealing with the unruly crowd outside the church, during which time the church had been closed. Tewdwr must have waited until Logan left the church before creeping into the nave and inserting the crucifix into Collie's mouth. He would have had plenty of time to accompany Collie to the church and ply him with bread and wine. In hindsight, it all seemed so obvious.

"So, now you know," said Tewdwr, bringing me back to my senses, "but now is the time for me to finish my work here. Mr Cheswis, I bear you no ill will, but I cannot let you go free, not yet at any rate. I also need to be assured that you will not make enough noise to raise the dead as soon as I walk out of here, so permit me, please."

With that, he untied the gag from around Hipkiss's neck and shoved it into my own mouth, tying it tightly around my neck.

"Someone will find you eventually," continued Tewdwr, "in the morning, but not before. Now, it is time for me to carry out the Lord's judgement."

In the dark, I watched as Tewdwr reached inside his cassock and pulled out a long dagger from a leather scabbard, before grabbing Hipkiss by the hair and wrenching his head to the side. Hipkiss tried to raise his knees in defence, but he was too slow, and Tewdwr stamped on Hipkiss's thigh, forcing the print worker to howl with pain. But then, instead of drawing the knife across Hipkiss's neck as I was expecting, Tewdwr started to pray softly.

"Holy Lord, almighty and eternal God. Hear our prayers as we entrust to you Jack Hipkiss, as you summon him out of this world. Forgive his sins and failings and grant him a haven of light and peace."

"Go fuck yourself, you insane bastard," groaned Hipkiss, aiming a globule of spittle at Tewdwr's face.

But just as Tewdwr began to draw back the knife, there was a flash and a bang from somewhere behind me, and a sharp scream from Tewdwr as he fell to the ground, clutching his knee.

For a second I thought St Chad had delivered his own judgement on Maredudd Tewdwr, but I quickly came to my senses at the sight of the middle-aged gentleman striding across the churchyard clutching a sword and a carbine.

"Colonel Hunckes, is that you?" Hipkiss was staring with incredulity at the newcomer as though he were a guardian angel.

For a moment, I thought Hunckes was going to take some steps towards me, but he seemed to change his mind at the last moment, and instead addressed Hipkiss.

"You are fortunate indeed that I was passing, Sergeant Hipkiss," he said. "Good God, how on earth have you become involved with such a nest of vipers? Here, let me undo your ties." Hunckes stepped over to Hipkiss and sliced through the rope tying the latter's wrists together with his sword.

"Well met, sir," said Hipkiss, who was not slow to grab the opportunity. "Your intervention is most opportune."

Whilst this was going on, Tewdwr was heaving himself to his feet and hobbling off through the gravestones to the edge of the churchyard, where he disappeared through a line of trees into a lane beyond.

"You are a lucky man, Hipkiss," said Hunckes, "he was about to slit your throat."

I tried to respond to that, but, thanks to the gag in my mouth, all that came out was a jumble of garbled nonsense.

"Be quiet, Cheswis," warned Hunckes, "your turn will come."

Hipkiss flashed a grin in my direction. "I think what Mr Cheswis may be trying to explain is that the man you just shot is the person responsible for the murder of Jakob De Vries, Ben Collie, and the others. I was about to be his next victim."

"That much is obvious," conceded Hunckes, "but it is not the whole story, I'll wager. I am most anxious to hear what Cheswis has to do with this. Yet first, take my sword and chase down our becassocked friend. I would hear his version of these events."

"Yes, Colonel," said Hipkiss, accepting the baldric Hunckes had lifted over his head and slipping it over his own. He then took Hunckes's sword and made off in the direction of Tewdwr's escape before the colonel could change his mind. No-one, I mused, could have accused Hipkiss of not being quick to take advantage of a situation.

For my part, I was unsure whether I was now better or worse off than before. At least with Tewdwr I was being held by someone who bore me no personal ill will. Hunckes, however, would most certainly arrest me for a spy, after which I could look forward to little more than sharing a cell with Saltonstall.

In the event, Hunckes seemed in no particular hurry to march me off to gaol. I could not say why – perhaps it was a desire on his part to savour his triumph, but instead of hauling me roughly to my feet, Hunckes loosened the gag around my mouth and leaned against the same gravestone Tewdwr had used.

"You have been a difficult man to break down, Mr Cheswis," he said, "but I'm afraid your arrogance has caused you to stay in Shrewsbury a little too long. Now I have you, and with God's grace your rabble of co-conspirators will not be far behind."

I was not exactly in a position of strength, I grant, but I was in no mood for this kind of talk. "I am the least of your worries, Sir Fulke," I said. "Do you realise you have just let two murderers escape, and armed one of them with a sword?"

"Two murderers? Poppycock," scoffed Hunckes, "what do you take me for? That was Charles Hipkiss, who served under me at Oswestry, a good and reliable soldier. He will bring back your killer, of that you may be certain."

I shook my head. "I fear you are wrong," I said. "Admittedly, he fooled a lot of people, but that was Jack Hipkiss, the rapist and murderer. Charlie Hipkiss died at Whittington. I doubt you will see his murderous brother again, although I concede you may see Maredudd Tewdwr, the other murderer, again, especially if Hipkiss catches up with him, in which case you are likely to be scraping his body off the street somewhere. I doubt Hipkiss will afford him much mercy."

My words had the effect of wiping the triumphant smile off Hunckes's face, at least temporarily. "I know not what game you are playing, Cheswis," he said, "but the truth will come out. I am sure the matter of the murders that have taken place in Shrewsbury these past days is something you will be called upon to help us with, and as for Tewdwr, he will not get far with an injured knee. In the meantime, however, I am more interested in finding out about your activities as an intelligencer in the service of that venomous toad, the arch puritan, Sir William Brereton. In particular, I would hear more about your co-operation with Alice Furnival."

I could do little else but laugh. "Alice?" I exclaimed. "Are you serious? You think I am in league with Alice Furnival?"

"There are too many unanswered questions. The nature of your escape from Dorfold Hall after January's battle in Nantwich, the strange events at Combermere, the revelation that you have known each other since childhood, and then there are your activities this past week, skulking around this town with each other. And everywhere you turn up, it seems, there is a dead body to be found. You can hardly deny you have been in Mistress Furnival's company this past week."

"It is true I was betrothed to her once," I admitted, "but that was many years ago. As for this past week, it is also true she asked me to help her identify the murderer of her employees, Jakob De Vries and Ben Collie, but that is all. Indeed, if it had not been for her, we would have succeeded in capturing the dies from the mint. In fact, I think you have something to thank her for."

Hunckes snorted derisively. "You cannot pull the wool over my eyes," he said, grabbing me by the coat and hauling me to my feet. "Come, it is time I took you to see the governor. Between us we will get to the bottom of this."

I own that at that moment my spirits were at their lowest ebb. I could not bring myself to resist Hunckes as he propelled me through the grim blackness of the churchyard. But then, all of a sudden, I caught sight of a lantern by the church entrance, and then another near the wall by The Sacristry. Then, four shadows, three tall and one short.

"Please do not take one more step, Sir Fulke," said a voice I knew well. "We will take over from here." And then, to my utter amazement, out of the darkness stepped Lieutenant Saltonstall, accompanied by Alexander, Ellis, and Gideon Townsend.

Chapter 26

Whilst the seething Hunckes was being gagged and bound to one of the gravestones with a length of rope by Alexander and Saltonstall, Gideon explained how he had managed to secure the lieutenant's release from the castle.

"Once we were free, we made our way along the river bank to the south of the town. On the common land outside the town walls, there is an old quarry, which offers good cover. We hid there until just before dawn, when we went straight to The Sacristry. There we hid until this evening, when Greaves took us to the safe house. We found Alexander already there, and he was able to explain the gist of the events that have taken place here these past days. Whilst he was doing so Ellis burst in and told us what had happened both here and at St Giles. We came immediately."

"And Greaves?" I said. "Where is he?"

"It is not safe to remain in the safe house any longer. Greaves and Mistress Eliza have taken the horses and left town via the Welsh Bridge. We will meet them in Frankwell later."

I felt sorry for Mistress Eliza. Despite her austere exterior, there was no escaping the fact that she had put her life at risk for us, and now she stood to lose her house too.

"Do not worry about Eliza," said Gideon, as if reading my thoughts, "she will accompany us to Wem afterwards, where I will make sure she is adequately recompensed for her loss. She will not suffer for the lack of a roof over her head, Mytton will make sure of that. In the meantime, we have other matters to attend to. What of Tewdwr and Hipkiss?"

"Tewdwr is injured, shot in the knee, and he has fled in the direction of the town walls to the south. Hipkiss is armed with a sword and has gone in pursuit of him."

Gideon clicked his tongue in irritation. "Then we must needs go after them," he said. "There is a gate in the wall that leads to the common, south of here. It sounds as if they have headed in that direction."

"Won't they get stopped by the sentries?" I asked.

"Of course, but they will have passes and will no doubt be known by the garrison soldiers. So long as Tewdwr can hide the seriousness of his injured leg, he should be able to get out onto the common, even at this time of night."

"But what about us?" I asked. "Alexander, Ellis, and we two are all suspected of being either spies or murderers, or both."

Gideon thought about this for a moment, the silence punctuated only by Hunckes's muffled protests. Gideon looked in irritation at the former governor and scratched his chin, but then his countenance brightened, and he offered me a conspiratorial smile.

"I think I have an idea," he said.

଄

Five minutes later, Hunckes, still protesting, was on his feet, his hands bound tightly behind his back. Gideon, now brandishing Hunckes's carbine, faced our prisoner, whilst Alexander held him by the shoulders.

"Now listen to me, Hunckes," said Gideon. "We have nothing to lose, so it's all the same to me whether you survive this night or whether I shoot you here and now with your own carbine. As such, I suggest you cease struggling and be quiet."

Hunckes flashed Gideon a look of pure hatred, but he nodded nevertheless, and so Alexander loosened the fabric that was holding his gag in place. Hunckes spat it out unceremoniously onto the floor.

"A pox on you, Townsend," he said, "you will pay for this, of that you can be certain."

"Perhaps," said Gideon, "but not tonight. Now, listen carefully. I will release your hands, but one false move, and I will shoot you in the back. Is that clear?"

Hunckes nodded, so Alexander untied the former governor's wrists.

"Now," continued Gideon, "this is what we are going to do. We are going to march down to the gate leading to the common, and you are going to secure passage for all five of us through the checkpoint. If challenged, you will say that you are seeking Maredudd Tewdwr and Charlie Hipkiss, who are both suspected of murder, and you have reason to believe they passed through the gate. Do not think for a moment that I will hesitate to use this gun. If you alert the garrison guards, we may well end up arrested, but you, Sir Fulke, will be dead. Is that understood?"

Hunckes gave Gideon a venomous glare, but eventually he answered in the affirmative, and so we made our way out of the churchyard and down the hill past Mistress Eliza's house, Hunckes in the lead with Gideon and Alexander close behind, and Ellis and myself taking up the rear.

At the gate, we were challenged by two burly pikemen and a sergeant brandishing a halberd. They stood at ease as soon as they recognised Hunckes, but insisted on an explanation as to why he wanted to leave the town at such an hour.

I could feel Gideon tense as Hunckes gave his answer, but fortunately the erstwhile governor followed the script as instructed by Gideon, and, despite a couple of suspicious looks, we were allowed to pass through the gate unhindered.

"Tewdwr and Hipkiss both headed towards the quarry," volunteered the sergeant. "You should begin your search there. If you wish, I can send a small detachment of men to seek them out."

There was a tense moment when I thought Hunckes was going to agree to this, and I swear he considered it, for I noticed the sudden flash of interest in his eyes, but a glare from Gideon appeared to change his mind.

"Thank you, Sergeant," he said, "but there is no need. The quarry is but a hundred yards away. If we need you, we will call for help."

"Very good, sir. Just wave your lantern from side to side if you require assistance. We will be keeping a lookout."

We headed downhill from the gateway across rough meadow land, towards a dark shadow in the distance, which I took to be a clump of trees surrounding the old quarry. Ellis and I carried the lanterns, allowing Alexander, Saltonstall and Gideon to make sure Hunckes did not make any false moves.

"Be careful through here," warned Alexander as we approached the trees. "It is a good hiding place in here, but it is treacherous, and there is a sudden drop once we get through the vegetation."

My friend was not exaggerating. Walking in a clockwise direction around the trees until we were on the opposite side of it to the town, he hesitated as though looking for something, before striking out through the trees along a narrow footpath. After a mere twenty yards or so, he stopped and put his hand in the air.

"Attention," he said, "we are right on the edge. There is a footpath down to the bottom, but the footing is uncertain and dangerous in the dark."

I held the lantern up to illuminate the landscape and immediately saw that we were standing on the edge of a wide amphitheatre, perhaps fifty yards or so in diameter, and thirty feet deep, entirely surrounded by thick vegetation, a perfect hiding place, as Alexander, Saltonstall, and Gideon had shown.

My eyes were suddenly drawn to a movement on the far side of the quarry, and, in the darkness, I could just make out two figures moving around the edge. Tewdwr, unsteady on his feet, was muttering something unintelligible whilst Hipkiss, waving Hunckes's sword at his enemy, was backing him towards the drop.

"Don't do it, Hipkiss," I shouted. "He cannot get far. He will face justice here in Shrewsbury and will hang for his crimes."

I do not know what I was expecting to achieve, but it was enough to make both men look up. Tewdwr, however, seemed to cry out in pain and made a grab for his knee, as though it had collapsed on him. Losing his footing, he fell backwards and landed on his side, before slipping out of sight down the deep slope into the depths of the quarry.

There was a five second interval when time seemed to stand still, but then Hipkiss threw Hunckes's sword into the darkness and disappeared into the trees.

"Quick, after him," said Gideon to me. "Hunckes, you come with me – Ellis, you too. We will clamber down and see if Tewdwr is still alive."

There was no time to lose. Alexander, Saltonstall and I rushed back out of the trees until we were once again on open heathland. Peering through the gloom, all that it was possible to make out was the fact that the ground fell away on three sides towards a dark semi-circular line that marked the broad sweep of the Severn. I held the lantern behind my back so that I could see better, and then it was just possible to make out a movement to my right to the west of the quarry, and I realised Hipkiss was making straight for the river.

The three of us charged down the hill after him, but the sergeant had a fifty-yard start and had not far to go to the river bank. Worse still, as we careered down the hill, I heard a sharp cry of pain behind me and swung round to find Saltonstall rolling on the ground in agony.

"By Christ," he groaned, "I've twisted my bloody ankle. Don't wait for me."

We continued to sprint down the hill, but we were too late. By the time we had reached the river bank, all that could be seen of Hipkiss was his head bobbing in the water as he swam across the river. Perhaps it was a sign, but as he did so, the thick cloud layer parted to reveal a half moon, which illuminated Hipkiss as he pulled himself up out of the water on the opposite bank, before turning around, waving at us, and disappearing into the undergrowth.

Trudging back uphill, we helped Saltonstall, now shivering with shock, to his feet and back to the place where we had left Gideon, Ellis, and Hunckes. There was no sign of them.

"Is anyone there?" I called into the dark depths of the quarry.

At first nothing, but then, all of a sudden, there was a scrabbling at my feet, and Ellis's head popped up above the rim of the quarry. I put my hand out and heaved him up. A few seconds later, Gideon appeared, and he hoisted himself up beside me.

"Tewdwr?" I asked.

"Alive," said Gideon. "Just. The place where he fell is not sheer, and he just rolled downhill into a pile of mud. Hunckes is sat with him. He is his prisoner now, and he will gain great credit for the arrest of a murderer."

I nodded and put my head over the edge of the quarry. In the darkness, I could just make out the gloomy outline of the prostrate schoolteacher lying at the bottom of the pit.

"That is good news indeed," I said, "but how in the name of God do we escape from here, Gideon? We cannot go back into town, as we are certain to be arrested without Sir Fulke, and we cannot leave him alone, as he will surely alert the guards on the gate as soon as we leave him."

There was a cough behind me, and I turned around to look at Saltonstall, who had propped himself up against a tree. I took a quick glance at his ankle and saw that it had swelled up to twice its normal size.

"There is but one solution," said the lieutenant. "I cannot walk properly and will only hold you up. And if I have to swim the river, I will certainly die. You must leave me here.

Give me the lantern and the carbine, and I will keep Hunckes at bay until you have made good your escape. Then I will alert the sergeant at the gate."

Gideon grimaced and shook his head vehemently. "We cannot do that, Lieutenant," he said. "They will hang you as a spy."

"No, they won't," argued Saltonstall. "I am too valuable to them. I am Sir Thomas Myddelton's great-nephew. They will lock me up for a while, that is true, but then they will use me for a prisoner exchange. And in any case, I cannot move."

I looked at Saltonstall intently for a moment, but I knew he was right. Neither Alexander, Gideon, nor I could stay behind, as we were of little value in an exchange. We were simply spies who would be strung from a gibbet within days. Saltonstall, on the other hand, was a gentleman. And Ellis? Well, leaving him behind was out of the question. I had made a commitment to return him to his family.

"That's all well and good," I said, "but how do we get out of here?"

"I have a solution," said Gideon. "There is a rowboat moored close to the Welsh Bridge. It is owned by one of the wealthier house owners in that part of town. I have always kept an eye on its location and availability precisely for eventualities such as this. If we make our way south of here and then back along the river bank, we will not be seen by the guards. We can then take the boat and let the current take us over to the other bank at the tip of the meander. From there we can walk to the village of Frankwell, where Greaves and Eliza will be waiting with our horses. We will be long gone before any hue and cry is raised."

"But where do we go from there?" asked Alexander.

"There is but one destination for us," I said. "It is where Sir Thomas Myddelton is headed, it is where Hipkiss in probably headed, and it is probably where Alice and Bressy are too. We have no option but to ride for Montgomery."

"You are a brave man, Saltonstall," said Alexander, whilst Gideon was relaying his instructions to Hunckes not to try any tricks and to wait for Saltonstall to alert the guards. "I misjudged you."

Saltonstall smiled. "There are no hard feelings," he said.

"Alexander is right, though," I said. "You can be sure that as soon as we reach Montgomery, we will alert Sir Thomas and make sure he prioritises your release."

"Godspeed," said Saltonstall, as Gideon's head once again appeared above the edge of the quarry. "Quickly," he added, shaking us each in turn by the hand. "There is no time for sentiment. You must go."

"Farewell, Lieutenant," said Gideon. "Good luck." And with that he plunged through the trees, followed by Alexander and Ellis.

I took one last look at Saltonstall, before giving him a quick salute and following my three comrades with the lantern.

Chapter 27

Alexander and I arrived in Montgomery early on the Thursday morning to find Sir Thomas Myddelton already there. We had said our farewells to Gideon and Ellis in Frankwell, where, as promised, Greaves and Mistress Eliza had been waiting for us with our horses. It had been good to see my bay mare Demeter again, and she had whickered in pleasure as I greeted her.

The landlord of The Sacristry, his cover still intact, had wished us well and seen us on our way before returning to his hostelry. Gideon, Ellis and Eliza, on the other hand, had ridden directly for Oswestry bearing a letter from me addressed to Evan and Hester Davies, explaining the nature of what had occurred in Shrewsbury, as well as a further communication to Colonel Mytton, alerting him to Saltonstall's situation, in the hope that a prisoner exchange might be arranged. I fully intended to raise the same subject with Myddelton once I located him.

Myddleton, it turned out, had enjoyed a successful few days whilst we had been dealing with Tewdwr, Hipkiss, and Sir Fulke Hunckes in St Chad's churchyard. The colonel had been approaching the Red Castle near Newtown, having received intelligence that a Royalist munitions convoy sent from Bristol had arrived in the town and was being guarded by a troop from Prince Rupert's Regiment of Horse under the command of a captain called Gardiner.

On learning this, Myddelton had sent a detachment of two hundred and fifty cavalry and dragoons under Lt Colonel James Till into the town, seizing the convoy, together with Gardiner, two junior officers and about forty men. The success meant the capture of thirty-six barrels of gunpowder and twelve barrels of sulphur along with various stocks of match and bullets, as well as some weaponry.

Myddelton had arrived in triumph in Montgomery on the Wednesday evening, having ordered Till to follow him with the munitions convoy, which was expected the following evening. By the time we rode into town, he had already made himself comfortable in the attractive town house owned by Lord Herbert's Royalist officer son, Richard.

Myddelton was, as expected, not best pleased to discover that the dies for the mint had been shipped down the river to Bristol, that the treasure was still in Jem Bressy's hands, and that his great-nephew had been arrested as a spy and was being held in Shrewsbury.

"Master Cheswis, Sir William Brereton has you for a reliable fellow, and yet from where I am standing, you and Clowes have performed like a pair of worthless wastrels," he thundered. "Either that or venomous miscreants. Which is it, sir?"

The only other person present in Richard Herbert's study was a red-haired and bearded captain called Samuel More, one of Mytton's men, who looked on with a hint of faint amusement in his eyes.

"We are sorry, Colonel," I said, "but Lieutenant Saltonstall injured his ankle as we tried to flee. Staying behind was the only course of action open to him, and it allowed Mr Clowes, myself, and three others to make good our escape."

"That may be so," retorted Myddelton, "but what do you propose to do about it? We cannot allow Philip to be executed as a spy."

"I believe I have a solution, sir," I said. "I presume you are about to commence negotiations with Lord Herbert regarding the surrender of the castle?"

"Indeed. That will be Captain More's responsibility. What of it?"

"Well, I have good reason to believe that the Royalist spy Jem Bressy sits in the castle as we speak, perhaps also with Mistress Alice Furnival, herself a pro-active supporter of the King, and probably also with most, if not all, of the treasure we were commissioned to recover."

"So, what do you propose?"

"Sir Thomas, I recognise Bressy, so if you allow Mr Clowes and myself to accompany Captain More during his negotiations, I will be able to ascertain if either Bressy or Mistress Funival are in the castle. If that is the case and we can negotiate the terms of the surrender of the castle, we may be able to capture both of them for use in a prisoner exchange, whilst also securing at least part of the treasure for return to Sir William Brereton. That way everyone wins."

☙

And so it was that Alexander and I ended up joining the negotiating party aimed at persuading Lord Herbert to surrender Montgomery to the parliamentary army. I have to say, it was no easy matter, for although London had already applied substantial pressure on Herbert to surrender the castle, Herbert, being, on paper, a Royalist, could not be seen to give into Myddelton's demands too easily.

More, being the son of a Shropshire member of Parliament, had been engaged by Myddelton because of his influence in the local area, but the negotiations went on throughout the day, and the captain was making little headway, to the point where matters were becoming increasingly awkward. A key point of disagreement was that, with the arrival of Lt Colonel Till and the munitions convoy imminent, More wanted to negotiate access to the castle's outer works to store the captured munitions. For security, he also wanted Herbert to stand down most of the thirty-strong garrison, which the latter refused to do.

At this point, having kept myself in the shadows for most of the day, I proposed to More that we approach Herbert together and try to gain direct access to the eccentric old aristocrat rather than having to pass messages through the garrison guards.

Eventually, around five in the afternoon, More and I were summoned to the gatehouse and led across the drawbridge to the castle's middle ward, before being led into Herbert's fine brick mansion. We were shown into a small drawing room, although not, I noted, into the library, which, Herbert had made clear, was sacrosanct.

Herbert was sitting in an upholstered chair by the window, a walking stick by his side, and I noticed how much older and careworn he looked compared to the last time I had seen him, no more than a few weeks previously. He appeared to recognise More and tried to struggle to his feet, but the captain gestured for him to sit down.

"Do not get to your feet, your Lordship," said More, "there is no need to put yourself out for me."

"Poppycock," said Herbert, "I have welcomed your father here on many occasions before. I would not be so uncivil."

More gave Herbert a thin smile, but said nothing.

"It comes to something, does it not," continued Herbert, "when a man has to surrender his house, against his will, even when he has done nothing against those who would take the house from him."

"It is true that you have been careful not to let Prince Rupert in here," conceded More, "and for that we thank you, but your sons fight for the King."

"That is their affair," said Herbert, "but let me be clear, Captain. I have no desire to stand in your way, but I cannot be seen to be surrendering this place without giving a modicum of resistance."

"That I understand, your Lordship, and that is why I have brought someone with me who might be able to smooth the way somewhat."

Herbert looked at me closely, and I saw a flash of recognition cross his face.

"I know you," he said. "You are the cheese merchant who came to Combermere with Roger Wilbraham. I think I can guess why you are here. The lady you seek is still here as my guest, but you knew that, of course."

"I did," I admitted, "but we also seek one Jeremiah Bressy, one of Rupert's intelligencers."

Herbert laughed jovially. "I thought you might," he said, "but I'm afraid you are too late. He escaped over the wall last night once he realised Sir Thomas Myddelton had arrived in town. A very impatient man – I was glad to see the back of him. Mistress Furnival, on the other hand, I am happy to entertain any time she chooses."

"Did Bressy take the silver with him?" I asked.

"The silver? No, he got fed up of me waiting to make a decision on what they were proposing, but he left it here with Mistress Furnival, who is in the difficult position of having control of the treasure, but not having control of it, as it were, because you are here, and I cannot leave. Are you suggesting a deal, Mr Cheswis?"

"I have been sent to make sure the silver does not find its way to the mint," I said. "I need to recover the silver for Sir William Brereton, but as for all the other valuables, I am sure a blind eye could be turned to their whereabouts. After all, Bressy could easily have fled with them. I would insist on one thing, though. Mistress Furnival is to be handed over to us."

Herbert frowned. "Why would you want her? I thought there was some kind of history between you and her. Surely you would not have her arrested as a spy?"

"That is exactly why I would have her taken into custody. I would see her safe. She also has some value to us, of course."

Herbert looked at me levelly. I could see he must have been a stern negotiator in his day, but I also saw that he knew when to cut his losses and run, and with More beginning to get impatient, I could see that this time had come.

"Gentlemen," said Herbert, "pray give me a few hours to consider my options. I will call for you when I am ready."

"Very well," sniffed More, "but don't take long about it. Our patience is not infinite. You have until nine o'clock tomorrow morning to make your decision.

CR

In the event, things moved quicker than expected. When Till arrived in Montgomery with the munitions convoy at around seven in the evening, More ordered the occupation of the castle outworks, and with the risk of the arrival of Royalist forces rising by the hour, the captain was becoming increasingly agitated. Myddelton too, by all accounts, for later that evening Sir Thomas gave More the order to force Herbert's surrender, and around midnight Till led a party of soldiers into the ditch below the raised drawbridge and fixed a petard to the main gate. They then stripped away some of the wood from the raised drawbridge and entered the passage leading to the main gate. The resistance was all but over. At two o'clock the gate was opened, allowing Till, More and myself to enter to negotiate the final surrender of the castle.

Once again, as I entered the mansion, accompanied by the two officers and several other soldiers, we were shown into the drawing room. This time, however, Herbert was not alone. Sitting next to him in a striking blue dress, trying her best to remain calm, was Alice Furnival. Two of the soldiers immediately made to grab her by the arm, but Herbert stopped them.

"I will have no violence here," he snapped. "In my house, you will behave with due deference."

"It is of no matter, my Lord," said Alice. "I will go quietly, if Mr Cheswis will accompany me." With that she got to her feet and linked her arm through mine, allowing me to lead her out of the mansion towards the remains of the drawbridge.

There had been times when I had dreamed of leading Alice like this along the aisle of St Mary's Church in Nantwich. What an irony, I thought, that it was I who was now leading her by the arm, but only as far as Sir Thomas Myddelton, and the inside of a prison cell. At least, I reasoned, she would not be there for long. If we managed to secure the castle for Parliament, it was highly likely she would be returned to the castle at the earliest possible opportunity.

"I promised you I would do something to help secure the release of your man, Saltonstall," she said, as I led her into captivity. "This was not exactly what I had in mind, but it seems I may end up being of some value in terms of an exchange."

I nodded my thanks, but suddenly baulked as the end of the drawbridge came into view, and two guards started to march purposefully towards us. I started to wave them away, but Alice put her hand on my arm to stop me, and gave me a single kiss on the cheek.

"Do not concern yourself for me, Daniel," she said. "Let them do their duty. I will survive, as I always do, and furthermore, fate will ensure that this is not the last we will see of each other. Of that you can be certain."

Chapter 28

Montgomery – Thursday September 19th, 1644

*S*ir Thomas Myddelton stood at the northern end of the inner ward of Montgomery Castle and stared out over the agricultural landscape, which had played host to the great Parliamentarian victory that had been achieved here the previous day. With more than four hundred dead and fifteen hundred captured, the defeat suffered by Lord Byron's Royalist army had been significant. Indeed, the only real logistical concern now being faced by the Parliamentarian commander, Sir John Meldrum, was what to do with the great hordes of Royalist foot soldiers who had surrendered en masse, for they almost outnumbered their captors.

The only other negative point had been the sad death of Major General Colonel Sir William Fairfax, Black Tom's cousin, who had died a hero's death, suffering many wounds, in a final victorious assault on the ditches surrounding the castle.

Despite these negatives, it was a great relief for Myddelton to have secured Montgomery for Parliament, for the past two weeks had been very difficult.

Following the success achieved by Captain More and Brereton's intelligencer, Cheswis, in negotiating the capture of the castle, Myddelton had been joined in the Welsh border town by Colonel Mytton, who had garrisoned the castle. However, on 8th September, whilst Myddelton and his party had been away *from Montgomery on a raid, Sir Michael Ernle had sallied out of Shrewsbury and attacked, leaving Mytton to defend a besieged castle. It had taken the combined strength of the Yorkshire horse under Sir William Fairfax, Myddelton's own brigade, Sir William Brereton's Regiment and the valiant Cheshire Foot under Major James Lothian to save the day.*

Now, however, having secured victory, Myddeton looked forward to re-uniting himself with his brave great-nephew, who, having been the subject of a prisoner exchange with the Furnival woman a week previously, and having recovered from his sprained ankle, had distinguished himself on the field as part of Sir Thomas's own brigade. The young man would join him at Lord Herbert's table that evening, together with Meldrum, Brereton and Lothian. After all, with Herbert having secured the safety of his personal possessions (including his precious library) a military escort as far as Coventry should he so desire, as well as a fair proportion of Abbott Massey's treasure, the old goat could well afford the hospitality.

Meanwhile, in Shrewsbury, Sir Fulke Hunckes collapsed on a chair in the front room of his town house and thanked the Lord that he had been fortunate enough to return from battle in one piece along with his regiment, for most of the Royalist foot had not, including Colonel Broughton, who was now a prisoner in Montgomery. With Byron's army dissipated and almost completely destroyed, Hunckes was wise enough to realise that times were about to become much more difficult for Royalists living in Shrewsbury. For now, however, things were tolerable. True, he had been forced to apologise to Alice Furnival for suspecting her of treachery, but the woman seemed to have forgiven him. Not only that, he was still riding a wave of gratitude from the townsfolk of Shrewsbury for having delivered them the murderer,

Maredudd Tewdwr. The schoolteacher was due to be hanged in a couple of days' time, so there was plenty of time to milk his enhanced standing in the town even further.

The mood in Bristol was very different. It would be a day or two before Prince Rupert received news of the defeat at Montgomery, but Jem Bressy knew that whatever happened, any chance of regaining the silver for Thomas Bushell's mint was long gone. Frustrated by Herbert's prevarications, Bressy had eventually realised he needed to flee for his life from Montgomery Castle while he still could. He had escaped over the wall with the help of a couple of Herbert's guards and slid down the steep escarpment, through the town, and into the fields beyond. To add insult to injury, he could have sworn he had seen that traitor, Daniel Cheswis, making his way up to the castle with a young captain. No matter, he thought, there was still plenty of fighting to be done in this war, and he would yet gain the upper hand over his enemy. He would make sure of that.

Back in Montgomery, Lieutenant Philip Saltonstall was well aware of his duty to attend to his great uncle later than evening, but before then he had a more important duty to perform. After weaving his way through the crowds of soldiers drinking in the taverns, he had made his way to the quieter area of Back Lane, where he entered an unassuming-looking blacksmith's workshop between a bakery and a private house. As his eyes grew accustomed to the gloom inside the building, he recognised the young teenage boy he had last seen in Shrewsbury. With him was an older youth, a dragoon from Sir Thomas Myddelton's brigade, whose name he knew was Skinner and whom he knew, despite his young age, had recently become betrothed to the other youth's sister.

Both the young men were staring in satisfaction at the sight of the Royalist soldier, a strong, well-built sergeant, who was being pinned to the floor by half a dozen soldiers directly under a solid wooden block, on which stood the blacksmith's anvil.

"Good morrow, Mr Hipkiss," said Saltonstall. "We have you at last, I see." The sergeant merely grunted and stared at the lieutenant with a look of hatred in his eyes.

"Today," continued Saltonstall, "I am the bearer of both good and bad tidings. The good news is that Maredudd Tewdwr, the murderer of Jakob De Vries, Ben Collie, Cornelis Smits, Joseph Finch and William Stubbs, dies in two days' time, convicted of murder. The bad news I have is that he has asked me to convey the following message to you."

Saltonstall reached inside his coat and extracted a letter, which he opened and read aloud – JH Exodus 21:24.

"Do you recognise that quotation, Sergeant Hipkiss?"

"I am not much of a one for Bible quotes," growled the sergeant.

"That is a surprise," said Saltonstall, with heavy sarcasm. "Then let me read that verse to you – 'Eye for Eye, tooth for tooth, hand for hand, foot for foot'. You get my meaning, I think."

Hipkiss said nothing, but his face turned pale and beads of sweat began to appear on his forehead. One of the soldiers pretended to make a move to grab the anvil and push it towards the edge of the wooden block on which it stood, which made Hipkiss flinch and emit a terrified gasp. Once the soldiers' raucous laughter had died down, Saltonstall spoke.

"You are lucky, Hipkiss. We do not do things Maredudd Tewdwr's way here. You will get a reprieve, but not for long I'll wager, for we will take you from here to Oswestry, where you will face justice in the time-honoured manner."

And with that, Hipkiss was hauled to his feet and manhandled out of the workshop and into the street in the direction of the gaol house.

Whilst all this was occurring, fifty-five miles away in Nantwich, the cheese merchant and his bellman friend were riding across the bridge at the start of Welsh Row. They had been on the road for almost exactly a month, and they were glad to be home. When they reached the junction of Beam Street and Pepper Street they brought their horses to a halt and looked at each other before simply nodding and riding their separate ways, the bellman to the chandler's workshop on the left side of Pepper Street, and the cheese merchant to the somewhat larger brick house not far from the earthworks at the end of Beam Street.

This time, mused the cheese merchant, he and Alexander had completed their mission successfully, at least in part. Although Bressy had got away and the dies for the mint had still found their way to Bristol, they had been successful in making sure that the whole of Abbott Massey's treasure had stayed out of Royalist hands, all of the silver had been recovered and was now in Thomas Mytton's hands, Lieutenant Saltonstall had been freed, and he, Daniel Cheswis, had received a commendation from Sir Thomas Myddelton for the role he had played in negotiating the surrender of Montgomery Castle.

He was exhausted, and Cheswis could have been forgiven for assuming he would now be allowed to live in peace with his wife, his child-to-be, and his adopted family. But he was no fool. In a town where Sir William Brereton's word was law, he knew this was something he could never rely on.

With a sigh, he dismounted from his bay mare and tethered her to the gate, before walking through his front door and into the arms of his pregnant wife.

Historical Notes

On 2 July 1644, on the very same day that Prince Rupert of the Rhine was riding across Marston Moor learning that he was only the second best military commander in the country, a smaller battle was taking place not far from the Welsh border at the village of Whittington, a couple of miles from Oswestry. It was a confrontation that would set the tone for the subsequent Parliamentarian push through Shropshire and the Welsh Marches under Sir Thomas Myddelton, which would culminate in the Battle of Montgomery on 18 September, 1644.

At the end of June, the new Parliamentarian governor of Oswestry, Colonel Thomas Mytton, having captured the town a week earlier from the Royalist commander, Colonel Edward Lloyd, found himself being threatened by a force of 2,000 foot and 600 horse under Sir Fulke Hunckes, the Shrewsbury governor.

Myddelton, aware of the threat to his brother-in-law (both Mytton and Myddelton were married to daughters of Sir Robert Napier, 1st Baronet of Luton Hoo), marched from Cheshire with the aim of relieving Mytton, but was attacked at Whittington by a cavalry force under Colonel John Marrow, apparently against Hunckes's direct orders. The Royalists were routed, and Hunckes was forced to retreat back to Shrewsbury.

Marrow, who by all accounts was a valiant and loyal officer, eventually lost his life, as this novel relates, during the skirmish at Sandiway, near Northwich, on August 18, 1644.

By late August, the severely weakened Prince Rupert, who had been in Chester since Marston Moor, had decamped, first to Shrewsbury and then to Bristol, whilst Myddelton was commencing his plans to cut a swathe through Montgomeryshire.

On 2 September, Myddelton advanced from Oswestry with a view to persuading the owner of Montgomery Castle, Edward Herbert, First Baron Herbert of Cherbury, to surrender the castle to Parliament. Herbert, by nature a Royalist, was in poor health and had prevaricated for months over which side to support in the conflict, even to the point of refusing a direct request from Rupert to garrison the castle for the King. Critical to Herbert was the protection of his valuable library.

On 3 September, Myddelton had the good fortune to overwhelm Sir Thomas Gardiner's garrison at Newtown, thereby seizing a munitions convoy, which was on its way from Bristol to supply the garrisons at Chester and Liverpool. Flushed with success, Myddelton proceeded directly to Montgomery, where he attempted to negotiate with Herbert for the surrender of the castle, whilst placing the convoy under the command of Lt. Colonel James Till, who was ordered to follow Myddelton to Montgomery.

Till arrived in Montgomery on the evening of 5 September, which precipitated an acceleration in the attempts to persuade Herbert to surrender, including tactics such as fixing a petard to the drawbridge and stripping away planks of wood from it. Unsurprisingly, Herbert, whose daughter Beatrice was with him in the castle at the time, capitulated without further delay, and the castle was placed under the governorship of Captain Samuel More.

Two weeks later, after an attempt to besiege the castle by Royalist forces under Sir Michael Ernle, the Battle of Montgomery was fought, which, as explained in the final chapter of the novel, resulted in the dissipation and defeat of John, Lord Byron's Royalist force, by a parliamentary army under the overall command of the Scottish career soldier, Sir John Meldrum.

Shrewsbury, during the late summer and early autumn of 1644, was a Royalist stronghold, initially under the governorship of Sir Fulke Hunckes. However, after arguing with the commissioners of array, Hunckes was replaced in mid-August by Colonel Robert Broughton.

Shrewsbury did indeed host a Royal Mint during the early part of the Civil War. Housed in the semi-derelict Bennett's Hall on Pride Hill, it was under the management of Thomas Bushell, who, on the King's orders, had moved the mint from Aberystwyth at the start of the war. In reality, though, the mint had already been relocated twice by the time the action described in this novel takes place, firstly to Oxford in 1642, and then, a year later, to Bristol. For the sake of the plot I have kept the mint in Shrewsbury until 1644.

Shrewsbury was notable at the time in that it also housed the only printing press outside London and Oxford, although it was not located in the old school buildings opposite the castle. Its probable location was Chorlton Hall, which was situated in the area bounded by St John's Hill, Cross Hill, Swan Hill and Market Street. The old school is now the home of Shrewsbury Library.

At the time of the Civil War there were four main churches within Shrewsbury's town walls – St Mary's, St Alkmund's, St Julian's and St Chad's. In addition, on the other side of the river, there was the Church of the Holy Cross (the old abbey church) and the smaller church of St Giles, located half a mile further up the road, which, at one time, had housed a hospital for lepers.

James Logan, Nicholas Prowd, Andrew Harding and Mr Lentall were all real people, being the ministers of their respective churches as described in the book. Logan's background as I describe it is of my own invention, but Nicholas Prowd did indeed become minister of St Mary's during the week at the end of August, 1644, as described in the book. I can only assume his first week in office was somewhat less traumatic than the one I describe. All four ministers were removed from office when the town was captured by Parliament in 1645.

St Chad's Church was the largest of the four main churches in the 17th Century, but only a small part of the original church is still standing, due to the well-documented collapse of the central tower in 1788, an event which triggered structural amendments also at St Alkmund's. At the time of the Civil War, St Chad's churchyard did contain a series of almshouses called the College.

The church's Sacristry, which later became a tavern of that name, still exists. Today it is called The Golden Cross Inn. At the time of the Civil War The Sacristry was known as a meeting place for Royalists.

The area of common land south of the town walls is now known as the Quarry Park and incorporates the old 'wet' quarry now known as the Dingle. The original quarry was cleared out in the 19th century and now houses ornamental gardens. My description of the quarry as being surrounded by thick trees is a creation of my own imagination.

The aptly named Grope Lane was, as the name suggests, originally so named because it was the location of many of the town's brothels. Indeed, the original name of the street was a rather more graphic variation of its current name.

On the other side of the river across the English Bridge, many of the abbey ruins were still standing at the time of the Civil War, but this area would have been much poorer than it had been before the dissolution of the monasteries. The abbey church, of course, still exists today.

Which brings me on to the subject of the use of Shrewsbury as a location for historical crime fiction. As everyone who is a fan of Ellis Peters' Cadfael series of novels will appreciate, writing a historical crime novel in Shrewsbury is a daunting task, because of the comparisons which will inevitably be drawn. Many of the locations in this book will be recognisable to Cadfael fans, although the town would have been rather different in 1644 to what it was three hundred years before.

Just in case anyone is wondering, the use of monkshood to murder Ben Collie was not an intentional tribute to Cadfael, although I'm happy for it to be seen as such. I simply needed a poison that worked quickly and which was available at that time, and when I googled it, monkshood is what came up.

However, having decided to have one murder victim despatched in a church bell tower, I confess that I could not resist being influenced by the brilliantly conceived ending to Dorothy L Sayers' *The Nine Tailors*, specifically the idea of a victim being finished off by the deafening noise of a peal of bells.

So, what next for Daniel Cheswis? He will certainly be back in Shrewsbury before long, but, with the 1644 campaigning season almost over, it is time for him to return to Nantwich for the winter and to enjoy the company of his family. Given the traumatic experience of Nantwich folk during December and January 1643/44, nothing could possibly happen to disturb the equilibrium of a Nantwich Christmas for the second year in succession. Could it?

Bibliographical Notes

As always, researching the historical background for *The Saints' Reckoning* involved the use of a number of key resources, which I have listed here.

The most important work on the history of Nantwich is James Hall's *A History of the Town and Parish of Nantwich or Wich Malbank in the County Palatine of Chester* (1883).

For information on the Civil War in Wales I used John Roland Phillips' *Memoirs of the Civil War in Wales and the Marches 1642-49* (1874) and *Sir Thomas Myddelton's Attempted Conquest of Powys 1644-45*, which is an abstract from the Montgomery Collections Vol. 57, Part 2 (1962).

The best-known work on Shrewsbury is *A History of Shrewsbury* by H Owen and JB Blakeway (1825). However, I found H Pidgeon's *Memorials of Shrewsbury* (1837) particularly useful, especially for the in-depth information on the town's churches. I also used *Shropshire in the Civil War* by Terry Bracher and Roger Emmett (2000) and *To Settle the Crown* by Jonathan Worton (2016).

Worton's recently published book, *The Battle of Montgomery, 1644* (2017) was absolutely invaluable for information on the lead-up to the Battle on 18 September, whilst for information on Northwich I read Tony Bostock's *Owners, Occupiers and Others: Seventeenth Century Northwich* (2004).

For the history of the Shrewsbury Mint I referred to articles by Lt Col. HW Morrieson called *The Coins of the Shrewsbury Mint, 1642* and by Geraint Morgan called *Making a Mint*, whilst information on Oswestry was gleaned from an abstract entitled *The Search for Oswestry Town Wall* by Derrick Pratt as well as various information from Oswestry Museum.

Acknowledgements

Thanks, as always, to Matthew, Tom, and Vanessa at Electric Reads, whose editing and design services I have used for all four Daniel Cheswis novels. Their input always makes for a significantly better book than I could create on my own.

I am also indebted to Colin Bissett of the Sealed Knot for checking the historical accuracy of my first draft, and to Jonathan Worton for the tour of Shrewsbury.

Thanks also to Nantwich Bookshop, Bookshrop, Nantwich Museum, Mike Molcher, and John Beardsworth, all of whom have helped in various ways during the process of bringing this book together.

And, of course, thanks to Karen, Richard, and Louisa for their love and support.

Printed in Great Britain
by Amazon